Christmas Trees & Weak Knees

Also by Katrina Emmel

Near Misses & Cowboy Kisses

Trail Rides & Starry Eyes

Christmas Trees & Weak Knees

KATRINA EMMEL

Delacorte Romance

Delacorte Romance
An imprint of Random House Children's Books
A division of Penguin Random House LLC
1745 Broadway, New York, NY 10019
penguinrandomhouse.com
getunderlined.com

Editor: Alison Romig
Designer: Michelle Canoni
Production Editor: Jamie Johnson
Managing Editor: Tamar Schwartz
Production Manager: Liz Sutton

Library of Congress Cataloging-in-Publication Data is available upon request.
ISBN 979-8-217-11766-6 (trade pbk.) — ISBN 979-8-217-11767-3 (ebook)

The text of this book is set in 11-point Sabon Next LT Pro.

Manufactured in the United States of America
1st Printing

The authorized representative in the EU for product safety and compliance is Penguin Random House Ireland, Morrison Chambers, 32 Nassau Street, Dublin D02 YH68, Ireland, https://eu-contact.penguin.ie.

Random House Children's Books supports the First Amendment
and celebrates the right to read.

To Samantha,
for being the best little sister a big sister could ask for

A-SIDE INTRO

Dust and Tears

Paisley

MAY

I CAN'T BELIEVE I agreed to this.

As I stand in the Omni Theater's wings, hidden behind a thick red velvet curtain, my heart pounds so loudly, I wonder if the microphone will pick it up like a drumbeat when I take the stage. It's frenetic and fast, completely at odds with the set list I've put together for my first attempt at performing in front of a crowd of strangers. The auditorium—filled with the quiet din of restless bodies—has a maximum capacity of five hundred people, and I doubt all the seats are full, but still . . . that number is daunting.

Don't lock your knees.

I shift my weight, but it doesn't stop me from feeling lightheaded.

"Deep breaths," I murmur. But my lungs are tight. My chest burns. I can only imagine how wide and wild my dark brown eyes look, my gaze bouncing all over the backstage area like

I expect monsters and ghouls to jump out at me from the shadows.

Performance anxiety is the absolute worst.

Clint Davis, the stage manager, saunters in from the hallway that leads to the greenrooms and gives me an encouraging grin as if he can't see the abject terror written across my face. Dressed in all black, from the brim of his cowboy hat to the tips of his scuffed leather boots, he practically blends into the walls, and it makes me wish I hadn't opted to wear the look-at-me bright green shirt Mom said would "really set off the auburn highlights" in my hair.

I've known Clint for as long as I can remember. Probably as long as I've known how to talk. And while it's nice to have a friendly face back here, it's not doing much for my rapidly rising blood pressure. Clint's a popular session musician at the Hideaway at Hidden Acres Christmas Tree Farm, my family's business, where he's often found playing his steel guitar or a Dobro for the bluegrass and blues musicians who record at the studio.

Gosh, if only I were at the Hideaway right now.

Maybe I can make a break for it?

Clint must sense my fight-or-flight instincts kicking in. He shuffles closer and whispers, "You've got this, Paisley," in his low, raspy voice.

I wish I had an ounce of his confidence and a hefty helping of his musicianship.

Heck, I'd settle for even the merest hint of confidence.

The knot in my stomach cinches tighter.

Unlike Clint, who is completely at ease with any sized audience (he was once a sideman for a show at Madison Square Garden), I'm most comfortable writing songs or messing around at the soundboard in the studio. I don't mind playing music with friends and family, or having a low-key jam session with the studio musicians, but the whole thought of standing on a stage, all by my lonesome, in front of an audience of strangers makes me shudder.

My teeth chatter and I force myself to loosen my jaw. If I don't figure out how to release some of this pent-up tension soon, I'm going to sound pitchy.

On the wall behind Clint is the poster for Ballad FM's May Music Showcase. It's difficult to make out in the dark, but I practically have it seared into my memory. Most of the space is taken up by an artfully grainy photo of the members of Six String Justice, a Nashville country-rock band with a rebel image and a new hit single.

ONE NIGHT ONLY!

Below it, in a smaller font:

WITH LOCAL GUESTS
Chet Bryant, Bluegrass Banjo
&
Paisley Morgan, Singer-Songwriter

I glance down at my left wrist, which is covered in beaded bracelets filled with inspirational song titles and meaningful acronyms. Little personal messages to help me focus and spark creativity.

My gaze lands on WWCKD. I allow myself a moment to wonder: What *would* Carole King do?

I close my eyes and her song "Beautiful" comes to mind.

Well, for starters, Carole probably wakes up smiling every morning, just like she advises in the lyrics to her song. I am *not* a morning person, so that's not happening. Carole's prepared to show the world every drop of love in her heart. Right now, all the love in my heart is being beaten to death as it pounds against my rib cage. I'd rather not show *that* to the world.

I blow out a sigh that's equal parts frustration and nerves. Carole King—one of my biggest musical inspirations—managed to conquer her stage fright to become one of the most influential female singer-songwriters ever. If she could do it, maybe I can, too?

Bile rises in my throat, and I force it back down.

Maybe not.

Chet Bryant, banjo player, ends his set with a flourishing finish to "Foggy Mountain Breakdown," and the emcee—local news reporter Kirk Hoenig—steps out onto the stage. Clint gives me a stiff nod. "Time to get out there," he whispers as he holds out my acoustic-electric guitar.

I stare at it for a minute, hoping I'll get lucky and a sinkhole will open beneath me. The ground under my feet wobbles . . . No, actually, that's just my trembling knees.

Reluctantly, I hand him my journal, which I've been clutching to my chest like a shield. They say the pen is mightier than the sword, but right now, my haphazardly scrawled lyrics aren't offering much protection in my current time of need. I take my Fender from Clint with shaky hands and pull the strap over my head, brushing my shoulder-length, wavy hair aside so it doesn't get caught.

"And now, it's time for Tennessee's Songwriter of the Year to take the stage. At only eighteen, Paisley Morgan wowed the Ballad FM contest judges with her unique blend of folk pop–inspired country music and heartfelt, poetic lyrics. Paisley's also signed on with Exit 12S Records' publishing arm as their newest, and youngest, in-house songwriter. There's sure to be more great things to come from her," Kirk Hoenig continues.

No pressure.

Kirk spreads his arms wide. "Let's give a warm welcome to Paisley Morgan."

My name rings out over the speakers like I'm being announced on *The Price Is Right*. My heart bounces around in my chest like it's a game of Plinko.

A small patter of polite applause filters backstage. The audience seems as excited for me to go onstage as I am. (Which is to say, not very.)

"I can't do this." My guitar hangs on me like a lead weight, the tooled leather strap cutting into my shoulder.

"Sure you can." Clint gives me a pat on the back that turns into a friendly nudge, and I half stumble onstage. Thank goodness I'm blocked from view by the heavy velvet curtains. My cheeks burn like I've leaned too close to a bonfire. I blink into the blinding stage lights that hit me when I walk forward and somehow manage to make my way to the microphone. My vision blurs. My ears ring. And my limbs feel like they're filled with Great-Aunt Betty's famous Christmas pudding. I might be having an out-of-body experience . . .

But at least I'm still standing. An image of Sir Elton John, decked out in fabulous jewel-encrusted sunglasses and a flamingo-pink feather boa, pops into my head. There's zero chance he's ever felt the level of stage fright that I'm feeling at this very minute.

I force down a swallow and run the pad of my pointer finger along the edge of my guitar pick.

I know I should look up from the scuffed stage—to channel some semblance of stage presence—but it's impossible considering how hard I'm focusing on trying not to puke. My fingers are clutching the neck of my guitar so tightly, they're starting to go numb. I force my left hand to loosen, and out of habit, I strum my right hand across the strings to double-check the tuning. Earsplitting feedback blares through the auditorium speakers.

I jump back like I've been electrocuted, and the speakers squeal again. A guy from the tech crew jogs onstage, lifts an arm in a friendly "just a sec" wave to the audience, and starts fiddling with the wireless pickup he'd previously attached to my guitar. A moment later, he gestures for me to step forward and I do, much to my regret. The jarring feedback makes my teeth ache.

It's probably only been a minute, but I feel like I've been standing here for hours. My mouth is parched. *Great.* I smile-grimace at the crowd I can't quite see beyond the glare of the stage lights, hoping I don't look like an unhinged serial killer. Even though I can't see them, I can feel them out there.

Watching.

Waiting.

The audience grows as restless as I feel. I hear them shifting and murmuring to each other, their whispers getting louder until they drown out the low, humming buzz from the speakers.

"... Six String Justice ..."

"... some local chick ..."

"... waste of time ..."

The tech guy signals to the person in the sound booth, and after a few snaps and crackles, there's a low hum. Suddenly, the speakers go quiet. "Sorry about that, folks," says the guy in the sound booth. "We just had a few technical difficulties there. Should be all sorted out now."

The tech guy ushers me back to the mic. Somehow, I manage to step forward on trembling legs, wincing as I wait for feedback or random audience members to jeer at me, but now all I'm met with is incredibly awkward silence.

"Hi. Uh . . . I'm . . . uh, Paisley Morgan." I clear my throat. Take a fortifying breath. And try to remember which lyrics go with which chords. "This first song is called 'Dust and Tears.'"

I remember strumming an E-minor chord, and after that, the whole performance is a blur. I might have warbled my way through my three-song set in a pitchy, reedy voice. I might have spoken in tongues. Or danced the Hokey Pokey. It's equally as likely I was abducted by aliens and had my memory wiped.

I'm not sure if this temporary blackout is a blessing or a curse.

I come back into myself with a start, to a smattering of polite claps and a group of overzealous hoots, which I'm pretty sure are from Mom and Dad—the only people here who love me enough to cheer for such a horrible flop.

If I weren't already so embarrassed for myself, I'd be embarrassed for them, too.

I should get offstage. But, for the life of me, I can't seem to get my feet to cooperate. Before, they functioned perfectly on their own even though they were unsteady, but now they absolutely refuse to move at all.

A rough cough.

A loud series of snickers.

My mortification is practically complete.

Kirk Hoenig walks out with a pained smile plastered on his face. "Let's hear it for Paisley Morgan."

"Uh, thank you," I manage to croak into the microphone to another tepid round of pity applause.

"Thank you," the emcee says, like he's just as relieved as everyone else that my set is finally over. Suddenly, my feet become unstuck and my guitar no longer feels like a crushing lead weight.

The lights dim and Kirk hustles me offstage as the set crew rushes on. My legs are as wobbly as a newborn reindeer's, and I'm on the verge of hyperventilating.

"That was—" I'm about to say "horrific," but Clint cuts me off.

"Truly something," he says, lifting his bushy eyebrows. "But you know what they say: The first cut is the deepest."

"I think that's supposed to be about your first broken heart," I mutter.

"Same thing," Clint says.

"If you say so." I've never been in love, so I wouldn't know.

I pull the wireless pickup from my Fender and hand it over to Clint before slipping my guitar into its beat-up case, covered in random stickers and Sharpie doodles. Once I've latched it, I take my notebook from him and run my fingers along the spine.

"The next gig will be easier, now that you've gotten this first one out of the way," Clint says.

"What makes you think there'll be a next one?" My voice

warbles and hot tears fill my eyes. Who would want me on their stage after this?

With all the jumbled feelings roiling in my stomach, now's the perfect time to channel them into an angsty song about getting knocked down and getting up again. Or maybe an epic breakup song.

And then my heart sinks even more. *Will Exit 12S still want me to write for them after this fiasco?*

One of the greenroom's doors bursts open, and a group of guys in faded jeans and dark, fitted T-shirts tumbles out, jostling each other as they make their way toward us.

"Talk about awful."

"Totally," one of them says with a laugh.

"Who even was that?"

"Probably some chick who thinks she's the next Taylor Swift."

"Don't they all?" one of them asks with a bitter edge.

"I think her name starts with a *P*. Penny?"

"Pansy?"

"Panties?"

That sends them into a round of riotous guffaws.

My cheeks flame hot, and I step aside to get out of their way just as one of the guys looks over at me from under a dark baseball cap. His gait changes and he moves closer with a Mick Jagger swagger and a smirk on his face. "Look, guys, we have a groupie."

I glance around, but no one else is back here, not even Clint. Oh . . . they think *I'm* a groupie.

Behind Swagger, a guy with a bandana tied around his wrist leers and waggles his eyebrows. "Hey, babe."

Eww, no.

I take another step back to give them more room to pass, but when Swagger gets close enough, he grabs my songwriting notebook from my hands, flips it open to a blank page, and says, "I didn't know they were giving out backstage passes to this thing." He shrugs and pulls a black Sharpie from his front pocket. Using his teeth, he tugs the cap off and then defaces my lyric notebook with his autograph.

"Stop," I whisper, reaching out to grab it back before any more damage can be done, but my fingers barely graze it as Swagger hands it to his bandana'd bandmate. The ringing in my ears intensifies while I watch helplessly as the second guy scrawls in my book. He hands it to a guy holding drumsticks, and after he's defaced it, he hands it to the guy in the back whose face is hidden beneath his cowboy hat.

Cowboy Hat takes the book, and I watch in horror as he pulls it open and the spine cracks. He swirls his signature over the page as Kirk Hoenig gets back on the microphone. "And now it's the moment you've all been waiting for, folks. Our headliner is ready to take the stage. So, without any further ado, let's hear it for Six String Justice!"

Swagger bumps into my shoulder as he makes his way to the stage. Bandana licks his lips. Drummer twirls his sticks. And Cowboy Hat tips his brim up to reveal striking warm brown eyes. For the briefest of moments, everything around us seems to fade away when our gazes lock. Speckled with flakes of gold, just barely perceptible in the darkness, his just might be the most beautiful eyes I've ever seen. Suddenly, all the sappy songs written about eyes make a lot more sense.

"That's us," Cowboy Hat says, shoving my notebook back at

me with a shrug. And then, as if signing my lyric book wasn't enough, he has the audacity to wink.

At me.

In an instant, the spell's broken. "I . . . That's my . . ."

I can't get the words out, but even if I could, it wouldn't matter. He'd never be able to hear me over the audience's applause. Without so much as a backward glance, he swivels away and jogs to join the rest of his band.

The hot, angry tears that have been threatening finally spill over. I watch them drop down onto the ruined page in my notebook, splashing next to the messy scrawls where the lyrics for my next song were supposed to go.

J. Foster

Johnny Lantz

Ryder Atkins

Ka$h Murray

A vibrant major chord blares and the audience cheers.

I hate them all.

INTERLUDE

6StringJustice:

Help wanted—a chick who can carry a tune.

6StringJustice:

Yikes, that's gonna be a tough act to follow. So much for warming up the crowd.

6StringJustice:

POV—When the opening act doesn't slay but you still gotta play.

B-SIDE INTRO

Rest Stop Ruin

Kash

JULY

"I THINK WE should try out some new material at our next show," I say, strumming a few strings on my Martin as the tour van bounces along the highway. Headlights glide past us in the dark. We've just finished up a two-night stint in Cleveland and are headed to Chicago by way of Indianapolis. We haven't had much time off the past few weeks—not that I'm complaining—but back-to-back nights of shows and being on the road take a lot out of you.

Thankfully, we have a few days off before our next gig, which means it's a perfect opportunity for us to rehearse some new songs. And grab some horizontal sleep.

"We don't have any new material." Justin, who's in the backseat next to me, glances up, his eyes narrowing. He looks like a ghost in the light radiating from his phone screen. "*I* haven't had time to work on anything since the tour kicked off."

"*I* have," I say, plucking a few random notes. It hasn't been easy, scratching down ideas on the back of receipts at rest stops or humming riffs into the voice memo app on my phone at two a.m., when inspiration strikes. All those bits and pieces have added up, and I think there's enough material there for at least a song or two. Maybe more.

Ryder, who's sitting shotgun, starts patting out a beat on the van's interior with his drumsticks.

Justin gives me side-eye and I suspect he snorts, but I can't tell for sure over Ryder's dashboard drumming. "Dude, you haven't written anything in ages."

"How would you know?"

We were in seventh grade when we started Six String Justice, fueled by Sour Patch Kids and impossibly large dreams. Back then, before the sold-out local gigs and our record deal, we'd all crowd into the rickety shed behind my house. I would share early versions of songs with them. Johnny'd come up with a great bass riff, and Ryder would tap out a sick beat with drumsticks on a rusty old shovel. After a while, Justin started writing songs, too, and then we had twice as much material to choose from. Back then, Justin and I had equal shares of the lead singer and lead guitar duties. Lately, though, it seems like our set lists include more songs that feature him than me.

I push the jealousy away as Johnny weaves the tour van through traffic, accelerating to get in front of a slow-moving semi. We're all jostled around thanks to the van's less-than-stellar suspension. Someday we'll have a proper tour bus. Sleep in five-star hotels. And have a team of roadies to haul our equipment.

"So, this song I'm working on," I say.

"What about it?" Justin's tone is bored and dismissive, like he's asking out of habit instead of interest. As if to prove his point that he couldn't give a crap about my song, he doesn't even bother looking up from his phone. His thumbs tap at the screen, which has all his focus.

I'm disappointed but not surprised. Justin's been running Six String Justice's social media for the past few months and is always looking for ways to make us go viral. Sure, growing followers is great, but so is making music. It kind of pisses me off that he's scrolling and captioning when he should be strumming and composing.

It's become a tug-of-war between branding and banding.

I miss when it was mostly about the music.

My other bandmates aren't as caught up in chasing likes and shares as Justin, but they haven't exactly been pressing for us to create new material, either. Ryder and Johnny are more live-in-the-moment guys, which was okay when we were just a few kids messing around. They'd be perfectly fine coasting along forever in this beat-up van with no plan.

While it seems sudden, there's been a slow and steady change in our band dynamics for the past year that I'm only just noticing. Some days, it feels like we only look up from our phones to play a gig. We barely have conversations anymore. I can't remember the last time we shared an inside joke or even had a good laugh. And Justin's been making a lot of decisions for Six String Justice that would have been up for a group vote only a few months ago.

I bristle again at how dismissive he's being about my new song idea and then force myself to take a deep breath. We've been packed into close quarters for weeks now, with hardly any privacy and barely any time away from each other. Add in a crap diet and lack of sleep, and it's sure to cause a little cabin fever. Just because I'm feeling irritable doesn't mean I should be.

My hand runs over the fretboard, cool beneath my fingertips, and I start strumming the tune that's been noodling around in my brain for weeks now. When the intro ends, I hum the melody over the chords. Bits and pieces of lyrics swirl through my mind, but the wisps of words are like bonfire smoke, drifting away before they form anything coherent. I finish the first verse, and the pre-chorus hits with a power chord progression.

Ryder shifts in the passenger seat and joins in with a building beat he taps out on the dash. He tosses me a grin and we drop into the chorus together, perfectly in sync. At the start of the second verse, Johnny jumps in by improvising a bass riff, which he changes around a couple of times until he settles on one he likes and gives a sharp nod of approval. His hands tighten on the steering wheel as he sings the bass line. He's locked in.

With only my acoustic guitar, Johnny's bass line humming, and the thumping of the tires on the highway blending with Ryder's beats, the song sounds more like a ballad than the country-rock song I envisioned. Still, the way it's coming together in this van, out on the road, reminds me of the shed days.

Everyone's into it but Justin, who's still scrolling on his phone. He's either oblivious or ignoring us, but either way, it sucks that he's not paying attention.

Just as we head into the song's bridge, the van approaches an actual bridge, which I take as a good sign. I'm here, on the road with my buddies, hustling to make our dreams come true. The music builds to a crescendo as we bump across the bridge. A chill races down my spine because we've recaptured that fleeting music magic again. Johnny and Ryder in the front, bopping along to the tune I'm strumming. Watch out, world, Six String Justice is just getting started.

I glance over at Justin. He's finally looking up from his phone and has a contemplative, faraway look in his eyes. He reaches for his guitar case and pulls out his Fender. A moment later, he's playing along with me. For a few bars, we're in harmony, but then he alters the strumming pattern, the chord progression, and just goes off and does his own thing, changing almost everything.

I stop playing. "That's not how it goes."

Justin glances at me and shrugs. "This version's better."

"It's completely different," I say.

"So?"

"So, I want us to play the song I wrote, the way I wrote it."

Why is he suddenly trying to take over everything?

"Whatever," he says in a bored tone, sliding his guitar back into its case. "You have lyrics?"

"I'm working on 'em."

"I'll write them," Justin says, like he's forgotten that I once wrote most of our material.

My jaw goes taut. "I said I'm working on it."

Justin opens his mouth like he's going to argue back, and I brace for a battle. "I need to pee," he says.

What?

My fingers falter on the strings of my guitar as Justin taps Johnny on the shoulder. "Exit. Now."

That took an unexpected turn.

And so does the van. We swerve onto the exit ramp and glide down to the stop sign. Johnny takes a right and pulls into a

McDonald's parking lot. Justin jumps out before the van's even in park, the door squealing as it lurches open. The rest of us get out to stretch our legs.

"So, what do you guys think?" I ask, rolling a guitar pick across my knuckles. Maybe if I can get Johnny and Ryder on board, they can help me convince Justin to give it a chance.

"I like it," Ryder says with a grin. He spins his drumsticks around in his hands and then pounds a short beat on his thighs.

Johnny holds out a fist for me to tap. "Good stuff, man."

"Do you think we can get it ready for the next show?" I ask.

"No." I turn to find Justin walking toward us.

I palm the pick and study him, surprised at how decisive he sounds. "No?" I huff.

"No," Justin repeats. He plants his feet and crosses his arms like he's the boss and we're just his minions. Like this is *his* band and we're just backing musicians.

I look to the others for reinforcement. Surely they can see what's happening. Ryder glances down at his feet and Johnny cops out with a shrug.

Stupid me for assuming they'd step up.

"Why not?" I ask, turning my attention back to Justin. "We used to test out new material at gigs all the time." There's a strange chill in the air that has nothing to do with the breeze.

Justin's jaw tightens. "That was before our record deal."

"So?" I ask. There was a lot of legal jargon in the contract we signed, but I don't recall it saying anything about us not being able to write new music or test it out at shows.

"So," he says with a sneer. "It's too rough. It needs lyrics."

"I'm working on the lyrics," I say, my tone acidic.

"It'll take me time to learn the melody."

"The melody's good," I say. "*I've* got it down."

Justin shoves his hands into the front pockets of his jeans and acts like he hasn't heard a word I've said. "Even if I can come up with a suitable arrangement and I manage to work out decent lyrics—"

I take a step back. "It's not your song, Justin."

He flinches. "Right. And I assume *you* want to take the lead on this one?" he asks, like it's a preposterous idea. Like we didn't once share the lead singer roles once upon a time and not so long ago.

"Yeah," I say. My blood grows hot. "Why not?"

Justin grimaces. "It's just . . . not the direction we're going in."

"What the hell are you talking about?" A vein in my neck starts to throb. I look to Ryder and Johnny to see if they're at all concerned about any of this, but neither of them will meet my eye.

"Look, Kash," Justin says, his face stony. "Your songs just aren't hit material. There's a reason we haven't been playing your stuff at shows lately. We're about to break into the big time and Six String Justice needs chart-toppers, not basic bull crap."

My hands fist at my sides and I'm one breath away from clocking him. Who the hell does he think he is? "You think my stuff is basic bull crap?"

I look to Ryder, who still won't meet my eye, and then Johnny, who casually spins the van's key fob around his finger while he stares off into the distance.

A semi roars by, filling up the growing silence that hangs between us.

"C'mon, Kash. It's nothing personal. It's just . . ." Justin's eyes go cold.

"Just what?" I manage as a ball of defensive anger coils in my gut.

"What do you bring to the table?"

"Excuse me?" I say, cocking my head because I'm not sure I'm hearing him correctly. My blood pounds in my veins and I'm pretty sure there's smoke pouring out of my ears.

"We have a bass player. And a drummer," he says, his voice dry and dismissive. "And I'm the lead singer and lead guitarist."

"Since when?" It's like I've been sucker punched in the gut.

"Since we signed with the label." Justin's so distant. So mercenary. So different from the kid I grew up with who used to TP our principal's house on Halloween and eat sour gummy worms after band practice until he puked.

"And you're cool with this? Letting Justin call all the shots?" I ask Johnny and Ryder.

Neither of them look my way. Traitors.

Even though most of our set lists have featured Justin's songs, I never considered that it was intentional. A lot of the songs I sing have more of a classic country-rock bent, and we've been playing stages in areas with a larger Nashville country fan base.

Or at least, that's what I thought.

But now it's got me thinking . . .

Of all the selfies Justin's posted on our social media lately.

Of all the solo calls he's taken with our label.

Of how I've been along for the ride but haven't really felt like a part of the band for a while.

It hits me suddenly. "Are you muscling me out?"

At least Ryder has the decency to look ashamed. Justin and Johnny, who've always been thick as thieves, are cold as ice.

Justin sighs, like I just told him it's his turn to take out the trash. "I'd planned to wait until we got back to Nashville to change the lineup," he says. "But if you aren't happy, no use in prolonging it, right?"

Looks like the trash is me. Damn.

"You can't be serious."

Justin doesn't blink. "Grab your gear."

He's serious.

"C'mon, guys," I say. "You can't just leave me here."

"Could we at least drop him at a bus stop?" Ryder asks.

Justin and Johnny share a look.

"It's not really on the way," Johnny says, as if he knows this area by heart.

I'm too stunned and dumbfounded to process everything as it's happening, and before I know it, my ratty old knockoff Samsonite and beat-up guitar case are tossed on the ground at my feet. I blink as a cloud of dust billows up around me when Johnny shifts the van into drive. From the front passenger seat, Ryder gives me a sympathetic "Them's the breaks" look.

I stare at the taillights as the tour van squeals onto the main road and chugs back toward the highway on-ramp.

My eyes burn. My chest pounds. And a streetlight flickers on.

I pull out my cell phone only to find there's no reception. Because of course there's not.

This pit stop is the absolute pits.

INTERLUDE

6StringJustice:

Someone got too big for his britches. IYKYK.

6StringJustice:

Pro tip—know when to trim the fat.

6StringJustice:

We're leaner, meaner, and our sound is much cleaner. Check out our new song!

TRACK 1

Back to My Roots

Paisley

JULY

THE FIRST FEW weeks of summer break pass in somber tones as I sink into myself. Picasso had his Blue Period. I guess this is mine. Most of the time, it feels like the only thing I'll ever successfully accomplish is soaking my pillow with tears of failure and frustration. But even that's growing old.

After my onstage meltdown, I returned home with a bruised ego, a broken heart, and only a week left before high school graduation. News of my disastrous performance had spread like wildfire, and it took all that I had left in me to pretend I didn't hear the whispers or see how everyone stared between me and their phones. Because of course someone in the audience was filming. Multiple someones. I did all I could to avoid the sympathetic looks from friends and the barely masked smirks of frenemies.

As the weeks went on, words and snippets of nebulous lyrics

raced through my mind, but I forced them away. Before the incident, I would have been racing to scrawl them in the margins of my physics notebook to be copied into my lyric book later. But not anymore.

Spring showers helped wash away some of my doom-and-gloom attitude, and now the summer sun is bringing wildflowers and new bud growth to the evergreens.

As Dad likes to say, "A little hard work never hurt anybody." And there's plenty of work to be found at Hidden Acres, even in the offseason. There are seeds to plant. Seedlings to transplant. Trimming and mowing and soil testing and fertilizing.

Unless it's thundering or pouring rain, my days are spent outside—the fresh air in my lungs replacing the lingering acrid scent of the ashes of my self-esteem. I work myself to exhaustion in the hopes that I'll fall into a dead sleep instead of lying in bed and staring up at the ceiling in the darkness of my room, unable to silence the what-ifs.

What if I hadn't crashed and burned at the concert?

What if I hadn't skipped out on graduation?

What if I hadn't deferred my acceptance to Tennessee State University?

(I'd wanted to drop out entirely, but Mom managed to convince me to press pause for a beat and take a gap year instead. "You shouldn't make any major decisions when you're sad or snacky," she'd said, wrapping me in a bear hug and handing me a Reese's peanut butter pumpkin left over from Halloween.)

All in all, I'm holding it together just fine.

Or as fine as can be expected, considering . . .

At least, that's what I tell myself as I hike back toward the farmhouse from the grove of Murray cypress I was tagging with different colors of plastic ribbon. Blue for trees less than three feet tall. Salmon for three- to four-footers. Orange, red, yellow, green, and white for the taller ones. The spools of soft flagging tape bump against each other in the canvas satchel at my hip. The scuff of my boots over the dirt adds a beat, and my brain starts filling in the rest of the song. A bass guitar comes in with a syncopated groove and then a driving riff from a rhythm guitar.

My fingers twitch as if looking for a guitar to strum. I swallow down the cottony lump building in my throat, suddenly in need of a cool glass of water. Or maybe something stronger, like Mom's fresh-squeezed mint lemonade.

I wrap my hand around the satchel's shoulder strap and stride toward the workshop. Though muffled, the music gets louder. Dad must be listening to the radio while repairing the old riding mower.

I pause in the doorway as the chorus of a Crosby, Stills & Nash song crackles from the tinny speakers of the old stereo that probably should have been scrapped for parts years ago. Dad's lying on a blanket on the cracked cement floor next to the mower, a raggedy red bandana wrapped around one hand and a socket wrench in the other. He hums along to the song with his soft baritone. The sound soothes me just like it did when I was younger, curled up in his lap with my ear pressed to his chest as he rocked me to sleep while humming "All the Pretty Horses" or "Blackbird."

"Hi, Dad. How's it going?"

Dad wipes his brow with the back of his arm and tilts his head toward me. "It's not," he says. He's got a smudge of grease on his chin. While his eyes are creased in frustration, there's a determined purse to his lips. "I think the bolt's stripped."

I've spent hours in the workshop with him: building things, repairing things, tearing things apart. I'm not particularly mechanical-minded, but I'm decent enough. A new song begins to play and I pause, listening to the solo drumbeat. My mouth hangs open as I'm about to volunteer to help, but all it takes is the three twangy chords when the guitar comes in to send my jaw slamming shut with such force, I practically see stars.

It's a Six String Justice song.

In an instant, I'm back on that stage, the bright lights blinding me. I can feel the heat of them on my face, burning my skin. My heart pounds as my memory conjures up the off-key notes I sang to mixed-up, mumbled lyrics. A memory I thought I'd lost but that has now reared its ugly head to haunt me.

It hurts to breathe in this musty, dusty workshop air. My legs wobble and I reach out and grab the door frame, my hands gripping it so tightly the weathered wood sends splinters into my palms. My heel slips off the threshold and I stumble back. The fresh air is like a slap to the face, jolting me out of the flashback. "I, uh . . . I gotta go."

Dad says something but I can't hear it over the pounding in my ears. I turn, the gravel crunching under my boots, and then I'm sprinting to the farmhouse.

My heart aches.

My throat's tight.

I'm pretty sure I'm spiraling.

As I pound up the stairs and collapse in a heap on my bed, I can't help wondering: Am I doomed to relive the worst moment of my life whenever I hear one of Six String Justice's songs?

A CROP OF FRECKLES has sprouted across the bridge of my nose, moving outward along my upper cheeks, in spite of the sunblock and hats I wear to shield my face from the sun. They remind me of constellations in the summer night sky. I brush my finger over a particularly large one that has a tail like a comet as if I could wipe it away. It makes me think of my older sister, Halley. Of course, she's named after the comet, and unlike me, she's bold and fierce. Unstoppable and unshakable. Halley left home for college at seventeen, and I'm not sure she's ever looked back. Just like Halley's Comet, she blazes into our lives periodically, each visit brief. A long weekend here, a holiday there.

My gaze goes to a set of clothbound journals on my bookshelf, each one wrapped in a different paisley print. I will inevitably get at least one paisley-themed gift for my birthday and Christmas, as if sharing the name with the design means that I'm a huge fan. I suppose I should be grateful I'm not Chevron or Gingham or Houndstooth. Instead, I was named Paisley for no other reason than Mom liked the word.

I suppose Paisley's a fitting name since my life feels a lot like a paisley pattern, swirls of teardrops and uncertainty. Though I've often been curious: How would things be if I was named Athena or Cassandra instead? Would I be bold and brave, holding my guitar onstage like a battle-ax? Or would I still be me, cowering behind my guitar the moment I step onstage?

My phone, which has been living at the bottom of my sock drawer lately, sits on my dresser, charged and ready for our scheduled call. As if she can tell I'm thinking about her, Halley texts.

Halley:

Grab your guitar. Karl's birthday FaceTime in 5.

My thumbs hover over the phone screen, about to type out a protest. I haven't so much as touched my guitar since May. The only reason it's even out of its case and propped in its stand is because Halley snuck into my room and put it there the last time she was home for a visit. There it sits, haunting me. Taunting me.

I reach out a tentative finger and brush it over the cool wooden body, leaving a trail in the thin layer of dust that's collected there. A faint tingle of anticipation skirts over my skin, but it's not powerful enough to dispel the anxiety that coils like a cobra in my gut. It used to be easy playing for my family, but now it feels anything but.

My phone buzzes with another incoming message.

Halley:

Don't make me drive home.

I can almost hear her lecturing me in her practiced bossy-pants voice.

"You're not the boss of me," I mumble, feeling like a little kid again. I guess no matter how old we get, I'll always be her little sister.

Still, my hand hovers near the neck of the guitar like it's the north pole and my arm is the magnetic needle of a compass, trying to guide my path forward.

Halley:

We're waiting.

It shouldn't be this hard. I shouldn't have to wage war with myself just to play "Happy Birthday" for our neighbor Karl, who's currently in an assisted living facility. Karl had a stroke last year, and while he still has trouble communicating, he responds well to music.

"For Karl," I say, like it's a battle cry. I suck in a deep breath and grab the guitar before I can talk myself out of it.

It's just one song. I can strum just one song.

Can't I?

TRACK 2

Ode to Oak Street

Kash

AUGUST

I'D ALWAYS IMAGINED my return to Nashville would be similar to a hero's welcome, coming on the heels of a wildly successful tour. My ego wasn't so blown up that I was expecting a mob of paparazzi or eager autograph-seekers, but I'd thought I'd get some recognition from strangers in Publix or an old teacher who'd have an "I remember when . . ." story. But here I am, stepping onto the shady, tree-lined curb on Oak Street, greeted only by the near silence of suburbia. Not even the USPS mail carrier glances over at me. This is nothing like I'd pictured.

From the first time I invited the guys to jam in the shed behind our old house, I'd known we were destined for something bigger. There we were, capturing lightning in a bottle with our music. It wasn't always easy, but it always felt right. Until it didn't.

The band was my idea.

The thought stabs me like a knife. If it wasn't for me, Six

String Justice wouldn't even exist. Maybe I should have fought harder to stay. Maybe I should have kicked Justin out of the band. Maybe I should have . . .

It doesn't matter. There's no going back now. My fingers clench into a tight fist.

It's not that *I'm* not good enough for the band. It's that *they're* not good enough for me. I don't need them. So what if I've returned to Nashville with nothing more than a ratty guitar case, a pair of worn-out boots, and all of twenty bucks in my wallet? Sure, my stubble's grown out and scratchy. My stomach's hollow from a diet of convenience store food. And my pride's taken a serious beating. But I've still got my guitar and the songs I've been working on. I've still got plenty of ambition and drive.

I'll show them.

I'll show everyone.

THE RIGHTEOUS FIRE IN my belly dies away the moment my boots scrape over the worn wooden steps that lead up to Granddad's front porch. It's bad enough I'm back in Nashville before I'd planned. It's even worse that I have no place to go. When Six String Justice started taking off, I had less and less time to chill with friends who weren't in the band. There are still a few guys who stuck around after graduation, but it's not like I can just text them to ask for a place to crash for a while.

Other options are limited. Dad's company transferred him to Austin last year, so he and Mom sold our house and moved to Texas. That meant I lost my bedroom and Six String Justice's practice shed. Luckily the band had just signed the deal with Wild Burro Records, and they hooked us up with a temporary apartment and rehearsal space until it was time for us to go on tour. At the time, I wasn't worried that I didn't have a home base to return to. That was a problem for future-Kash.

Thanks a lot, past-Kash.

A few months ago, I didn't dream any of this would happen. I was picturing packed auditoriums and sold-out gigs. Groupies and autograph signings. Heading into the studio to record some new stuff with the band. I thought I had plenty of time to figure out a living situation later. But later's already come and I'm out of time.

My knuckle connects with the wooden door, the glossy forest-green paint cool beneath my skin. *Knock, knock.*

I step away and take a deep breath.

Granddad's a cool guy, but he also sided with my parents whenever they tried to push me away from music toward "a more stable job" in corporate accounting. Like my dad, Granddad was in finance until he was forced into early retirement a few months ago. I'm not sure what's so stable about a job that leads to forced retirement or cross-country transfers. But then, who am I to talk? I just got punted in a fast-food parking lot by the band I founded.

The door swings open. Granddad gives a slow, surprised blink as he takes me in. While I probably look like I've hit rock bottom, Granddad looks like he's been living his best life. His salt-and-pepper hair is trimmed, he's clean shaven, and he's dressed in a pair of pressed khaki pants and a polo with toucans printed all over it. He looks like he just finished a round of golf at the local members-only country club.

"Hi, Granddad," I manage before I have to force a swallow down over the uncomfortable lump in my throat.

His lips press into a tight line for a moment; then he opens his mouth to speak. "You're a few months early, aren't you, sport? But then, you were never one to stick to someone else's schedule. You look hungry," Granddad says with a grunt.

"I could eat." With all the couch surfing I've been doing the past few weeks, it's been a while since I've had a home-cooked meal. Or anything resembling a square meal, for that matter, because I'm pretty sure soggy gas station hot dogs and blue raspberry Slurpees don't count.

Granddad steps back and motions me to follow him. "C'mon in, then."

I heave a relieved sigh. While I hadn't expected Granddad to turn me away, I've lost trust in the people I thought I could count on most. Shouldn't I have known that the guys I considered my band of brothers were nothing more than a bunch of good-for-nothing backstabbers? All the blood, sweat, and tears I put in to the band. And to have it just tossed away, as if I hadn't played an integral part in getting them—getting us—a deal with Wild Burro Records.

My teeth gnash together and I force myself to take a deep breath. The whole experience has messed me up. Will I ever be able to trust anyone else again?

In the entryway, I kick off my boots so I don't track miles of disappointment into the house. Before I can set down my guitar and suitcase, Granddad says, "Take it upstairs. Don't want all that stuff cluttering up my front hall like this is a bed-and-breakfast."

The guest room's on the second floor, tucked in between

Granddad's office and the upstairs bathroom. The large multi-paned window overlooks a small backyard where Granny used to grow roses before dementia took her away. The garden is wild now, reclaimed by nature, but still full of lush green plants dotted with bright pops of color.

I'm not prepared for the grief that kicks me in the gut. Granny's been gone for years, but with everything else going on with me, the loss feels as fresh as if it were yesterday.

"Soup's on," Granddad hollers up from the kitchen.

I blink away unshed tears. *Pull it together, Kash.*

"Be right down," I call back.

After washing my hands and splashing some water on my face to rinse off the travel grime, I head downstairs. The savory scent of ground beef, spicy peppers, and earthy spices greets me by the time my foot hits the bottom tread, and I follow it to the kitchen like a tracking dog. Granddad sets a steaming bowl of chili on the place mat where I usually sit. He turns back to the Crock-Pot on the counter and dishes some out for himself.

"I hadn't planned on company, so it's nothin' fancy," he says.

This is practically five-star cuisine, as far as I'm concerned.

"It looks great," I say, digging in.

Our spoons clank against the sides of our bowls as we eat. After a few minutes, Granddad sets his spoon down and sits back in his chair. "You gonna tell me what happened?"

Fortified by comfort food and familiar surroundings, I take a deep breath and lay it all out for him. Granddad listens without interrupting, keeping his expression neutral. When I finish, I slump back into my seat, as exhausted as if I had just finished playing a two-hour set.

There's a short pause, and then he says, "Well, that sucks."

I'm not sure what I expected him to say, but that wasn't it. Talk about the understatement of the century. Our eyes meet, and suddenly I burst out laughing. All the emotions that have been building up in me boil over, and I let them out until my stomach hurts and tears stream down my face. Granddad joins in and soon we're both roaring with laughter and fighting for air.

It takes a few minutes for us to be able to look at each other without breaking out into another fit of laughter. My sides are sore, my eyes are red, but I feel lighter than I have in weeks. I still have a lot to unpack, but maybe I'm not carrying as much baggage as I thought I was.

I push the chair back and stand to collect our dirty dishes. When I lift my bowl from the table, there's a house key lying underneath it. When I was little, Granny used to leave little treats under my plate for me to discover after a meal. Usually it was a five-dollar bill, but sometimes it would be a new guitar pick or a gift card to our favorite ice cream shop. I glance up at Granddad, my eyes growing watery at the memories.

"You can stay as long as you'd like," he says, his voice rough with emotion.

"SO, WHAT'S NEXT?" GRANDDAD asks.

"I dunno." I shrug and toss the damp sponge into the sink. "I'm waiting for my manager to call me back. I think he's still my manager? But as far as Six String Justice is concerned, I'm done."

Granddad reaches out and gives my shoulder a squeeze. "Sometimes you have to find your own way."

"I guess I'll have to get a job."

Not just any job, Mom's voice whispers in my head. *A stable job.*

Now I can't help but wonder if pursuing a career in music *was* really the mistake my parents warned me it would be. They'd pressed me to apply to Haslam College at the University of Tennessee so I could get a degree in accounting.

Just like Granddad.

Just like Dad.

I'd promised to fill out the online application. And I had. Thing is, I never promised I'd submit it. Which I hadn't.

If I'd applied and been accepted, there's a good chance Mom and Dad would've convinced me to quit the band before we got the offer from Wild Burro Records. I'd probably be sleeping through Accounting 101 right now instead of watching my music career spin out before it even hit the racetrack. I'm not sure which is worse.

My pointer finger traces along the beveled edge of the counter. "I'll have to call Mom and Dad and tell them they were right." I cringe as a bitter taste fills my mouth.

Granddad frowns. "Right about what?"

"Oh, you know," I say, crossing over to the table and sinking back down into the kitchen chair with a weary sigh. "Music is a creative outlet, not a career. If I don't go to college, I'll regret it. I'm throwing my future away for an unrealistic pipe dream."

Granddad takes his seat across from me, his graying eyebrows furrowed. "You know, I never thought you had the makings of a good accountant."

"No?" I glance up into his earnest brown eyes. He's never said anything about it before, despite numerous opportunities.

He shakes his head, the edge of his mouth tipping up into a subdued smile. "When your dad was a kid, he was always counting his pennies. I knew right then he'd end up an accountant like me. But you?" He gives a short bark of a laugh. "You'd take your allowance right down to the corner store, pick out your snacks, and hand your money over, hoping you had enough to cover the cost."

"Yeah, that tracks." Math has never been a strength of mine, and I sit with this a minute. I've gotten better with the concept of money since then, but I still hired one of Granddad's old colleagues to handle my accounting as soon as I started earning money. "Why didn't you try to stop them from pressuring me?" It's hard to keep the frustration out of my voice. Years of arguments over what my parents wanted versus what I wanted might have left me feeling less on my own if I'd known Granddad was on my side.

Granddad rubs the backs of his knuckles. "It wasn't my place. I'd already raised your father; it was his turn to raise you. To be fair, your parents are doing their best. They only want what's best for you." He narrows his eyes at me. "But I don't know," he says after a beat. "Maybe they were right. Maybe music *is* just a creative outlet for you."

My jaw tightens. "So you think being a musician's a stupid career choice, too?" I try to keep my voice even, but I can't quite mask the acid that burns the back of my throat.

"I didn't say that," Granddad says. "But here's the thing you need to consider." He holds my gaze for a moment until he's sure I'm paying attention. "Is music your passion? Are you willing to do whatever it takes to get where you want to be? Or is it just a creative outlet? It's okay if it is," he says, holding his hands up. "Hobbies are important. But if music's more than a pastime . . . if being a working musician is what you really want . . . then you can't let any of *this* be what stops you."

He's right. I know he is. And I can't let what happened with Six String Justice derail my dreams completely. I want to be a musician. I really do. But what am I supposed to do now?

Granddad interrupts my thoughts. "If you want to get a job, get a job. But if you want to be a musician, you gotta find a way. Life's too short for what-ifs, sport." He stands up and strides over to the pantry. "What you need right now is a good, old-fashioned MoonPie."

TRACK 3

Feelings to Fall Into

Paisley

OCTOBER 31

"HOPE TO HAVE you back again next year," I tell Lorna as I take the bronze key attached to a carved wooden eighth-note key chain from her outstretched hand.

"Sure thing, sugar," she says with a gleaming grin. Lorna's short brown curls frame her face, and without her layers of makeup and teased, bleached-blond wigs, she hardly resembles Dolly Parton. In fact, you'd never know just by looking at her that she's one of the most popular Dolly impersonators in the Nashville area.

A fabulous singer in her own right, Lorna Meade is one of the most talented musicians to spend time at the Hideaway at Hidden Acres Christmas Tree Farm. She and her husband, Dave, are two local Nashville musicians who reserve the studio and the home-away-from-home cabin next door for a week to celebrate their anniversary. Every year for as long as I can remember, they've spent the last seven days of October hiking around the farm and recording songs.

One year, Lorna brought a bunch of her old costumes and Dolly-ed me up for Halloween. Out here in the boonies, there's nowhere to trick-or-treat, so Mom and Dad, Lorna and Dave, and Halley and I piled into the farm's old delivery van and went into town for the night. I felt so bold when I stepped out onto Main Street, hidden beneath a face full of makeup and decked out in rhinestone-covered clothes. Clutching my kid-sized acoustic guitar in one hand and an old milk pail in the other, I wanted nothing more than to fill my bucket with enough sugary treats to last me until Christmas.

The dented milk pail was about halfway full by the time we made it to the corner of Main and State. That's where we ran into Mr. Barker, a Halloween legend. Mr. Barker always handed out giant candy bars from the front stoop of his hardware store, making his place a must-stop along our trick-or-treat route.

"Evenin,' Miss Dolly," he said, tipping his pirate hat to me with his silver hook. Instead of a fearsome seafarer, Mr. Barker's character was jolly.

"Trick or treat, Mr. Barker," I said, grinning up at him as I held out my milk pail.

He pulled a candy bar from his bowl, but instead of handing it over like usual, he said, "How about a song for a Snickers?"

Aside from guitar lessons and a few friends-and-family gatherings, I'd never played in front of anyone before. Just thinking about people watching me try to remember the chords and strumming patterns sent a pang of unease through me. Beneath the layers of foundation, blush, and copious amounts of eye shadow, I felt my face grow warm and red.

Dad placed a reassuring hand on my shoulder and gave it a comforting squeeze. "Show 'em what you got, Paisley."

"I dunno," I said, stepping back against my father as if I could melt into him and disappear.

"Why don't you play 'Jolene'?" Mom gave a nod of encouragement.

Lorna winked at me and Dave gave me a thumbs-up.

My nerves vibrated like the chainsaw Dad used to cut firewood.

Just thinking about it has my pulse racing like a frantic metronome now.

"You gonna come on down to the city for a duet at one of my shows?" Lorna asks with a glimmer in her eye. She's been trying to get me to join her onstage, for what she thinks will be a "real hoot."

I blink away memories of my first real showdown with stage fright and offer up a weak smile. "Maybe," I mumble half-heartedly.

In reality, there's absolutely no way I'd risk it. Tanking my last show was bad enough, but I couldn't do that to Lorna. Or to Dolly.

"It would be so much fun," she continues, apparently oblivious to my discomfort.

Lorna might have witnessed my one and only attempt at busking when I was eight, but she wasn't in the audience this past spring, when I crashed and burned onstage at eighteen. I have zero desire to put myself back in the spotlight ever again.

Especially not now that I've settled into the quieter, safer Christmas tree farm kind of life.

I peer out the window at the gently sloping, tree-studded hills that surround our farmhouse. The breeze sends fading maple leaves swirling across the ground. I have everything I need here, in my own little hideaway at Hidden Acres.

Lorna wraps me in a tight hug, her signature floral scent surrounding us in a comforting cloud, and squeezes me extra close for good measure. "Stay sweet, sugar," she says, squashing all the air out of me. An air-kiss dusts my cheek.

Before I can even catch my breath to reply, Lorna's bounding out the door in bedazzled Keds. The storm door creaks shut behind her, and I watch through the screen as she hoists herself into Dave's old Chevy pickup. The engine rumbles a deep bass, and then they're bumping down the potholed dirt driveway on their way back to Nashville.

When their taillights disappear behind a thicket of American arborvitae at the bend in the road, I inhale deeply and breathe out a sigh of relief. While I'm always sad to see the Meades go, I savor the rare quiet moment. It's the calm before the Christmas storm, with only a few weeks left before the tree lot opens for the season.

Between planting seedlings, shaping trees, and monitoring for pests and disease, there's always something happening on the farm. Things ramp up considerably in the weeks before Christmas. There's still plenty of prep work to do, but now that the last reservation for the Hideaway is over for the year, I can have the studio to myself. No one needs to know I'm working on anything.

The bright lights of Nashville might be meant for Lorna. But it turns out, anonymity is my jam.

HIDDEN ACRES IS MANY things:

A homestead.

A Christmas tree farm.

A reindeer rescue.

And, for the past few months, my refuge.

I've spent most of my free time holed up in the barn loft or the Hideaway. Writing music for myself. Recording instrumental jingles for local businesses. These are the things that fit perfectly into my comfort zone. Who needs center stage when you can be front and center with an old Neotek Elan 28 inline studio console or a digital audio workstation?

And here, in the Hideaway's recording studio, I can do exactly that—hide away. I slide on the studio monitor headphones, plug in my guitar, and lose myself in the music that's just for me. Behind thick, padded walls, I don't need to perform or be perfect. I can just be.

I've definitely needed the quiet solitude of the Hideaway. After strumming "Happy Birthday" for Karl at Halley's insistence, it was impossible to resist the siren song of my guitar. I've found comfort in the soft acoustic reverberations. Still, my lyric notebook sits on the corner of my desk, taunting me whenever I look at it. And when I do, the spiral of doubt builds inside me until it hurts to breathe.

But even so, I couldn't keep the melodies at bay. They crept up on me when I was trimming trees, gliding over the *snip-snip-snip* of the pruners until I found myself humming along. They filtered in on the breeze that rattled the tree branches and whispered through the field grass, sending my fingers tapping a beat on my thigh as I hiked up to the ridge to survey the groves. They echoed along with the cool autumn rain pattering against the farmhouse's metal roof, dripping with syncopated lyrics that begged to be written.

As I was swatting at mosquitos a few weeks ago while checking trees for aphids, a new jingle for the tree farm came to me.

Hidden Acres Christmas trees are sure to be . . .

The very best trees in Tennessee.

Sure, it's not big or splashy, but it's something.

Something I've been desperately trying to ignore.

But earworms, like pesky tree-killing bagworms, are persistent little buggers. I read somewhere that the most tenacious earworms can last up to a year.

I believe it.

And I just know this earworm won't let me go until I write and record it, even if the last thing I want to do is put myself back in front of a microphone again . . . audience or no audience.

I've put it off as long as possible, but I can't do it anymore. Grudgingly, I tap out the jingle on the Yamaha portable digital grand piano just to get a little peace and quiet.

It starts small, with that jingle.

But the peace and quiet don't last.

Twenty acres of tree farm and even that's not enough space for me to hide from the melodies and harmonies that continuously pop up, so insistent that I pay attention. Just like I have no control over my dimples or slight widow's peak, writing music seems to be in my DNA.

TODAY'S RECORDING SESSION'S BEEN productive. I've managed to get most of the percussion finished, so the only thing left to do is record a jingle bell track. I reach for an old sleigh bell strap from the hook in the instrument storage cabinet. The tooled leather's worn from years of use. The metal is dull and dented, but the sound is bright and cheery, conjuring up visions of the season's first fluffy snowflakes and jolly old Saint Nick driving his sleigh.

Which reminds me . . .

I glance up at the wall clock and sigh. The reindeer are waiting for dinner and it's my turn to feed them.

Giving the sleigh bells a little shake, I put them away and power off all the recording equipment. I should be able to finish up the tree farm jingle tomorrow, and then I can check one more item off my holiday prep to-do list.

Cool air glides over my skin when I step outside, and I wish I'd thought to grab a sweater before I headed over to the Hideaway.

Thankfully, most of the buildings are grouped together in the southeast corner of our property, so it doesn't take long to make my way from the studio to the stable. Twilight darkens the clear blue sky, and the birds are busy with their evening songs. My eyes track the flight of a northern mockingbird, and I pause as it alights on a tree branch above me. It whistles a short song that sounds a lot like the earworm I had last week, and it makes me wonder if I taught it the melody or if it taught it to me.

Feeling playful, I whistle back. The mockingbird cocks its head at me and ruffles its feathers, but it doesn't fly away in horror, so I guess that's something. Maybe I only perform terribly for humans.

Dunder and Blixem must have heard me whistle. They rush over in a flurry of hooves and happy grunts to meet me at the corral gate.

"Good afternoon, ladies," I say, giving each one a muzzle rub.

Their names come from the original published version of C. C. Moore's "A Visit from St. Nicholas." Dunder is slightly shorter and grayer than her sister, Blixem, but what she lacks in height, she makes up for in spunk and a stubborn streak. As I step into the enclosure, Dunder nuzzles into my side, sniffing my pockets to see if I've brought a handful of moss for them as a treat.

"No dessert until you've finished your dinner," I say, sounding a bit too much like my mom.

Blixem, the taller, tanner reindeer of the pair, snorts and gives me a judgmental side-eye.

"You're right," I agree. "I need to loosen up."

I stifle a shiver and scratch Blixem under her chin. A jealous Dunder knocks her antlers into her sister's. They remind me a lot of me and Halley when we were younger, always vying for our parents' attention.

As I head into the barn to get reindeer feed, my fingers automatically glide over the beaded friendship bracelet I'm wearing today, the message inspired by Sara Bareilles: REWRITE THE LINES.

I have at least one bracelet for every mood, outfit, and occasion. I suppose they're my version of worry beads or a worry doll or whatever worry talisman people use to get over their fears and make things happen. My beaded bracelets are meant to inspire, encourage, and remind me that I'm part of a sisterhood of songwriters.

Only problem is, I'm not sure the bracelets are working.

TRACK 4

Blank Page Malady

Kash

NOVEMBER 1

I'VE GOT A blank page.

Actually, a whole legal pad full of 'em. And they're taunting me relentlessly.

One day . . .

Two days . . .

Three days . . .

Four.

I'm not sure how long I've been staring at the college-ruled yellow sheet of paper in front of me. Long enough, that's for damn sure.

Long enough that I can still see the red margin lines slicing across the black writing lines when I close my eyes.

Long enough that I've dreamed about them in my sleep.

And still, I've got nothing more than a few crumpled-up wads of paper from failed attempts and an unfortunate coffee spill.

The uppermost page remains blank and time marches on, bringing me closer and closer to a deadline that will make or break what's left of my music career. It's not looking good.

A few months ago, I couldn't stop random riffs and bits of melody from living rent free in my mind. Now I'm lucky to hear the buzzing of a neon vacancy sign in the empty vastness that remains.

Writer's block is the absolute worst.

Tick, tick, tick, tick.

Granddad's old kitchen clock reminds me I'm running out of time. The kitchen chair squeaks when I lean back and toss my hands up in frustration. This shouldn't be so hard. When I signed the solo artist deal with Exit 12S Records in September, I was elated. My luck was finally turning around. But now I wonder if I've signed on for a fresh new round of hell. How many times will I be *thisclose* to my dream, only to have it ripped away before I can grasp it?

The ticking clock is going to drive me bonkers. Guitar in hand, I head to the back porch. Fresh air might do me some good. Settling into my usual chair, I survey the yard. Granny's coneflowers are in bloom and are buzzing with bees and the occasional butterfly. The butterfly weed in the corner has really taken off since I moved in.

I'd spent the first few days here moping around and feeling sorry for myself. But after an "it's time to get your act together" pep talk/ultimatum from Granddad, I got off my ass and started playing as a solo act at open mics all over Nashville. If there was an opportunity to perform, I was there. Coffee shops, honky-tonks, in-the-round sessions, karaoke. I even spent a day busking in Printers Alley.

I'd been honing my chops, doing my best to show the music world I'm not done yet. Mostly I was playing stripped-down versions of country-rock classics by Creedence Clearwater Revival and the Eagles, intermixed with old songs I'd written for Six String Justice. I even tested out a few different versions of that song I'd pitched in the van that fateful night of my dismissal.

And then, one hazy, hot, and humid afternoon, Barry Winslow showed up.

Barry's a well-known talent scout who's been on the Nashville music scene for ages. Before a heart attack forced him into semiretirement, he was affectionately known as the "One in a Billion Bloodhound" for being able to sniff out a star on the cusp of an epic rise.

Like a man that time forgot, Barry wears his black hair swept up into a pompadour and pairs it with thick sideburns. On some guys, it would look sketchy, but on Barry, it works. And somehow, he still manages to get lost in the crowd until he wants his presence to be known.

A few years back, he'd popped into a Battle of the Bands event during a Six String Justice set. He'd just gotten out of the hospital and wasn't actively looking to sign anyone new. I'd barely hopped offstage when he pulled me aside and said, "You got skills, kid, but you're still finding your groove. I'll see you around." At the time, I was still too green to know who he was or what it might mean that Barry Winslow shook my hand.

In August, we ran into each other again at the Dusty Boot Bar and Grill, a small establishment patronized mostly by Nashville locals. Known for its hot chicken and cold drinks, it's popular with starving artists for offering up a free meal to any musician who plays a full fifteen-minute set. The waitlist is long, but I was hungry for an opportunity to play (and for a fried chicken sandwich), so I kept submitting my name for a chance in the lineup. Finally, I got the call.

"Your set's at 3:45. Three-forty-five. You have a fifteen-minute limit. Don't be late."

I arrived early and played my heart out. I had no idea Barry was there until he came up to me after my set. By that time, my mouth was full of chicken and my hand was coated in hot sauce.

"Hey, kid, remember me?" He pulled out the seat across from me and sank into it like he was an old friend meeting me for a late lunch.

I nodded like a bobblehead as I tried to swallow the hunk of chicken in my mouth. No one forgets Barry Freakin' Winslow. But the fact that he remembered me? My mind was blown.

"Have you written any new stuff lately?" Barry clasped his hands in front of him on the table like we were sitting in his office and not at a wobbly table at the Dusty Boot.

"Some," I managed to reply after taking a giant swig of sweet tea.

Barry studied me for a moment. "You been playing any of it?"

Um, no. Most of the crap I'd come up with since my return to Nashville would have gotten me booed offstage. Sure, country music is full of the "lost my dog, lost my car, lost my wife" sad songs, but my version—where I'd lost my band and been backstabbed by guys I thought were my bros—was just too pathetic. It was safer to stick with old standards and the early Six String Justice songs I knew by heart.

"Not really," I admitted. I wiped hot sauce from my fingers onto a paper napkin, wishing I could wipe away some of my discomfort, too.

Barry pressed his palms down on the table and stood. "I gotta think about it."

Think about what? I hadn't asked him for anything. He'd approached me, after all.

Bottles clanked and forks scraped over plates, and it felt like I was supposed to say something back to him. "Okay?"

"Look, kid," he said, leaning closer as he pushed his chair in. "Covering old songs is great. But it's not going to get you where you want to go. My advice: Work on some new stuff. Find your musical voice."

So I tried. I worked on pathetic breakup songs. I tried my hand at a country-rock anthem. The attempts went all cattywampus. At the end of the day, I was more comfortable performing covers than originals. It didn't help that Justin's version of *my* song was gaining traction.

But it was *his* version, and that gave me pause. Was he right about my songwriting? Was my stuff not hit material?

Barry kept popping up where I was playing. Open mics led to short-set opportunities to open for better-known local acts. Soon I was playing gigs that required original compositions. All my stuff sucked, but at least I was trying.

After a show at the Drowsy Cow one night, Barry came up to me and said, "Okay, kid. I've made up my mind. Today's your lucky day."

Everything after that was a blur. Exit 12S Records offered me a recording deal for a solo EP. All they needed were six original songs by December 31, and as soon as I signed, I got a small advance to make it happen. I was back to being a legitimate paid musician again.

Much to my father's disappointment, I'm sure, given that I'm still not an accountant. But I did the math and the math looked good. Real good.

Six songs in four months = one and a half songs per month = easy peasy.

I inked the deal in a heartbeat, ready to take Nashville by storm.

Except . . .

All those songs I've been dreaming about, all the memorable, catchy lyrics I've been conjuring up, all the stuff that's wanted to pour out of me for months now seemed to vanish before the ink on the contract was even dry.

Now here I am, staring at the same blank page watching the minutes tick by, and I am totally, absolutely, monumentally screwed. I have until December 31 to deliver an album demo and I have zilch.

Nada.

Nothing.

Well, maybe not nothing. I have a lot of crap and that one semi-decent song from the van that sounds nothing like the song Justin created from it.

My hands ball into fists. If that song wasn't good enough for Six String Justice, what makes me think it'll be good enough for Exit 12S Records?

As if he can sense trouble brewing across town, my cell phone lights up with a call from Barry. "Hey, kid," he says in his reedy, raspy voice. I'm pretty sure he knows my name, but I'm not sure he's ever actually used it. "How's the songwriting going?"

I gulp down an uncomfortable swallow. "Good. Great." The lie is as hollow as the body of the acoustic guitar in my lap.

"That so?" Barry says in a way that lets me know he's not buying what I'm selling. "I don't want to add any more pressure, kid, but we need you to deliver."

He makes it sound so simple, like the label's expecting me to drop off an extra-large pepperoni pizza with a side of garlic bread and not six solid songs fit for radio play.

"I, uh . . ." I squirm and run my fingernail around the edge of the pick guard. Should I try to convince him that I can still deliver, or should I go ahead and admit defeat? When I signed the agreement, I was full of ideas and something to prove. Now I'm just a has-been musician mooching off my grandfather, a hop, skip, and a jump away from being a complete washout.

"Lemme guess. You have a case of writer's block." He sounds unconcerned and there's not even the slightest hint of judgment that I have nothing to show for the passage of two months' time.

"You could say that." Admitting it relieves a bit of the pressure that's been steadily building inside, but it doesn't stop me from feeling like the biggest loser in Tennessee.

"It happens to every songwriter," Barry says. "Even Willie Nelson said so. Did you ever read that book of his?" He doesn't wait for me to answer. "He said—and I'm paraphrasing here—'the secret to getting over writer's block is to wait.' Now, Willy's an icon, so he knows what's what for sure, but unfortunately for you, kid, you aren't Willie. You don't have time to wait."

Tell me something I don't already know, Barry.

My body tenses, bracing for impact. This is it. This is where Barry's going to tell me that the label's changed its mind. That they made a mistake. That they're headed in a different direction. That it's time to part ways.

That I owe them money.

I'm sitting in a wicker rocking chair on the back porch at Granddad's place, but I might as well be standing in a fast-food parking lot watching the tour van drive away. I'm about to get axed all over again.

"You still there, kid?"

I blink and mumble, "Yeah."

"Good," Barry says. "So, here's the deal. Exit 12S's publishing arm recently signed a local songwriter to do some for-hire work. I think the two of you should work together to write your demos. She helps you. You help her. Exit 12S gets the demo on time. It's a win-win-win for everyone involved."

Is it, though?

It was hard enough working with a bunch of guys I grew up with, and I'd known them forever. Does Barry really expect me to form some kind of insta-trust with a random songwriter I've never met?

Barry must sense my hesitation, because he goes into sales mode. "She's eager to be a working songwriter, and she's been building some real buzz. A few awards and accolades." He pauses as if to consider what he's about to say next. "Some attention on social media earlier this year. But you two shouldn't have any trouble working together."

"Oh."

"It'll go like this," Barry says. "Tomorrow, you'll head up to this farm about a half hour, forty-five minutes from Nashville.

It's an out-of-the-way place with a recording studio, so you shouldn't be too distracted to work. The label's rented out the neighboring apartment for the rest of the year, so you have a place to stay while you're songwriting. You can work with her a little or a lot. That part's up to you."

Even so, I'm not sure I can get on board with this. Can I really put my music career in someone else's hands again? Shouldn't I be able to do this on my own?

"I don't know what to say."

"Look, kid," Barry says, his tone going serious. "This call is really just a formality. I'm asking you, but I'm not really asking you. Catch my drift?"

Here it is. The line in the sand. If I say yes and step up, I'll still have a shot of making it happen. I could write the songs and get the demo turned in. But if I say no, I'll sure as hell watch another opportunity get away from me.

I close my eyes and see the red taillights of the van leaving me in a cloud of dust.

"Any other questions?" Barry asks.

Yeah, I think as my fingers curl around the guitar pick in my hand. *What the hell have I just gotten myself into?*

TRACK 5

Imperfect Strangers

Paisley

NOVEMBER 1

"HIDDEN ACRES CHRISTMAS Tree Farm," I say after picking up the receiver and tucking it between my shoulder and ear. The smooth, heavy plastic is cold against my skin and I stifle a shiver as I reach for the memo pad we use to mark down Christmas tree and wreath orders.

Mom and Dad insist on keeping the old wall-mount rotary phone, an artifact from the past that probably should have retired with the previous farm owners. It's not as old as the farmhouse—at least, I don't think they had phones back when it was built—but it's definitely an antique, with its yellowing ivory case and perpetually tangled coiled handset cord.

It's not that we don't all have cell phones or get bad cell service out here or anything. Mom's phone is always tucked into a pocket, and Dad likes to wear his in an indestructible case on a belt clip. Right now, my cell phone's upstairs in my sock drawer, where it's spent most of its time lately.

While videos of my disastrous performance initially only went viral at school, spreading like a bad case of the stomach flu, my embarrassment was mostly contained to the greater Nashville area. At least, it was until my nemesis, Seth Carpenter, got it into his head that it would be a great idea to create a bunch of remixes and heavily edited clips of the worst day of my life. He posts a new version every so often, as if he thinks I need a regular reminder of my failure.

Seth and I have had an academic rival relationship going all the way back to elementary school, but he's really had it out for me ever since seventh grade, when my science fair project on the effect of country music on the growth rate of Norway spruce seedlings took third place in the district, narrowly defeating (by two points) his project on 3D-printed optical illusions, garnering him honorable mention and preventing him from moving on to the Robertson County competition.

Now I'm a meme.

And it seems like I'm getting tagged in every post and group chat whenever another video drops. Every time a notification pops up on-screen, it feels like I've just been zapped by an electric fence.

I think it was Oscar Wilde who said, "There is only one thing in the world worse than being talked about, and that is not being talked about." No offense to Oscar, but he's wrong. In the modern, internet-powered world, being talked about can be brutal. And once something is online, it has the nasty ability to haunt you forever. I just can't with it anymore.

It doesn't help that Mom and Dad refuse to cancel my cell phone plan because "this too shall pass" and "we need a way to get ahold of you when you're out and about."

Not only is that *super helpful*, but I have zero desire to ever leave the farm again.

Yo ho, yo ho, a hermit's life for me.

In fairness, I don't think they're torturing me on purpose. Mom and Dad also refuse to cancel our landline, even though Halley and I have been trying to persuade them to get rid of it for years now. They insist on having a backup just in case the local cell towers go down in an ice storm or some other unexpected crisis hits.

"Like . . . an emergency Christmas tree order?" I once asked, before pretending to make a call. "Hello, Hidden Acres Christmas Tree Farm? We're going to need a six-foot white pine over here, stat."

Halley laughed so hard, milk shot out her nose.

I suppose I can see their point. It can't hurt to keep the landline just in case. The number's been used in countless advertisements for the tree farm over the past fifty years or so. Some of our most die-hard Christmas tree customers probably have the number memorized. In fact, I wouldn't be surprised if Mrs. Larson, our local octogenarian and oldest customer (literally), has it on speed dial. She calls us at least four times between Halloween and Thanksgiving to make sure we have a tree reserved for her.

I blink away my thoughts and continue answering the phone the way Dad drilled into me when I was a kid. "This is Paisley speaking."

A scratchy, baritone voice from the other end of the line says, "Paisley. Just the person I'm looking for."

Me?

It takes me a second to place the voice, and when I do, the

pen I'm holding at the ready drops to the memo pad with a dull *thwack*.

"Barry," I say, my mouth going suddenly dry.

My skin gets cold and clammy, just like it does before I'm about to vomit . . . or step onstage. It's been a while since Barry and I last spoke, not since before *before*.

Way back in March—what feels like a whole lifetime ago—I signed an agreement with Exit 12S Records Publishing to write five country songs on an as-needed basis. This was right after I was crowned Tennessee's Songwriter of the Year. (I wasn't actually crowned, but I did get a star-shaped crystal trophy, which I guess is sort of the same thing.)

I never expected to hear from Barry again after my tanked performance in May. I guess I kind of figured my contract with Exit 12S would either be canceled or they would ghost me. As more time passed and I didn't hear anything, I figured maybe they forgot about me. The agreement was a payment-on-acceptance deal, so it's not like they were out any money, and I didn't have a timeline attached to deliver any songs.

My heart skips a beat, and not in that good, excited, just-saw-that-special-someone kind of way. This is more like the beat-skipping that happens just after you lose your footing on black ice, in that split second before your tailbone cracks against the cold, rock-solid ground.

I drop onto the cushioned stool at the kitchen counter, grabbing hold of the phone cradled against my ear so it doesn't fall. My fingers wrap around the plastic.

Why's Barry calling me now?

I bet it has something to do with that stupid mash-up video Seth made last week, where my head's been replaced by a cat head wearing sunglasses. Because yes, I did sound like a cat being dunked in a bathtub in the video. No creative editing required there.

I stifle a groan. Has Exit 12S finally decided to give me the ax? Are my dreams of being a successful songwriter about to be crushed completely? If only I'd never stepped foot on that stage. One bad decision and look where it's gotten me.

I sit up straight and brace myself for the bad news.

"How the heck are you, kid?" Barry says like we're old friends catching up. Like he doesn't know what a flop I am. Or that I'm still reeling.

My heart races like a cornered animal. I wipe a sweaty palm over my thigh and force myself to release the death grip I have on the phone.

"Did you change your number? You haven't been answering my calls," he says.

Wait, what calls?

"Sorry," I manage to warble as my mind spins with worry and worst-case scenarios. I force down a swallow over my desert-dry throat. "I, uh, didn't hear my cell phone ring."

Technically, that's true, given that the ringer's off and the phone's been shoved into a fuzzy green Grinch sock and buried at the bottom of my sock drawer for the past few days. I'm not even sure it has any battery left.

Barry grunts and then says, "Busy time on the farm, I imagine, with the holidays coming up. Hard to believe it's already November. The year's really flown by."

Has it, though?

"Yeah," I say, but not with much conviction. The past few months have felt like the longest decade of my life.

"Anyhow," he continues without missing a beat, "I've got a bit of a situation over here, and I'm hoping you could help me out."

"Uh . . . maybe?" I coil the phone cord around my pointer finger as my stomach twists and turns into a heavy knot like a string of Christmas tree lights that've been haphazardly shoved into a box.

"Okay. Here's the deal, kid," Barry says. "I signed this country musician a couple months ago. He's got the talent. He's got the looks. And," Barry sighs, "he's got a bad case of writer's block and a looming deadline."

"Oh," I say to fill the silence that follows.

Barry sighs harder this time. "Look, I've got corporate breathing down my neck. Our flagship artist is in rehab, Donnie and Marlene are in the midst of a bitter divorce, and Macy McRae is about to have her baby. Normally, we'd give Murray an extension to make music magic happen, seeing as how he's new to this solo-artist thing, but we need to kick off the new year with a strong new talent." Barry pauses. "Which is where you come in."

"Me?" My eyebrows lift.

"You wanna be a professional songwriter, right? Well, this is your chance to show us—show the world—what you really got. And you don't even have to do it alone. Help Murray write some original songs for his demo by the end of the year, and we'll double your contracted rate per song."

Wow, I *did not* expect that.

"How many songs?" I ask.

"He owes us six. But you two can decide how many to co-write together."

Six original songs?

I stand and the floor is cool beneath my feet. My pulse kicks up again as temptation whispers to me while I pace around the kitchen. I want to say yes. I want to realize my dream of being a legitimate working songwriter. I want to join the ranks of other incredible women who've inspired me over the years: Carole. Dolly. Taylor. Lucinda.

"The label's already rented out the Hideaway apartment and studio space. Murray will be there tomorrow to start working on his demo." Barry cuts into my thoughts. "I'd feel a whole lot better about it if he had some help. So, what do you say, kid?"

It's on the tip of my tongue to say yes. But then that good ol' self-doubt rears its ugly head and whispers, *What if you screw up again?*

My reflection in the windowpane over the kitchen sink stares back at me. The way the phone is tucked between my chin and shoulder, it looks like I'm tethered to this spot. Or maybe anchored is more like it.

I glance down at my DO IT LIKE DOLLY bracelet, the gold-stamped letters glittering up at me from pastel beads.

Dolly Parton once said, "You'll never do a whole lot unless you're brave enough to try." There's no doubt in my mind that, presented with this exact opportunity, she would primp her hair, give a sharp, decisive nod, and say in her perky drawl, "Okay." And then she'd wake up the next morning and write two hit songs before breakfast.

Could I ever write songs as epic as "Jolene" and "I Will Always Love You" in my lifetime, let alone on the same day?

Dolly did it.

I glance back at my reflection in the window.

Do it like Dolly.

Be brave enough to try.

I toss my wavy, dark auburn hair. Give my reflection a slight, not quite decisive nod. I'm no Dolly Parton, but . . . "I guess I can try," I say as if I'm attempting to convince myself. While the tone of my answer inspires zero confidence, Barry doesn't seem to mind.

"That's all I'm asking for, kid." There's a loud smack followed by a muffled noise, like Barry's clapped his hands and is rubbing them together like he just won the jackpot. "And, hey, no pressure, but if you help Murray finish even one original song, I'll make sure you're the go-to in-house songwriter for Exit 12S Records. You and Murray come up with a hit single? The sky's the limit. This opportunity here is what they call a career-maker, kid."

My mind snags on *career-maker*. I've already given up any and all thoughts of being a performing musician (not that I ever really wanted to be), and even though I postponed enrolling at Tennessee State this year, I did it with no formal guarantee that they'll hold my spot for next fall. I'm not even sure what I want to do with my life anymore.

But this . . . this would bring me one step closer to achieving my dream.

Even though there's a heck of a lot riding on this, maybe I can use this opportunity to put the past behind me. Prove to the world that just because I'm not meant for the stage doesn't mean I don't belong in the music industry. Prove to myself that I'm more than one bad onstage experience. There are so many talented, brave, inspiring female songwriters who have come before me. It's all I've ever wanted, to be like them. So many of them had to fight and claw and scratch their way to the top, it would be ridiculous of me to look this gift horse in the mouth. The ones who came before me paved the way; it's time for me to buckle in and take the wheel.

I'll do it like Dolly: be brave enough to try. As I spin the DO IT LIKE DOLLY beads on my bracelet, a glimmer of courage sows itself deep inside me and the roots of determination take hold. Yes, there's still an underlying current of uncertainty and doubt slithering beneath my skin, but if I dig down deep enough to the meat and bones of me, I'm feeling almost . . . hopeful?

"So, we start tomorrow?" I ask.

TRACK 6

Five Miles Has Never Felt So Far

Kash

NOVEMBER 2

THE TOWN CAR Barry sent picks me up bright and early, as promised.

Unfortunately, an accident on I-24W has us at a standstill. Bleary eyed and bored, I unlock my phone and pull up Six String Justice's social media posts to see what they've been up to.

6StringJustice:

Inspiration comes and . . . dead weight goes. #newlineup

6StringJustice:

Heading back to Nashville! Exciting things to come!

6StringJustice:

We just want to thank everyone that helped us get "Better Without You" to number one on the Nashville country charts.

I growl and lock the phone.

Eventually, the Town Car turns down a gravel road and bumps over ruts, potholes, and washed-out areas. Every jostle and jerk over the dirt drive sends a spike of pain to my temples and rattles my bones. It reminds me of riding around in the tour van with its worn-out shocks, minus the backstabbing ex-bandmates.

Neatly trimmed green shrubs line the drive, and in the distance I see rows and rows of carefully planted trees of all different shapes and sizes. We pass by a large white farmhouse with a wraparound porch. A little farther on is a weathered shed with a riding lawn mower parked outside and then a small red barn with an attached corral.

We come to a fork in the road with a signpost. The arrow pointing to the right says CHRISTMAS TREES. The arrow pointing to the left says THE HIDEAWAY.

We veer to the left and travel down a narrow lane surrounded by oak and maple trees whose gnarled branches reach toward the crystal-blue sky. When the driver finally stops the car in front of a log cabin, I push the door open and step outside on stiff legs. The fresh fall air is clean and crisp, and I blink at the sudden brilliance of the afternoon sun, too bright for my eyes after sitting in a car with dark tinted windows. It doesn't help that my head is throbbing and I feel like I might puke. I throw on a pair of dark sunglasses, pull my suitcase and guitar from the trunk, and make my way up the short gravel walkway to the covered porch. Nailed to one of the posts is a hand-painted sign: THE HIDEAWAY AT HIDDEN ACRES.

The stairs are well-worn but are surprisingly sturdy beneath my boots as I stride up to the front door. A black wall-mounted mailbox hangs beside it, and when I flip up the lid, there's a key inside, just like Barry said there would be.

So much for security.

But then again, this place is pretty remote.

Maybe the check-in process at a place like this is a bit more relaxed. Or maybe the owners got sick of waiting around for me to arrive? I am a few hours later than expected.

The carved wooden music note on the key chain bounces against my wrist when I shove the key in the lock. The moment I step inside the cabin, I'm greeted by the scent of fresh-baked cookies. It's larger than I expected, with vaulted wood-paneled ceilings and farmhouse-country decor. The main living space is open and airy, with a stone fireplace on the far wall. A wooden stairway leads up to what appears to be a loft, where I assume the bedroom is. The whole space has a warm, inviting, homey vibe that instantly makes me feel more at ease.

The scent of baked sugar and vanilla makes my stomach grumble. Like a moth drawn to a flame, I set my things down next to the door and make my way to the kitchenette tucked into the far side of the main room. On the butcher block counter is a plate with half a dozen fresh-baked chocolate chip cookies along with a typed note:

Welcome to the Hideaway at Hidden Acres!

Whether you're here to relax, refresh, or rock out in the studio, we hope your stay is unforgettable.
Please note:

- *Extra linens are in the closet upstairs.*
- *The fireplace flue damper must be opened before use.*
- *The studio has a separate entrance, located around back.*

If you need anything, please call the farmhouse from the landline by pressing the reception button.

We hope you enjoy your stay.
The Morgans

Beneath it is a handwritten note in blue ink and ridiculously neat penmanship:

Sorry we weren't able to get started on your demo today. I'll meet you in the studio tomorrow at 9 a.m. Bring your guitar. ~P.M.

"I'm not sorry," I mumble, reaching for a cookie.

I'm still not sold on the idea that I need anyone's help writing music, let alone some random stranger Barry's lined up for me. And what kind of musician is up at nine a.m., anyhow? No one I want to know. Plus, Barry said it was my choice whether I was going to work with this chick. It's a bit presumptuous of her to just assume I'm going to show up to the studio at her beck and call. I've written stuff before and I can do it again. I don't need anyone's help this time around.

I devour two more cookies and then grab another before hauling my suitcase upstairs. The bedroom is cozy, with a king-sized bed taking up most of the space. The fluffy white comforter looks as soft as a cloud. I kick off my boots and lie back, hoping a bit of rest will help with my headache.

My mind wanders as I relax, but I can't ease all the tension that has my neck muscles in knots. I'm carrying a heavy weight that I won't be able to put down until I deliver those songs.

I only need to write six songs.

Just. Six. Songs.

TRACK 7

I Ain't Waitin' Around for You

Paisley

NOVEMBER 2

MOM AND DAD are thrilled that Exit 12S Records has reserved the Hideaway for the rest of the year. They're even more excited when they find out that Barry's asked me to help our guest, Murray, with his demo.

"It'll be good to have another musician your age around," Mom says as she dishes a helping of mashed potatoes onto her plate. "You've been spending too much time on the farm. You should be spending time with your peers and focusing on your songwriting again."

I can't help but bristle. If my *peers* weren't such jerks, maybe I'd want to spend time with them. But not a single one of my so-called friends showed up to support me when I won the Songwriter of the Year Award, and they sure as hell didn't offer me much consolation after my disastrous stage debut. Most of the ones who've stuck around town continue to share and tag me in those stupid videos Seth's been making, and who wants to spend time with people like that?

When I look back at most of the interactions I had with my classmates over the years, I realize I always gave more than I got.

Study groups? I was always invited so people could copy my notes.

Pool parties? Sleepovers? Friday night movies? Not so much.

It was all about what I could do for them. And now I have to do what's best for me.

"I'm not sure he even wants my help," I say, taking the mashed potatoes from Mom. I scoop some out and plop them on my plate.

Dad glances over at me. "Who wouldn't want your help?"

"Right?" Mom says. "You're a fantastic writer."

While I appreciate their support, they're my parents and they love me unconditionally. I don't think they have the ability to give anything I do honest criticism. I mean, they still rave about the first song I wrote when I was five. It was about mushrooms. And I don't even like mushrooms.

"Yeah, well, he missed our first session today—"

"That wasn't his fault," Mom says, cutting me off. "The state police had I-24 closed for hours. I had no idea lithium-ion batteries could cause such trouble."

"Okay, fine," I concede. "But he also hasn't shown up to introduce himself."

"Maybe he's shy," Dad says.

"Maybe he's tired," Mom says.

"Maybe he's seen the videos."

Mom and Dad share a "here we go again" look. I know they think I should just get over it. I'm trying. It's just not so easy.

None of their epic failures have been recorded and shared and immortalized on the internet. When they were my age, they could mess up and move on. When they share the stories of their youth, they get to control the narrative. It's not the same for me.

We sit in awkward silence for a few minutes, forks scraping against our plates.

"So, there's this new riding mower I've had my eye on," Dad says, and I have never been more grateful to John Deere in my life.

I'VE JUST FINISHED LOADING the dishwasher when the phone rings.

"Hidden—" I start to say, but an unfamiliar male voice cuts me off before I can finish the greeting.

"Yeah, I'm looking for reception."

What?

"Uh . . ."

"Look," the guy says on the other end of the line, his tone grumbly. "The sheet on the counter here says that if I need anything, I'm supposed to press the reception button on the phone. And that's what I did."

Oh, now it all makes sense. Murray's calling from the Hideaway. See, this is a great example of why we need caller ID.

I plaster a customer service smile on my face because Mom says it helps brighten your phone voice. "Right, and what can I help you with?"

Most of our guests call over to ask for more pillows or firewood.

But not Murray.

"Yeah, I'll take a cheeseburger and fries, extra crispy. No mayo. Extra pickles. Large Coke. And maybe some more of those chocolate chip cookies. Charge it to the room."

And then he hangs up on me. I stare down at the handset for a moment before I return it to the cradle.

Well, that was something. And boy is he going to be disappointed when he finds out we don't offer room service here.

TWENTY MINUTES LATER, I'M walking up the path from the farmhouse toward the log cabin. The original five-hundred-square-foot building was constructed sometime in the 1800s, but it's been renovated and expanded over the years to include the large main living area with an updated country kitchen and the recording studio.

The front porch is dark and I wish I'd thought to bring a flashlight with me. Even my cell phone would come in handy if it weren't still tucked inside my sock drawer. I carefully make my way to the front door and knock. All the lights are off and there doesn't seem to be any movement inside.

I knock again and wait. And then wait some more.

Is Murray even here? And if not, where did he go?

I turn to study the woods behind me, hoping he didn't decide to wander off by himself. The area around the farm is fairly safe, but there are plenty of pitfalls and caves out there that are best to leave for daytime discovery. I've lived here most of my life and I still wouldn't wander beyond the Christmas tree groves after sundown.

The longer I wait, the more irritated I get. What kind of person has the nerve to order room service from a farmhouse that is clearly not a hotel or restaurant, and then not answer the door?

I knock again, louder this time, and debate leaving the bag on the doormat. The food that I carefully packaged inside is probably lukewarm by now, so it's not like it matters. It's tempting, but I also don't want to wake up in the morning to find out that the local raccoons had a party on the porch.

Just as I'm about to give up and head back to the farmhouse, the log cabin's door creaks open just wide enough for the paper bag I'm carrying to fit through. I can barely make out a shadowy human form behind the door. All I can tell is the guy's taller than me.

"Room service?" he asks in a gravelly, groggy voice that makes it sound like he just woke up from a nap.

"Yeah, uh . . ." It's kind of weird talking to a shadow behind a door. But okay. I'll go with it, since it doesn't look like I have any other choice. "We don't really do room service here. But I packed you some of our leftovers from dinner."

The guy clears his throat and a hand emerges to take the bag from me. I assume it's Murray's, because it's too dark to see his face, or much of anything really, and we haven't officially met. Our fingers brush during the transition, and his skin is cold.

Maybe he's a vampire?

I rein in my overactive imagination. "Mom made meat loaf, which is kind of like a hamburger, right? I threw in a few slices of cheddar and some pickles, too, in case you wanted to dress it up a bit. There's mashed potatoes and green beans to go with it. Oh, and a few of those chocolate chip cookies you asked for. Unfortunately, we don't have any Coke, but there's sweet tea."

"Thanks," Murray says dryly. I can't tell if it's because he's parched or because he's a jerk. My guess is he's a little of both. His shadowy figure steps back and disappears into the cavernous darkness of the log cabin.

"The record label arranged for a grocery—" I start to call after him, but the door clicks shut before I can finish what I was about to say. "Delivery."

Welp, we're definitely not off to a good start.

NOVEMBER 3

MOM'S ALWAYS GIVING PEOPLE the benefit of the doubt, so I do my best to channel her energy and put last night behind me. It's a new day, and if we're going to make this co-writing thing work, Murray and I need to get started on the right foot.

I roll out of bed early to finish my morning chores before our nine a.m. meetup at the studio. There's a pleasant chill in the air that has me tugging the sleeves of my flannel shirt down as I make my way to the stable to feed Dunder and Blixem their breakfast.

"Good morning, ladies," I say.

They greet me with animated snorts and gentle muzzle-butts.

After cleaning out their water trough and refilling it, I add some feed formulated for late fall to a bucket.

"Big day for all of us. I've got a writing session coming up with our latest guest, and then you need to get camera ready for the kiddos."

Later today, we have a few preschool groups stopping by the big red barn to paint holiday picture frames with Mom. Then the kids will have photos taken with the reindeer. So after my morning session with Murray, I'll come back to get the girls gussied up in their fancy harnesses, the ones with jingle bells.

"Think we can pull it all off?" I ask.

Blixem sighs, but Dunder nudges her nose against my hip as if she's saying, "We've got this."

"I appreciate the vote of confidence."

My fingers sink into her thickening light gray coat. She and Blixem have put on a bit of weight in preparation for winter, and their coats are denser than they were this past spring. Unlike their first year at the farm, when they were mangy and underfed after they came to us as rescues, they're healthy now.

I pull two small McIntosh apples from my pockets and offer one to each of the reindeer.

"Wish me luck."

They munch happily as I walk away. Above me, the mockingbird sings our song, and I whistle back. It's our thing now, this back-and-forth melody, and I hope Murray and I can come up with a similar give-and-take as we work on songs for his demo.

I show up at the studio a few minutes before nine so I can get everything set up. I pull open the curtains to let in some natural light and flip on a few of the ambient lamps scattered about the room.

It's hard not to pace across the studio while I wait for him to show. I'm anxious and worried and excited and hopeful and about a million other feelings I can't quite name. I've never been on a blind date before, but I imagine it feels a lot like this. Wondering if you and the other person will hit it off. Equal parts worried if they'll like you and worried if they won't.

I set out freshly sharpened pencils and empty notebooks and sheaves of blank sheet music. Will he want to start with the music or the lyrics or something else entirely? I think of my lyric book tucked carefully away on the shelf above my desk, wondering if I'll be ready to use it again when this is all said and done.

After fifteen minutes of bouncing around the room, I decide to reorganize the percussion cabinet. Then I dust the mixing console and try my best not to keep checking the time every ten seconds. Eventually, thirty minutes pass and he's still not here. A flame of irritation licks across my skin.

Surely he'll come.

I sweep the floor and readjust the throw carpets, but Murray still hasn't arrived by the time I'm finished.

I'm no longer sure he's going to show. I watch the minute hand of the wall clock tick over to 10:00 a.m. and then sink into a chair like a deflated balloon, slowly releasing the anticipation and excitement that had been building up inside. I feel like an idiot, waiting around for someone who clearly doesn't give a crap. Or maybe he does, and it's me who's the problem?

I switch off the lamps and close the curtains. Snuff out the smoldering embers of hope. I should have known when Barry called that the offer was too good to be true.

TRACK 8

Take a Pic (It'll Last Longer)

Kash

NOVEMBER 3

THANKFULLY MY HEADACHE'S gone when I roll out of bed at noon. The combination of a home-cooked meal and ibuprofen did the trick. I haven't exactly been taking the best care of myself lately. I'm sure the added stress of my deadline and lack of sleep haven't helped. Still, it's been a few months since my last tension headache spell, so I thought I'd gotten past them. For it to happen now, well, the timing couldn't be worse. Every day I don't focus on writing music is wasted time. If I don't get my ass in gear . . .

I grab the glass of water on the bedside stand and guzzle it down. It was ice cold when I set it there last night, before I crashed into bed. Thankfully, this is one of the most comfortable mattresses I've slept on in months. No wonder they call these things king beds, because when you wake up, you feel like a king.

I stretch and peel the thick blackout curtains away from the window. The brilliant fall sun casts everything in a soft golden hue, and I feel like I should be out apple picking or hiking or something seasonal and outdoorsy.

After a hot shower and a quick raid of the kitchen pantry, I'm ready to get on with the day. I suppose that means finding Paisley and introducing myself. Barry didn't tell me much about her. Just that she's about my age and writes music. Since she lives on the farm, it shouldn't be too hard to track her down.

My boots scuff over the porch stairs. I take a moment to orient myself and then head around back to the studio. It's locked up tight, but when I cup my hands and peer in through the narrow window next to the door, I see a cozy-looking room with plenty of equipment. I've never recorded myself—that was always Ryder's thing—but it can't be too hard to figure out, especially if it's just me and my guitar.

When I reach a curve in the road, I hear an excited squeal and then what sounds like a group of boisterous children talking and giggling. Heading toward the noise, I follow a dirt path to the small red barn we passed on our way in.

A group of pint-sized humans is standing in front of a whitewashed split-rail fence, holding their hands out toward the two fuzzy-antlered creatures inside. Are those . . . ?

"Reindeer are ruminants," says a good-looking girl about seventeen or eighteen years old. She's standing in the corral with the reindeer, her attention focused on the kids lined up at the fence in front of her. Dark-washed jeans are tucked into the tops of her leather boots, and her emerald-green flannel shirt looks festive with the red-and-white cowboy hat she's pulled down over her dark wavy hair.

This must be Paisley.

There's something so familiar about her, but I can't figure out how I know her. I'm not great with faces.

"Ruminants," she repeats, enunciating the word carefully, "only eat things like plants. So, you don't have to be afraid—they won't eat you." She gives a dimpled smile to a little boy holding an older woman's hand. He gives a somber nod and lets out a giant sigh of relief.

"Does anyone know how many reindeer Santa has?" she asks. She holds up her hands and ticks them off on her fingers as she names them. "There's Dasher and Dancer and Prancer and Vixen. Comet and Cupid and Donner and . . ."

"Blitzen," finish a few of the more enthusiastic kids.

One of the reindeer paws the ground and snorts. Paisley reaches out and gives the reindeer a comforting pat on the back. "Easy, there," she says.

"What about Rudolph?" pipes up one of the kids.

"We can't forget about Rudolph," she agrees.

I'm not sure which of the kids starts it, but soon the whole group is singing about reindeer games. Their enthusiasm is contagious and makes me want to join in. I can't remember the last time I sang a Christmas carol. It's impossible to miss the pained expression on Paisley's face and the way her fingers curl into the thick fur of the reindeer standing next to her. Her smile is tight and she swallows hard when they finish with the line about being part of history.

When she speaks again, her tone is overly bright. "These two reindeer are sisters. This reindeer here is Dunder. And this one is Blixem. Their names are the Dutch words for *thunder* and *lightning*."

Paisley's gaze sweeps over the group as she speaks. Our eyes lock for an instant, but her attention doesn't linger. I'm hit once again with a sense of recognition. I'm sure I've seen her before. I just wish I could remember where.

PAISLEY'S OBVIOUSLY BUSY, SO I wander around the farm for a while. Rows and rows of Christmas trees ripple over the soft rolling hills. I can picture myself sitting out here on a blanket, strumming my guitar. Maybe Barry was onto something when he shipped me out here to work on the demo.

The sun warms my skin, and by the time I make my way to the large red barn, I'm parched. A car pulls into the gravel parking lot across the road, and a group of women my mom's age emerges from the car. "Just wait until you see the gift shop," one of them says. "The spiced cider is to die for."

Spiced cider sounds good right about now.

I wait a beat and then follow them down a short hedge-lined redbrick path that leads to a giant courtyard. Across the way is a large single-story building that looks like a gingerbread house. A sign on the door says HIDDEN TREASURES GIFT SHOP, OPEN HALLOWEEN TO CHRISTMAS EVE. The women head inside, but I take a few minutes to survey my surroundings. I feel like I've wandered onto an empty set for a holiday movie, minus the snow.

On the left side of the courtyard, nestled between two hulking Christmas trees, is a hot cocoa stand with a walk-up counter and a peaked roof. A blackboard sign hangs down from the rafters with CLOSED artfully written across it in white chalk. A few black wrought iron café tables and matching chairs are spaced out nearby.

To the right of the gift shop is a rustic stall with a sign that says FESTIVE & FREE. It reminds me of the roadside farm stands that pop up with seasonal harvests, but instead of tomatoes or apples or sweet corn, the bins of this one are filled with pine cones, round slices of wood with the bark still on them, and a jumble of green, orange, and white gourds.

Granny would have loved it here.

I force down the feeling of grief that threatens to surface and head to the gift shop. The thick scent of cinnamon hits me smack in the face as soon as I open the door and step inside. The walls are lined with floor-to-ceiling shelves filled with holiday decor, and wide tables down the middle display bins of Christmas tree decorations. There's a scented candle and essential oil display near the counter that seems to be the focus of everyone's attention.

"I'm sorry," sobs a little girl as giant tears roll down her face. "I didn't mean to."

At her feet are the shards of a broken glass bottle, and a translucent brown liquid oozes across the scuffed wooden floorboards. She clings to her mother and hides her face as her shoulders shake.

"I told you not to touch it," the mom says, but her voice isn't without sympathy. She wraps her arm around the girl and sighs.

The woman behind the cash register gives her a knowing smile. "Accidents happen."

There's a red velvet curtain hanging on the wall behind the counter that must lead to a storeroom. From within comes a series of thuds and bangs followed by "Found it."

Paisley steps through the curtain with a container of kitty litter and a dustpan and brush. She's no longer wearing a hat and her dark hair is pulled up into a ponytail. I realize I'm staring and force myself to look away before it gets weird.

Most of the shoppers go back to their browsing, but one of the women from the car keeps looking over at Paisley, too. "Does she look familiar to you?" she asks her friend in a loud whisper.

The other woman peers at Paisley through glasses with thick lenses. "A little, I guess."

"I know her from somewhere," the first woman says, shaking her head as if it'll knock the memory loose. "I'm sure of it."

"Maybe she just has one of those faces," the other woman suggests.

Paisley sweeps the kitty litter and broken glass into the dustpan. She gives a momentary wary glance at the two whispering women before surveying the other customers. "All set."

When she turns, I quickly look away so she doesn't catch me staring. I'm not sure what it is about her, but I can't shake the feeling that I've seen her somewhere before.

But maybe the woman is right.

Maybe she just has one of those faces.

TRACK 9

I Wish I Could Forget You (Like You've Forgotten Me)

Paisley

NOVEMBER 3

THE OIL-CLUMPED KITTY litter and glass ping against the sides of the trashcan as I dump it inside. It's never fun to clean up after a customer, but at least I can be grateful it wasn't vomit. I spend some time reorganizing the stockroom, hoping by the time I'm finished, that group of older ladies will have left.

It's always disconcerting when a stranger seems to recognize me. Pretending I don't see or hear them is one thing, but not letting it get to me is another thing entirely. It's hard to brush it aside when it feels like every move I make is being judged, like I'm performing some gymnastic routine at a competition and not going about a random day in my life.

See how she sweeps the kitty litter with her broom? Seven points for execution, but only five for effort.

"Hey, Paiz," Mom calls through the curtain. "I could use your help out here."

“One sec.” I sigh and adjust a box of tissue paper so that it’s aligned with the box beneath it. Lately, my life feels askew like that box was. Will I ever be able to straighten it out and get back on track?

It’ll take more than a nudge to get me centered again, that’s for sure.

I brush my sweaty palms over my jeans, hoping that the women are gone.

Luck is not on my side.

They’re still in the shop, but it gets worse. Standing in the corner, by a display of wooden nutcrackers, is my worst nightmare.

Kash Murray.

Okay, technically being onstage performing is my worst nightmare.

But Kash Murray, or any of the members of Six String Justice, comes in at a close second. What the hell is he doing here?

I stare at all six feet and one inch of him, dumbfounded. The one and only other time I saw Kash Murray in person was after my set, when I listened to the band make fun of me and then watched helplessly as they defaced my lyric book. I’ve spent half a year playing back the entire fiasco in my mind, from my disastrous solo act to the backstage aftermath. I realize I can’t blame Six String Justice for what happened that day—not entirely—but I can’t ever forgive them for their crude comments, what they did to my notebook, or for the cruel social media snipes their official account posted about me.

Another one of their diss posts comes to mind.

6StringJustice:

Everyone in the audience who had to sit through the act before our set last night should get a refund. Or earplugs.

I freeze, wondering if maybe I can disappear back behind the curtain and hide out in the storeroom until he leaves. But of course Mom spots me first.

She gently tugs on my arm to get my attention. "Can you work the gift-wrap station, please?"

"Yeah, sure," I say. Too late for a disappearing act now.

I glance back over at Kash Murray.

What is he doing here?

Maybe this is some PR stunt? Is he here to blow up my spot? I wouldn't be surprised if Six String Justice planned some stupid scheme for cheap likes and views. They're the kind of guys who would do anything to get ahead. I glance around for hidden cameras, but nothing seems staged, and I don't see any other members of the band.

Hmm.

Maybe he has a doppelgänger?

He glances up at me, and though I quickly avert my gaze, there's no mistaking that it really is Kash Murray. I'll never forget those eyes.

The last time I saw him, he was wearing a cowboy hat that shaded most of his face. In the bright store lighting, his dark hair has light brown highlights. His nose is straight and his jaw has just enough definition to keep it soft instead of chiseled.

His lips curl into a smile, and I hate how he doesn't look anything like the jerk I know he is.

There's a small queue growing at our gift-wrapping station, and of course the lady who was whispering about me earlier is first in line. She watches me like a hawk as I make my way over to a table surrounded by racks full of holiday paper, ribbons, and bows.

"How can I help you?" I ask, doing my best to keep all the irritation and anxiety I'm feeling out of my voice.

It's not easy, though. The last thing I need is to cause a scene, and I absolutely hate confrontation. A vein in my neck starts to throb.

"I'd like this wrapped, please," the customer says, setting down a large gingerbread-scented candle in a brown-and-white tin decorated like a gingerbread house.

It's one of our most popular candles, and I've wrapped so many of them over the years, I could probably do it blindfolded. Still, I keep my eyes trained on the task at hand, hoping that if I avoid eye contact with her, I won't be drawn into a conversation.

It doesn't work.

"You look so familiar," she says, dipping down a bit to study my face.

I force a smile. "I get that a lot."

"Really?" asks her friend.

I nod and focus on making crisp folded edges with the wrapping paper. Inside, though, my stomach feels like a piece of wrapping paper that's been torn from a package and then squeezed into a tight ball.

"Maybe you know my granddaughter, Kelsey?"

She's not going to let this go, is she?

"I don't think so," I say.

I glance up quickly and notice that Kash has moved from the nutcracker display to a closer spot, near the German Christmas pyramids.

"Did you take ballet lessons at On Pointe Dance Academy?" the woman asks.

"Nope."

I've just finished taping the very last part when she sets her soft, warm hands over mine.

"I have it," she says like she's Sherlock Holmes and she's just solved the Mystery of the Mysterious Mademoiselle. She leans closer and whispers, "You're that girl from those videos, aren't you? From that concert . . ." The delicate floral perfume she's wearing clashes with the cinnamon scent that lingers in the store, and I worry I might have been too optimistic about not cleaning up puke today.

I learned a few months ago that the fastest way to defuse a situation like this is to meet it head-on, no matter how painful or uncomfortable it is. As soon as someone knows something bothers you, it's like an open invitation to keep picking at it. If you pretend it's no big deal . . .

"You got me," I say, and give her a conspiratorial look, like I'm counting on her to keep it our little secret. This method works about 75 percent of the time. I hold my breath and wait to see if she'll announce her discovery loud and clear for all to hear. Thankfully, she takes the smile-and-wink route.

Unfortunately, Kash has made it closer, to the holiday bakeware section, but there's still a sizable line at the wrapping station. It's all I can do to focus on our customers and not jackrabbit out the door.

A porcelain angel tree-topper.

A collection of cocoa tins and festive mugs.

I'm midway through wrapping up a set of hand-embroidered tea towels when *he* sidles up to the side of the counter. The tips of his dark black boots, scuffed and worn, slide into my peripheral vision, and I feel my hackles rise.

"The back of the line's over there," I say with a nod and without glancing up. I have patience for many things, but line-cutting isn't one of them. Especially not if the line cutter is Kash Murray.

My fingers quickly crease and fold the paper, which is bright red with glittery gold polka dots. The faster I finish, the faster I can get out of here.

I *need* to get out of here.

"Yeah," Kash says. "I was hoping we could talk." His voice is confident and husky, and I'm tempted to look up, but this line's not getting any shorter, and my anxiety is through the roof.

"I'm kind of busy at the moment," I say as I tear a piece of clear double-sided tape from the dispenser and use it to secure the flap. I swivel the gift and glance up at the customer who's patiently waiting for me to finish. "What color ribbon would you like?"

We pretty much have an entire craft store ribbon aisle to choose from. I think there are way too many, especially when a handful of rolls of standard holiday colors would suffice, but Mom thinks our customers deserve as many options as we can give them.

"This'll only take a minute," he continues.

The customer selects a gold ribbon, and I grab a pair of scissors to cut it with.

"Please," he persists. "You're Paisley, right?"

Does he seriously not know who I am?

I pause mid-snip and look up into a face that's painfully familiar. It ought to be, since it's haunted me since May. Thick eyebrows sit over warm brown eyes that twinkle just like they did before. Back when I thought they were the most beautiful eyes I'd ever seen. I hate that they still are.

"I'm Kash," he says.

"Yeah, I know." I can't help but be short with him.

"Barry said I should introduce myself," he explains. "So, here I am."

"Barry?" I ask, my fingers fumbling with a fresh roll of tape. I bumble it and it bounce-rolls across the table, sailing over the edge. The roll hits the floor at the exact same time realization hits me.

"Barry said your name was *Murray*," I say, mostly for my own benefit, as if that explains this horror show.

Kash Murray is Murray.

Oh. My. God.

"It . . . is. Well, it's my last name," he says with an easy laugh.

The customer waiting at the gift-wrapping counter clears their throat. My chest burns with residual embarrassment and white-hot fury. This farm is my safe haven. And now Kash Murray is here, sullying it with his presence. And Barry, of all people, sent him.

I grab a new roll of tape and snap it into the dispenser with more force than necessary.

I probably can't get my parents to kick Kash out of the Hideaway, but maybe it's not too late for me to back out of the co-writing arrangement . . .

And to think, I was actually disappointed when he didn't show up at the studio this morning.

The customer coughs to get my attention, and I hand them their package. In spite of my lack of attention and bubbling ire, it's perfectly wrapped. Maybe I could become a professional gift wrapper, since it doesn't look like being a songwriter for Exit 12S is going to work out for me after all. "Happy holidays," I say, but it comes out strangled and angry.

Keep it together.

Maybe if I ignore Kash, he'll take the hint and go away. He's about to find out how frigid my cold shoulder can get.

Still, it's not that poor customer's fault that the Ghost of Paisley's Past has just arrived on the scene. I dig deep for some of that hidden Christmas spirit Scrooge managed to find and force my lips into a smile for the next customer in line. "Next."

Kash doesn't take the hint. "Look, Paisley, maybe this isn't the best time for introductions."

"You think?" I slice off a fresh sheet of wrapping paper and set a box of holiday coasters on it.

He shifts, thrown off by my attitude, but continues, undeterred. "I know you're busy."

This guy is unbelievable.

"What else do you know?" I ask, infused with a boldness I wasn't aware I possessed and unable to hide the snippiness of my tone. Ordinarily, I would keep my mouth shut and dip out ASAP, but I feel like a feral animal backed into a corner, and my claws come out on their own.

For the first time, I hear the confidence in his voice waver. When I look up, his brow is furrowed in confusion. "About?"

"Me."

He blinks. "Um . . . Your name's Paisley. You're a songwriter. You live on a tree farm . . . ?"

I wait for him to say something about how awful I was as an opener for Six String Justice. How bad he feels that they mistook me for a groupie and disfigured my book with a Sharpie. Or even snark about how many laughs the band shared at my expense after the show.

"Um . . ." he says. "Barry tells me you're making a real name for yourself?"

That's not exactly how I'd put it, but people have said a lot worse over the past few months. "Anything else?" I ask.

"Should there be?" The blank look on his face seems real enough.

It's crystal clear to me in this moment that Kash Murray has absolutely no idea we've previously met.

"I guess not."

"Look, I don't want to disappoint you," he says, shoving his hands into the front pockets of his jeans. "But I just wanted to let you know that I don't really need your help. I know Barry wants us to work together, but I can do this on my own."

"Oh," I say, taking a moment to process. "Okay. Fine by me."

And I should be relieved about it, right? Not only am I so inconsequential to him that he doesn't remember interacting with me backstage, but he doesn't even remember the way his band made fun of me on social media. Moreover, this is the guy who showed up late, ordered room service, barely thanked me for bringing him dinner anyway, and then stood me up at the studio. Not having to work with him on his demo is a gift.

"I guess I'll see you around," he says.

"I sure hope not," I mutter under my breath.

"Oh," he replies, sounding surprised that I'm not dying to spend time with the likes of him. Sounding a lot like someone who thinks the sun comes up just to hear him crow.

I breathe a sigh of relief when the gift shop door closes behind him.

I've spent so much time letting the memory of our last interaction live rent free in my head, and he hasn't even thought about me once. And yet I remember it like it was yesterday. How he laughed at his bandmates' jokes about my name and the fact they thought I was a groupie. How he lifted his chin when he strode toward me, tilting his cowboy hat to reveal his warm brown eyes. The way our gazes locked and the air seemed to absorb all the sounds around us. How he winked as he handed my lyric book back.

It's stupid to be upset that he doesn't remember me now. Completely bonkers. That night was the absolute worst night of my life. I wish no one could remember any of it.

And even more, why would I ever want to be memorable to someone like Kash Murray?

TRACK 10

I Don't Know How I'll Make It on My Own

Kash

NOVEMBER 4

I'VE BEEN IN the studio for a few hours, and I have nothing to show for it.

A song? Nope.

A melody even? Nope.

Not even a string of words that could be considered the start of some lyrics.

I've got zip. Zilch. Nothing.

I glance out the window. The midmorning sunlight filters down through the maple trees. Some of the leaves have started to fall, but a lot of the maples still have some foliage left. The fire-engine red and vibrant orange leaves sparkle in the breeze.

Something's got to change, because I'm never going to make any progress if I keep spinning my wheels. A change of scenery, maybe.

I grab my guitar, shove it back into its case, and head outdoors to look for some inspiration. When I get to the reindeer barn, Paisley's not there. Not that I'm looking for her. At least, that's what I tell myself.

Passing by the small gray shed, I head in the direction of the Christmas tree lot. Maybe being surrounded by orderly rows of fir trees will help me organize my thoughts. As I slip between two giant cone-shaped trees, I hear the soft sounds of someone humming punctuated by the sharp snipping sound of a pair of shears. I peer around the trees and spot a bright orange jacket a little farther down the row. When the person moves into view, I realize it's Paisley.

She's wearing large, old-school headphones and bobbing her head to a tune only she can hear as she shapes the tree. I should continue on my way . . . The last thing I need is a distraction, no matter how cute (and confusing) it might be, but then she starts to sing.

I'm transfixed.

Paisley's singing voice is clear and expressive, infused with a powerful, velvety undertone. Even though I've only heard a few notes, I know for a fact that I could spend hours listening to her.

She shifts around the tree to trim another side, and without thinking, I slink back into the next row like I'm some kind of secret agent spy, hoping not to be spotted on a stakeout. My breath catches in my chest.

Crap, what if she sees me?

I wait a moment, my heart pounding, but Paisley doesn't stop singing. She finishes the last few bars of "Harvest Moon" and then moves on to a countrified version of "She Used to Be Mine." Her sound is as incredible as it is nuanced. I can't believe Barry hasn't signed her as a singer-songwriter.

Paisley pauses and pulls away one side of her headphones. I

hold my breath, worried that if I make any noise, I'll give myself away. She tilts her head toward a slender gray bird perched at the top of the tree and whistles.

The bird whistles back and then takes flight.

I follow the bird's lead. Not wanting to intrude on her personal space any longer, I head farther into the grove in search of inspiration.

I'M BEGINNING TO THINK it's not location or scenery or communing with nature that will help me get this done. Even out here, with the blue skies above and the green grass beneath me, I haven't written a lick of anything.

The problem is one hundred percent me. And I don't know how to solve it.

A blue jay squawks like a hawk as it flies over and then disappears into the top of a pine tree. Mimicry must have been one of its adaptions for survival, and that gets me thinking about what I need to do to survive in this business.

Going solo after years with the band has been tough. Even though our music was evolving, we'd developed a signature sound that linked our stuff from the early country-rock days to the more recent Nashville country days. But now I wonder: Have I been trying so hard to distance my music from Six String Justice that I've forgotten what *I* sound like?

I stretch my legs out in front of me and readjust the guitar in my lap. When I play the opening chords of the first song I ever wrote, I'm back to being that naive kid again, full of big dreams and endless energy.

I don't think, I just play. My left hand glides along the fretboard as my fingers find the chords while my other hand strums.

"This ain't all it's cracked up to be,
So take my hand and come with me,
We'll go to where the mountains meet the sky."

I haven't played this song, let alone sang it, in almost four years, but I remember coming up with it like it was yesterday. Sitting upstairs on the double bed in my old room, pressing the pads of my fingers into the secondhand Epiphone's strings until they ached. I'd been playing old country-rock standards but had decided to mess around for the fun of it. When I'd played that particular chord progression, something inside me clicked. I can't explain it, but the song just made sense.

I'd come up with other songs after that, and then suddenly I was in a band and we were jamming in the shed. Those were the early days, when we were honing our skills playing old songs by Johnny Cash and John Fogerty and newer country stuff by Chris Stapleton and blues/roots by Larkin Poe. We tried straight-up country, Southern rock, and Americana and settled on being a country-rock band. Eventually, I shared some of the other songs I wrote with the guys. We worked on them together and they became ours. At least, until we shifted into the Nashville country sound and we started playing more of Justin's stuff.

But this song? I've always kept this song just for me.

Could I revamp it for the demo?

The thought has me sitting up straighter. It's tempting, especially since I haven't got anything else. But it also feels like sharing this song would be like selling a piece of my soul. I'm not that desperate yet.

I keep playing, letting the chorus build, and sing the last few lines.

"You know we could be good together,
We'll withstand the wildest weather,
Baby, don't you turn and walk away."

When I first signed with Exit 12S Records as a solo artist, I had something to prove. I wanted the guys to regret kicking me out of Six String Justice. I wanted my success to be my revenge. I was looking for a little six *song* justice.

The I'll-show-them fire's still there, but it doesn't burn as hot as it used to. If only I could have channeled it into songs right away, back when it was fresh and raw and my wounds hadn't started to scab over. Distance and time have dampened the hurt. Although self-doubt is rising all over again.

What if Justin was right? What if I wasn't contributing anything to Six String Justice? What if I can't do this?

In the back of my mind, I hear Granny's twangy voice reminding me *Can't never could*. It was one of her favorite sayings.

I can't do it, Granny, I'd say.

Can't never could. Now, try again, she'd reply.

I shift my legs beneath me crisscross applesauce, lean forward into my guitar, and close my eyes. The body of the guitar is warm from the sun, the nylon strings familiar under my fingertips. I listen to the wind rustle the trees and the birds chatter as they dart from branch to branch. The soft scent of pine floats in my direction, and I can almost taste the smoke of a campfire, though I can't tell if someone's really got a fire going or if it's just my imagination.

I take a deep breath and focus on letting my diaphragm expand.

I don't think. I just play.

And play.

And play.

I'VE BEEN SITTING OUT here for hours and all I've managed to come up with is a boring melody and six pathetic lines:

Taillights bleed into the dark
I'm left alone in this car park
I wasn't ready for you to let me go.
After everything that we've been through
I didn't mean that much to you
And I don't know how I'll make it on my own.

I'm drained and hungry and feeling more defeated by the minute. I'd hoped that being outside would inspire me, but the only thing the fresh air and sunshine have accomplished is tuckering me out.

It doesn't help that I can't stop wondering about Paisley. Why was she so short with me when I introduced myself? I know she had things to do, but her attitude started before I even said so much as "hi." And then to hear her voice? If she's that good at singing, I can only imagine how incredible a songwriter she is.

She has to be if Barry signed her to write music for Exit 12S. Which I guess makes her quick agreement that we wouldn't work together sting. Especially since she didn't seem to mind. Does she think I'm not good enough for her?

So much for sending me to a place with no distractions, Barry.

I make my way back through the maze of Christmas trees. When I come around the corner, there are groups of families milling about in a clearing. The woman who was working the cash register at the store yesterday is handing out clipboards and pencils. Her resemblance to Paisley is undeniable, so I bet she's her mother. I realize that I probably should've introduced myself to the owners right after I first arrived. Better late than never, I suppose.

She finishes passing out the supplies and then says, "The clues will lead you to different stamps we've hidden around the farm. When you find one, use it to mark the correct box. Once you've completed the scavenger hunt, you can bring your sheets to the cocoa stand to collect your prizes. There's still plenty of daylight left, so don't rush."

I hang back until the groups have all wandered off. "Mrs. Morgan?" I ask.

She turns to me with a smile. "You must be our guest, Murray."

"Kash Murray," I say, holding out my hand. "It's good to meet you."

"Jenny Morgan." She gives my hand a firm shake. "You settled in okay over at the Hideaway?"

"Just great," I say.

Mrs. Morgan glances at my guitar case. "Are you looking for

Paisley? I thought she said the two of you were going to meet up to write in the mornings. It'll be hard to pin her down now. As you can see, the afternoons get awfully busy here."

I'm not *not* looking for Paisley, but I really have no reason to find her other than to satisfy my own curiosity. "I, uh . . ."

"Paisley's probably with the reindeer." She points in the general direction of the small red barn. "Before you head over there, I should introduce you to my husband, Travis."

She leads me over to two men who are standing next to the same large riding mower I saw parked outside the shed the day I arrived.

"Excuse me, gentlemen," she says warmly. "I hate to interrupt a meeting of the minds. Are you making any progress?"

Both men look over at her with a frown.

"Could be the alternator," says the shorter man with a crew cut and a tan Carhartt jacket.

The other man wipes his hands on a rag. "Or the starter solenoid." He's taller than me by a few inches, and his work shirt and jeans are covered in grease and oil stains. He looks at me and asks, "You're the expert. What's your professional opinion?"

"I, um . . ."

"Stop your teasing, Travis," Mrs. Morgan says, slapping his arm. She rolls her eyes at me and says, "This joker here putting you on the spot is my husband. Travis, this is Kash Murray, our guest."

Mr. Morgan smirks. "You mean, he's not the lawn mower repairman?" He kisses the top of her head and turns his attention back to me. "Good to meet you," he says with a nod. "I'd offer to shake your hand but . . ." He waves the dirty rag he's holding.

"No worries," I say.

"This is our neighbor, Jim Atchley."

Jim and I shake hands.

"So you're here for some studio time, huh?" Mr. Atchley asks, gesturing to my guitar case.

"Yep." My hand clenches the handle. I hope to hell no one asks me how it's going.

'Cause it's not.

"Kash is here to record an album," Mrs. Morgan says, like she's proud of this fact.

"Demo," I correct.

"I was just telling Kash that he can probably find Paisley over by the reindeer," Mrs. Morgan adds.

"Is Paisley writing songs again?" Mr. Atchley asks, looking to Mr. Morgan for confirmation. He looks surprised, with his brows raised about as high as they can go. "I thought she'd stopped after . . . well . . ."

Both of Paisley's parents shift, and I get the sense they're uncomfortable.

"She just took a bit of a break is all," Mrs. Morgan says. The reassuring smile she gives me is tight.

"Well, I'm glad to hear she's back at it. That girl of yours has talent," he says to her parents. "And you're a lucky fellow to be working with her, that's for sure," he continues, patting me on the back.

It doesn't seem like the best time to clarify that Paisley and I are definitely not working together. I'm set on doing this on my own. And after the attitude she gave me yesterday, it's more than clear she isn't keen to work with me, either.

TRACK 11

Things I Didn't Know

Paisley

NOVEMBER 4

AGAINST MY BETTER judgment, I unearth my phone from the sock drawer and plug it into a charger. I've been avoiding the internet for weeks, but now that the outside world seems to be colliding with my zone of safety at Hidden Acres, I want to know why.

I chew on the inside of my cheek as I wait for the phone to power up. I'm not sure I'm prepared for what I'll find.

Unanswered calls.

Missed messages.

Tags to social media posts of more stupid videos Seth's probably made.

It's not easy for me to look up Six String Justice's social media accounts. I know they've moved on from making fun of me, but the hurt is still there. Still, I'm driven by insatiable curiosity and an inexplicable urge to channel my Nancy Drew alter ego in *The Clue at the Christmas Tree Farm*.

The home screen lights up and I steel myself for what I'm about to do.

"Just get in, get the info, and get out," I whisper to myself, like I'm planning an information heist. Except the clues I'm looking for should be hidden in plain sight, on what is essentially a giant electronic bulletin board.

I set my jaw and scroll back a few months in Six String Justice's timeline, to the end of July, until I find what I'm looking for.

6StringJustIce:

Someone got too big for his britches. IYKYK.

6StringJustice:

Pro tip—know when to trim the fat.

6StringJustice:

We're leaner, meaner, and our sound is much cleaner. Check out our new song!

Yikes!

Based on the biting tone of these posts, Kash was dumped from the band.

I don't feel as much satisfaction as I thought I would at the discovery. Even though I'm not a fan of any of the members, breakups always suck, especially when you're the one getting your feelings hurt. And being kicked out of a band you helped found . . . that definitely has to hurt.

The tone of the posts hasn't changed since he left in July, so I guess that means Kash probably wasn't running their social media account. How involved was he with that stuff when he was in the band? Are his personal posts snarky and cutting, too?

I search for Kash's social media account.

Interesting. It was first created in July and there are only two posts.

Kash$Murray:

Six String Justice and I have decided to part ways. I'll always be grateful for the good times we shared. Wishing them all the best.

And then a few months later:

Kash$Murray:

Stay tuned for an upcoming announcement with @Exit12SRecords.

NOVEMBER 5

SOME PEOPLE HAVE A sixth sense about things.

Before my grandparents moved to Arizona, Grandpa always knew when it was going to snow by the way his knee ached.

Mom has something we like to call deer-dar. She can sense Bambi by the side of the road before anyone sees him, which is a useful skill to have when you're driving out here on the back roads of Tennessee.

Apparently, my secret superpower is sensing when Kash is nearby.

What a letdown.

I'm scooping some reindeer feed from a bin in the barn when something compels me to look up. Just then, Kash passes by the open barn door, his head hanging low and his guitar bouncing against his side. The two times I've seen him, he's always seemed so sure of himself. But now, with his shoulders sagging, all he looks is dejected.

What is he doing here?

That question's been running nonstop through my mind since our conversation in the gift shop. Initially, I felt like an idiot that I hadn't realized Murray and Kash were the same person. But why would I even make the connection in the first place? As far as I knew, Kash Murray was in Six String Justice and Barry was talking about some new solo artist he signed. In my avoidance of all things social media, how was I supposed to know the band had given him the boot?

Kash glances my way, and what used to be a delicious sparkle in his eyes has faded into weariness. He nods and gives me a polite smile. Before I can decide whether to return it or not, he looks away and continues on, the soft sound of boots on gravel disappearing as he heads toward the Hideaway.

NOVEMBER 6

I HEAR HIM PLAYING before I see him, dressed in black jeans and a black jacket, leaning back against the trunk of a red oak tree. Kash stands with his boots crossed at the ankles, guitar in hand, a cowboy hat dipped down over his face. I refuse to admit how good he looks. Standing there, he resembles one of those leaning cowboy shadow silhouettes that people affix to their fences. Except the effect is so much sexier when it's captured in three-dimensional flesh and blood.

I can't see much of his face, but his tight-lipped frown is unmistakable. Beneath his hat, the wind ruffles the hair at the nape of his neck. He looks every bit a brooding cowboy. I hate that I don't hate it. In fact, this image of him would probably make a great album cover, sending all his fans swooning.

Kash works his jaw as he strums a few notes while he sings the melody. The sound carries down the row of Leyland cypress that separates us. It's not a bad chord progression, but it could use a little something more. I wonder how it would sound if he started on the relative minor chord?

Kash must sense that it's not working, too, because he stops playing with an angry grunt and bangs the side of his fist against the body of the guitar.

Clearly, it's not going well.

A spark of sympathy flares to life, but I smother that real quick. Even after everything I've recently discovered, Kash Murray doesn't deserve a bit of sympathy from me.

NOVEMBER 7

KASH HAS A HARMONICA.

Fantastic.

The wheezy, whiny notes coming from it make me cringe as I busy myself with restocking the Festive & Free stand.

He sits across the courtyard at one of the café tables near the cocoa stand, elbows on his knees, doing his best to scare away our customers and any unsuspecting wildlife in a fifty-yard radius. Thankfully it's a slow day, or I'd feel compelled to break my self-imposed vow of silence and ask him to move along.

The longer he attempts to play, the more it sounds like there's a dying duck being tortured in the courtyard. I'm sorely tempted to march over there and show him how to play it the right way just to save my eardrums.

A note blares from the harmonica and the hair on the back of my neck actually stands up. Of all the days for me to have left Mom's old MP3-player headphones on the charger. I'm irked that they don't have the same battery life as my phone, which I'll probably have to start carrying around again so I can listen to music for more than an hour at a time.

Eventually, Seth will lose interest in posting meme-ified videos of my set, right? He can't be upset about the science fair forever, can he? A low growl gets caught in my throat, drowned out by the squawking harmonica.

As frustrated as I am with Seth and his social media posts, I'm even more peeved that Kash is sitting over on that wrought iron chair watching me work as he murders "Twinkle, Twinkle, Little Star."

I can't take it anymore.

"Use your diaphragm," I call out loud enough for him to hear.

The harmonica gives a final bellow, and then there's blessed silence.

"What?" His voice is low and gravelly when he responds, like he hasn't gotten much sleep. He sounds a lot like he did when I delivered dinner to him that first night, when he was just a dark shadow.

"Your diaphragm," I repeat, pointing to my midsection. "Don't huff and puff like the big, bad wolf. Control your breathing as you play."

"Oh," he says, his eyes widening. He glances from me to the harmonica and back again.

Trust me, dude, I'm equally surprised I'm talking to you, let alone helping you out.

He breathes deeply and brings the harmonica to his mouth. This time when he plays, it's slightly better.

"Thanks," he says.

I nod and walk away.

NOVEMBER 9

I'M STILL NOT READY to pull my lyric notebook down off the shelf, but the temptation to write music again in earnest is too great to ignore. Just because I don't want to work with Kash (and he doesn't want to work with me) doesn't mean I don't want to be a working songwriter at all. Even if I don't have any co-written songs to turn in by the end of the year, it couldn't hurt to come up with some material for Barry. It'll do me good to flex my writing muscles.

I grab a fresh paisley-print notebook from the shelf, a blue gel pen, and my guitar case. There's an old hayloft in the big red barn that's a good, out-of-the-way spot to write without interruption.

The ladder is less rickety than it looks, and it only takes a minute for me to make my way up to the loft. We mostly store extra holiday decorations and old junk Dad doesn't want to throw away up here. There's even an antique Portland Cutter sleigh, with a black body and red tufted upholstery, that I like to curl up in to write.

Small windows set high in the barn's walls let in enough ambient light that the space is cozy like a cocoon, not creepy like a crypt. Dust motes float through the air, and I breathe in the comforting old barn scent.

Settling into the sleigh's bench seat, I turn sideways and prop the empty notebook on my leg in case inspiration hits and I need to jot down notes. After running through some warm-up scales, I play a few bluegrass-y verses of AJ Lee & Blue Summit's version of "Tear My Stillhouse Down," and then I get to work.

That chord progression Kash was working on the other day has been on my mind. It hasn't been as persistent an earworm as the new Hidden Acres Christmas Tree jingle was, but it's still there. Waiting for me. There was nothing fancy about it, and I strum through the chords like Kash did to get a feel for them while I hum the melody he was singing over it. I pause, the gears in my mind turning as I adjust my fingers on the fretboard and start with the relative minor chord. It's better, but there's still something missing.

If I was writing the song for me, I'd slow it down and add arpeggios to give it more of a folksy feel, and I'd leave some space for fingerpicking. But for Kash . . .

I picture his dark eyes peering out from beneath his cowboy hat with confidence. I've never seen him onstage, but I bet he has presence. He's definitely not scared of the spotlight like I am. Add his scuffed old work boots and his black leather jacket, his in-need-of-a-trim hair and the shadowy stubble along his jawline, and Kash embodies more of a country-rocker vibe than that of a classic country artist.

What Kash needs is a song with power chords.

I drop the third note and only play the root and fifth notes of the chords. Now we're getting somewhere. I hum the melody again, and this time, it's like magic. It just fits.

I can't quite remember the lyrics, so I make some up as I go, just to give it a test run. "Something, something about taillights. And then there's a parked car. I can't remember the words to the song," I sing, already hearing in my mind how the melody will sound with some folk-style harmonies layered in to really lean into the country side of things.

"Is that my song?"

I yelp like a cat whose tail just got stepped on and reflexively kick out my leg. I've never taken self-defense lessons before, and I'm most definitely not a ninja, so all I manage to do is pull a muscle as my notebook goes flying into the sleigh's dash with a dull thud. "Ow."

Kash climbs the rest of the way up the ladder and steps into the loft. "You okay?" There's dust on his knees and a piece of straw on his shirtsleeve, but otherwise he's the epitome of a hot, broody musician.

"I'm fine," I reply automatically. "You just startled me."

But, no, I'm not *okay*. What is he doing here? My already racing heart doesn't slow, and the air up here feels a billion times warmer than it did a few minutes ago.

"Didn't mean to scare you." With apparent lack of awareness that he's just intruded into my personal space and scared the living daylights out of me, Kash wanders around the loft, glancing between the heaps of decorations and the exposed rafters. When he reaches the sleigh, he sets his hand on the dash and studies me with dark, soulful eyes.

I can't seem to look away, but I absolutely refuse to focus on his eyes. I look at his mouth instead. Big mistake. Why does he have to have such tempting lips?

"Hey," he says.

"Hey," I reply.

TRACK 12

I Ain't Got the Time or the Talent

Kash

NOVEMBER 9

SO, THIS IS awkward.

Paisley sits up as straight as a board in a sleigh that's been pushed up against the wall, under the barn's eaves. She holds her acoustic guitar out in front of her like a shield. Unlike the open and earnest expression she had with the schoolkids the other day, her eyes are narrowed and her lips are pursed, as they've been the last few times I've interacted with her. She's tense and defensive, and I feel about as welcome as a porcupine at a balloon factory.

What is it about me that pisses her off so damn much? From the minute she first saw me, she's had a big ol' chip on her shoulder. Like she despises me just for existing.

For being Kash Murray.

Yes, okay, maybe I could have done a better job introducing myself. She was busy and working, so I should have chosen a better time and place. But I was anxious to make it clear I wasn't looking for a writing partner. I don't know what all Barry might have told her, but I didn't want her thinking we were going to meet up at the studio to work when I had absolutely no intention of being there.

But I was a little taken aback at how quickly she dismissed me. At how glad she seemed that we wouldn't be working together.

"Thanks for the harmonica help," I say.

"Don't mention it," she replies, but unlike some people who say it as a quick, rote response, I actually think Paisley means it by how razor sharp her tone is. It's like she doesn't want to be reminded of doing something nice for someone she despises.

Someone like me.

This is going downhill fast, and I'm no skier. Or snowboarder. Or much of an outdoorsman, really. Music's always been my thing. And now I'm watching it slip away from me in real time.

Fifty-two days left.

"So . . . um." I rub my hand over the back of my neck, trying to release some of the tightness before it builds into a tension headache. "I wasn't tryin' to intrude, I swear," I say. "I just heard you singing my song . . ."

If I thought she was tense before, I was wrong. She flinches and every muscle in her body goes taut like she's bracing for impact.

Her eyes get flinty. "So?"

I'm over here, cool as can be, considering, and she's giving me attitude? What right does she have to be upset, as if she's the one who's been wronged here? She took my song . . . just took it and . . .

Well, made it better. But I told her I didn't need her help.

I don't want her help.

And what's with everyone wanting to completely change what *I* write? First Justin. Now Paisley.

Except . . . it's better.

It's a heck of a lot better. For the first time since I started strumming the chords, I don't hate it. In fact, I could see myself performing it onstage.

And unlike Justin's revamp, which was clearly rewritten to suit his style, Paisley's managed to make this song sound more like *me*.

"So . . . it sounds good," I admit.

The critical voice in the back of my head taunts me. *It's better than anything you could come up with on your own.*

"Oh," she says, tucking a strand of her dark auburn hair behind her ear. She relaxes into the sleigh's worn-velvet back cushion in apparent relief. "I was just"—Paisley focuses her attention on the tuning pegs of her guitar—"messing around."

I brace my forearms on top of the curved dash with its chipped black paint and lean forward so I don't bang my head on the rafters. "Must have been at it for a while."

Paisley peers up at me from beneath dark eyelashes, her bottom lip caught between her teeth. I try not to stare.

She lifts her shoulder in a slight shrug. "Not really."

"C'mon. It must have taken you a few hours, at least."

Her cheeks grow rosy, almost like she's embarrassed, and she looks away. "I've only been up here for an hour or so."

"And you weren't working on it at all before?" I give an incredulous laugh. My knee knocks into the metal crossbar that connects the runners and I wince.

Paisley shakes her head.

There is no way Paisley took my basic bull crap and turned it into *that* in less than an hour.

"I don't believe it. Not possible," I say, my tone filled with honest-to-goodness disbelief.

"You can believe whatever you want," she says dismissively. She leans down to pick up a cloth-covered notebook from the floor of the sleigh, then flips it closed and sets it on the seat beside her.

"Look," I say, holding up my hands, palms out and fingers pointing to the sky. "I appreciate the effort, but—"

She glances up and fixes me with a steely gaze. "I didn't do it for you," she says. The way her nose scrunches in irritation is incredibly cute. "You made it perfectly clear you don't need my help."

"I did," I say.

Except that was before . . . and now?

Now I'm not so sure.

Paisley's done more for my music in less than an hour than I've managed to accomplish in over three months. I can't help wondering how much she could do for my demo in the time that I have left.

I wanted to do it on my own to show the guys that they made a huge mistake. That I could survive and thrive without Six String Justice. But what'll happen to my career if I completely punt it because I'm too stubborn to see straight?

Even if I manage to get a demo to Barry in time—and that's a major *if*—it won't have anything on it as good as what Paisley just came up with.

Your songs just aren't hit material.

. . . basic bull crap . . .

What do you bring to the table?

Justin's words play on repeat in my mind.

Paisley grabs her guitar by the neck and slides out of the sleigh. I'm more than a few inches taller than her, so she has to tip her chin up to look me in the eye. I stare down at the freckles that dust her nose and lean in. She smells like fresh air and pine sap, with a hint of butterscotch. I inhale and wonder what it might be like to kiss her smooth, pink lips.

"Just so we're clear," she says, fixing me with a stony expression. "I have zero interest in helping you write anything. Ever."

DUST SWIRLS AROUND THE loft in Paisley's wake. I blink and massage my neck, wondering if it's possible to get whiplash from a conversation.

I don't know that I've ever inspired such hostility from anyone before. She doesn't even know me. I sure as hell have never been interested in anyone who had that much animosity for me. I may not want to work with her on my demo, but I can think of plenty of other things we could do to get better acquainted.

Keep dreaming, dude.

Forget dreaming. I have to get focused. Problem is, I don't know how. Back in the old days, I'd start playing a song I was working on and Ryder would grab his drumsticks and come in with a solid beat. Justin and Johnny would grab their guitars and we'd jam. Hearing the other instruments helped me figure it all out. But now it's just me and my guitar.

There's an old wooden chair next to a bin of green and red

bulb ornaments as big as grapefruit. I use my palm to brush the dust off and then sink down into it. It creaks but holds, and I sit back and stare at the sloped ceiling above me.

Putting together a six-song demo is looking pretty impossible right about now. I don't have the time or the talent. Unless things change, I'm destined to blow my music career to smithereens in fifty-two days. If I can't deliver, word will get around and no one else will take a chance on me again. Nashville's a big city, but it's not that big.

I wanted to do this solo, but I've never felt more alone.

No band.

No muse.

No Paisley.

I take a deep breath, hoping to catch a whiff of pine sap or butterscotch, but there's no trace of Paisley left in the loft. Still, the way she played my song echoes around the rafters with how it's seared in my memory, her voice soaring over the melody even as she messed up the lyrics.

My phone buzzes in my pocket and I pull it out.

Today, 3:14 PM

Barry:

Hey kid, how's the demo coming?

Perfect timing, Barry.

I run a hand through my hair in frustration and give the ends a little tug. What am I supposed to tell him? I don't have the guts to admit to Barry that I'm no closer to having a demo now than I was when he sent me up here. It's not going great, but there's time to turn this around. I've still got fifty-two days.

Today, 3:16 PM

Kash:

👍

Today, 3:16 PM

Barry:

You record anything yet?

A scratch track?

Today, 3:17 PM

Kash:

Been focused on writing.

Today, 3:18 PM

Barry:

Paisley's easy to work with, right?

I wouldn't know.

Crap, I never actually told Barry I didn't want to work with her. And I guess Paisley hasn't let him know about it, either.

I stand and pace over to a box filled with wooden blocks of all shapes and sizes. I pick one up and twist it in my hand while I consider how to respond. Barry initially said it was up to me if

I wanted to work with her a little or a lot, so I didn't think I had to keep him updated. Although, I suppose she did help me improve my harmonica playing, which is music-writing adjacent, so technically I worked with her a little. Who knows, I might decide to put a harmonica track on a song for the demo.

Today, 3:20 PM

Kash:

👍

I toss the wooden block back into the heap and a clattering sound fills the loft.

Today, 3:20 PM

Barry:

I bet you're cooking.

I just knew you two would be perfect collaborators.

I grimace.

I'm not sure I'd go that far, Barry.

Still, Paisley did take a song I was writing and work on it, too. So, you could call that a collaboration.

Today, 3:23 PM

Kash:

👍

Today, 3:24 PM

Barry:

Not to add any pressure, but the folks in management would like to hear a sample.

A short sample.

Can you get me something by the end of the week?

Can I get Barry something by the end of the week?

I release a maniacal laugh.

I haven't managed to put two decent notes together in weeks. There's not a snowball's chance in hell I can make anything happen by the end of the week, even if it's just a short sample.

Then Barry decides to really twist the knife.

Today, 3:27 PM

Barry:

I expect the sample in my inbox by noon on Friday.

Good luck, kid!

Say hi to Paisley for me.

TRACK 13

A Plate Full of Humble Pie

Paisley

NOVEMBER 9

"PAISLEY."

I turn to find Kash jogging toward me. His dark hair falls into his face, and he brushes it back from his eyes when he catches up to me. Slightly out of breath, he flashes me a grin that's part contrite and part calculating.

I don't have to be clairvoyant to know where this is going.

"No," I say, spinning around so quickly, the pom-pom tail of my sparkly Santa hat almost whacks him in the face.

"Wait," he says, hustling to keep up with me. Our boots crunch over gravel and send small pieces of stones scattering. "You haven't even heard what I have to say."

I pick up the pace. Nothing he has to say interests me. Well, that's not true. An apology would be interesting. Admitting he's a jerk would pique my curiosity. I suppose if he were here to tell me I won the lottery, I'd hear him out. But realistically, he's tracked me down for one reason and one reason only: He needs a favor. And I'm not in the mood. "It doesn't matter. The answer's no."

"Please?" he asks, and he actually presses his palms together like he's begging.

"No."

"Pretty please?"

"Still no," I grumble.

Kash follows me into the courtyard like a piece of gum stuck to the bottom of my shoe. It's my night to work the cocoa stand. It's not as crowded as it'll be after Thanksgiving, but Mom's running a drop-in cornucopia craft night over at the big red barn as one of our pre-Thanksgiving events, so there are enough people milling about to justify firing up the electric stainless steel water boiler.

"Pretty, pretty please with a cherry on top?"

There's a desperate look in Kash's big brown eyes, and I bet he doesn't hear no an awful lot.

"What are you, like, six?" I pull open the hip-height saloon door to the cocoa stand and unlock the cabinet where we store the single-serve cocoa packets. Then I grab a wicker basket from the shelf and set it on the counter.

"Paisley," he says with an impish grin that is most definitely *not* adorable. "Please just hear me out."

"Why should I?"

His smile falters and his brows furrow. "Because I was wrong."

Well, that gets my attention. It takes a lot to own up to something.

I stop setting out stirring sticks and paper cups and take a good, long look at him. I look past the shape of his jawline and notice the firm, determined set of his jaw. I ignore the golden flecks in his deep brown eyes and focus instead on the sincerity in their depths. It takes a second for me to convince myself that I'm not getting taken in by his good looks or a manipulative lie.

"I'm listening," I say.

"I shouldn't have been so quick to decide not to work with you. I should have shown up to that first session in the studio the morning after I arrived, and I should have made an effort. It was rude to blow you off and then show up while you were working to tell you I didn't need your help. I can imagine how it felt to be treated like that. To have wasted your time. And I'm deeply sorry."

It's a good start, and honestly, I'm kind of impressed. I didn't think he had it in him. But there's still so much hurt I'm carrying around. I'm not sure it's enough.

"Is that all?"

He scrunches up his face and closes his eyes. A muscle in his jaw ticks as he thinks. He opens his eyes and fixes me in his gaze. "I'm sorry about the whole room service thing. I shouldn't have been so demanding, and I should have been more grateful that you brought me anything to eat at all. For what it's worth, it was really good." The edges of his mouth tip up. "Look, I messed up. And you and I both know I'm in a bind. I have a deadline for this demo, and I . . ." His brow furrows like he's in pain. "I've never been great about asking for help and sometimes my ego gets in my way. I'm pretty sure that's part of the reason I'm not in the band anymore."

I cross my arms over my chest and arch my eyebrows.

"Thing is, I can't do it on my own. I thought I could. I can't.

And so here I am, asking for help. And I know I'm asking a lot of you," he says. He reaches out to grab my hands and dips down so that we're eye to eye. "But I need your help. Please."

Somehow, I manage to extract my hands from the comforting warmth of his skin on mine. The calluses on his left hand brush over the back of my right hand, and I let out a slow, measured breath. I take a step back and swallow.

Turns out, I'm a sucker for baby animals and quality apologies from Kash Murray.

"Meet me in the loft tomorrow at nine a.m.," I say, shaking my head in disbelief because I can't believe the words coming out of my mouth. "Bring your guitar and whatever you've been working on."

"I'll be there," he says in a raspy voice. He reaches out and gives my arm an excited squeeze. His eyes twinkle in the white Christmas lights. "Thank you."

A group of people wander over and I direct my attention back to getting everything ready to make the hot cocoa. He nods goodbye and turns to go.

"Hey, Kash," I say before he walks away. "Don't make me regret this."

NOVEMBER 10

SINCE AGREEING TO HELP Kash, I've had a field day with my doubts. Was agreeing to co-write his demo a wise business decision or just another choice I'll come to regret?

I guess there's only one way to find out for sure.

The ladder to the loft creaks as I climb up to the ledge. I'm almost to the top when Kash greets me. "Morning."

He stands in the loft, his dark hair post-shower damp. Light from the window behind him casts a golden halo around his head, and in his dark T-shirt and black jeans, he might as well be standing on a stage. It's incredibly sexy and disconcerting. He steps forward and reaches down to help me up, like he's picking me out of a crowd to join him onstage. I hesitate, wondering how many times he's done this before. Is that why he didn't recognize my face?

I can't go there. What does it matter how many groupies he has? I should grit my teeth and just get over it already. I can't expect Kash to show up, ready to work, and then not give it my all because of my own hang-ups. If we're going to pull this off, we both need to give one hundred percent.

"Thanks," I say, reaching for his hand.

His grip is sure and steady. He tugs me up the rest of the way, and I stumble when the toe of my boot catches on an uneven floorboard. Kash braces me before I slam into his chest. His eyes widen, and then his gaze goes to my mouth. There's a definite charge to the air around us, and for the first time, I'm glad the loft is no longer used to store hay. One spark and it would all go up in flames.

Kash drops his hands from my upper arms where he was steadying me and steps back to give me space. The cool air of his wake brushes over my heated skin, and I give myself a little shake. Just because he's hot doesn't mean I should let myself go all weak-kneed for him. We're here to work, and with everything already on my plate, I don't have time to lose focus.

I follow Kash toward the barn's long wall, where some of

the boxes and crates have been reorganized and stacked to create a cozy nook around the sleigh and two mismatched wooden chairs. An old, braided rug is spread in the center.

"You've been busy," I say, setting my guitar down so I can unwrap the scarf wound around my neck.

It's kind of cute how his spine straightens with pride. He does a little bounce on the balls of his feet and then strides over to his guitar case.

The old ladder-back chair wobbles a bit when I sit down and set my acoustic guitar in my lap. Kash settles into the Windsor side chair across from me. I check the tuning on my guitar and then turn my attention to Kash. "Ready to get started?"

WE START BY PLAYING the chorus of Kash's song "I Don't Know How I'll Make It on My Own" a couple of times. Kash makes a few small adjustments to the lead guitar part, but otherwise it sounds a lot like the version I was playing the other day.

"What about this for the intro?" he asks, his lips pressed together in concentration.

"Okay," I say. "I like where you're going. What about this?"

We fall into an easy back-and-forth pattern, building off each other's suggestions. It's almost too easy. Still, I don't hate it.

"One more time from the top?" he asks, fidgeting with the pick in his hand. "I want to see how the lyrics fit."

Up to now, we've been humming the melody line over the guitars.

"On your count," I say.

"A-one, two, a-one, two, three, four." Kash's hair has dried into an unruly mop and it bounces over his brow as he nods in time to the beat.

Despite all attempts to the contrary, I've heard enough of Six String Justice's material to know what they sound like. I guess I expected Kash to have that same polished, almost pop-country sound as his former band. But there's a definite edge to his voice when he sings, and the way he goes from warm to raspy is remarkable. I can see why Exit 12S signed him. Country music fans are going to eat his stuff right up.

When the song ends, there's a hopeful glow in Kash's eyes, like he can see it all coming together and he's happy with how it's turning out. I'm glad, because I feel that way, too. Kash has told me about Barry's request for a sample, and I think we can do better and have a full stripped-down song to him by the end of the week.

Soft beams of light illuminate the nook, giving it almost an otherworldly feel. My breath catches in my chest and I force myself to look away before I lose all sense of reason and start mooning over Kash's soft, kiss-me lips or his dark, soulful eyes.

"Can we work on the harmony now?" he asks.

I nod. "I have a few ideas."

"Let's hear them."

We take it from the top again, and when Kash starts singing, I layer in some hummed harmony. We're barely through the first verse when he abruptly stops playing. My strumming hand freezes over the strings.

"What's wrong?" I ask. I thought it was sounding pretty good, but Kash's forehead is creased.

"I can barely hear you," he says.

I can try to hum louder, I suppose.

I reset my fingers to the opening chord and Kash counts us in. This time, he stops playing three words in. He presses his fingers to his temple and gives me an uncertain look. "Um, do you think maybe you could sing the harmony?"

The loft grows cold and dark like a giant cloud is passing over. Every muscle in my body tenses. "I don't sing," I say.

Kash sits back in his chair. "You sing. I've heard you sing."

That sends a spike of anxiety through me. Was Kash really pretending this whole time that he didn't recognize me from the show?

"You were singing this song up here the other day," he continues. "Butchered the lyrics something awful. But you were singing."

Oh. Right. That.

I swallow over the lump in my throat. "I don't sing in public," I clarify.

"What? Why?" he asks with genuine surprise, as if he thinks my singing voice is something people would actually want to hear.

"I have my reasons."

Stage fright.

Residual embarrassment.

Fear of becoming a laughingstock all over again.

Kash is probably the only person in Robertson County who has no idea that I was the worst opening act in Six String Justice's history. That my onstage flop has given Seth Carpenter endless material for his stupid videos as he seeks his revenge over a stupid science fair. That it almost deep-sixed my dream of becoming a working songwriter. What's even more incredible is that he was *there* that night. He heard me sing.

It's so rare and strange to have someone look at me without sympathy. Without making me constantly wonder if they're replaying my failure in their mind. I'm relieved, in this moment, that Kash has no clue. But it also feels like I'm standing under the Sword of Damocles.

I shift and the chair creaks beneath me. I should just tell him and get it out of the way. Kash's lips part and I brace myself for another question I don't want to answer but know that I should.

The question's on the tip of his tongue. He leans in and I catch a hint of his cedarwood-scented bodywash.

"Okay," he says before proceeding to scoot his chair closer to mine. "You don't sing in public. Can you just try to hum a lot louder, then?" The chair legs scrape over the old floorboards, and his knee knocks into mine when he sits down. I expect him to shift away, but instead he leans even closer and gives me a "let's do this" nod. "A-one, two, a-one, two, three, four."

TRACK 14

When the Odds Are Stacked Against You

Kash

NOVEMBER 13

PAISLEY GIVES ME a thumbs-up, presses a button on the laptop, and sets her acoustic-electric guitar in the floor stand next to her. "I think that went well," she says.

Holy smokes. We have a complete song to send to Barry.

It still needs to be mixed and we don't have time to do any mastering, but there's a vocal, lead, and rhythm guitar track in the digital audio workstation. That's not nothing.

Even though we've just finished our one-take recording of "I Don't Know How I'll Make It on My Own," I still can't quite believe we did it. A few days ago, this song was barely a crumb, and now it's a full cake, minus the frosting. It's a holiday season miracle.

I glance at the wall clock over the mixing console. It's 10:30 a.m. and Barry wants the sample in his inbox by noon.

Paisley's gaze follows mine. "We still have time if you want to record another take. Ready to give it a listen?"

I swallow and nod, my nerves on edge.

Paisley reaches over and presses the play button. She leans her hip against the table, crosses her arms over her chest, and closes her eyes. There's a moment of silence, and then I hear the crisp, clean intro Paisley played on the acoustic guitar, rhythmic chords accented with hints of melody. After about ten seconds, I come in on vocals and lead guitar.

"Taillights bleed into the dark . . ."

My singing voice is darker and deeper than it used to be, and there's a bit of a raspy catch when I get to the end of the first verse. I've managed to capture a lot of the raw emotion that's been building up inside me.

"There's not as much reverb on the electric guitar as I'd like," I say, but Paisley holds her finger to her mouth in the universal hand gesture for "shhh."

She furrows her brow, eyes closed in concentration, and listens like she's hearing every individual note. The corner of her mouth twitches every time I add in some vocal fry on the track, and her head bobs gently to the beat. A satisfied smile plays across her lips when we get to the bridge and discover we successfully made it through the complicated strumming pattern we had trouble playing in sync yesterday.

Her eyes fly open and she mouths, "We did it." I love the way her nose wrinkles over her wide smile. The way she emits pure, unbridled happiness. I want to capture this moment and bottle it up.

After a short electric guitar solo and some power chords, the intensity ebbs and I sing the final lines of the song. The rich, driving chords of Paisley's acoustic guitar fade, and then there's silence.

"Wow," I say, stunned at how good it sounds for a stripped-down sample.

"Wow," Paisley says, nodding in agreement.

She sinks down into the office chair in front of the laptop and turns her attention to the digital mixing program. "I agree with you," she says. "The electric guitar could use some reverb." She taps the laptop's track pad to toggle a few switches and spin some dials until she has them set where she wants them. "We should probably adjust the EQ." She glances up at the clock. "I don't think I have time to do it manually, but I have a filter we can use."

Paisley is a boss and knows her way around the studio. It's super sexy, watching her work. My neck heats and I look away.

Don't make it awkward.

Thank goodness she's so focused on what she's doing that she doesn't catch me staring.

"And now to add some compression." After a few more clicks, she says, "Ready to give it another listen?"

"I was born ready."

She grins back at me and hits play. I'm blown away with how much better it sounds after mixing.

"It's amazing," I say.

"It's good, but I wouldn't go as far as amazing," she says in a teasing tone. "You got a little pitchy there in the middle, and no amount of mixing can fix that."

"Hey now," I say, my heart thumping faster at the way she laughs in response.

This feels dangerously close to flirting and . . . I don't mind. In fact, I'm already looking forward to our next songwriting session together. Who would have thought?

Paisley swivels her head and peers over at me from beneath fringed eyelashes. "Let's send this off to Barry. And then I have to get back to work."

NOVEMBER 14

I DON'T KNOW IF it's the emotional roller coaster I've been on for the past few months, all the pressure I've been under to deliver a sample, the fresh country air, or the cute girl I've been spending time with, but I slept like a log last night. I roll out of bed just after one, feeling refreshed. As soon as I make some real money and have a place of my own, I'm going to buy myself one of these plush, king-sized mattresses.

Paisley gave me the heads-up that weekends at Hidden Acres keep her busy with a steady stream of customers, so we decided to take the weekend off from songwriting. I start out grateful to have a quiet day to myself. I lounge around the apartment for a while, checking in on my folks and Granddad, and watching college football on Saturday (go, Volunteers!), but by halftime, I find I really miss being around Paisley. I've never really missed anyone like this before.

It's funny: She's out there on the farm, in the pine trees, and here I am, holed up in the Hideaway, pining for her.

I wonder if I can write a song about that?

Eventually, boredom gets to me. I haven't lurked on Six String Justice's social media lately, but all this extra time on my hands has me pulling up their latest posts.

6StringJustice:

Don't believe the rumors. The three of us will be just fine.

6StringJustice:

Check out Nashville Music Scene's interview with band leader Justin Foster.

6StringJustice:

Lineup change! Let's give a warm welcome to Bryce Skeen, our new drummer.

Whoa. Looks like trouble is brewing and I'm not entirely sure how I feel about it.

NOVEMBER 16

I'M DUE TO MEET Paisley in the loft in an hour, so it comes as a real surprise when she shows up out of the blue banging on my door at eight a.m.

I throw on a pair of pants and rush downstairs to find her

standing on the front porch wearing jeans under a plaid button-down jacket with a festive red scarf tucked under the collar and carrying a large white bucket with a metal handle. Her hair is pulled into a loose braid and some of the strands have worked themselves free in a very appealing way.

"Morning," I say as I open the door. I blink at the sunlight and rub the lingering drowsiness from my eyes with one hand while I lean my shoulder against the doorjamb.

Paisley looks up, her eyes going wide at the sight of my bare chest. She quickly averts her gaze and steps back, and I notice her cheeks have turned a rosy pink. I barely contain my grin.

"Something came up and I won't be able to work with you today. I'm sorry."

If I was thinking straight, I would be worried about how another lost day of work will affect me delivering my demo by the deadline, but my first thoughts are about how I hope it's nothing serious and how much I've missed spending time with Paisley over the past two days.

"I'll see you tomorrow?" Paisley's dark eyes flash over me before she looks away again.

Tomorrow feels like a long way off. "Is there anything I can do to help?"

"Actually," Paisley says, the sparkle of an idea lighting up her face. "Put on a shirt, grab your boots, and come with me. I think we can multitask."

"WHAT IS THAT?" I stare down at the walnut-sized brown ball hanging on a fir tree.

"*That* is a praying mantis ootheca," Paisley says with a frown.

"Say what now?"

"It's an egg sac. And they're all over the trees in this grove."

As far as I can tell, the egg sacs look a lot like tiny, harmless pine cones. "What's the big deal?"

Paisley sighs and chews on her lip as she surveys the trees around us. "Have you ever seen the inside of a house covered in hundreds of tiny praying mantis babies?"

"Uh, no." But I can definitely imagine it and it sounds like the start of a horror movie.

"Yeah, well, it's not great. Customers don't really like it." She gives me a frown. "I usually go around picking them off the trees before the lot opens for the season. But I've been so busy with the songwriting stuff, I forgot to check the trees for them until this morning. And there are . . . a lot." Her shoulders droop.

"So what's your plan?" I ask, giving her a nudge with my shoulder.

Paisley momentarily leans into me, her temple brushing against my upper arm. I'm tempted to reach out and wrap my arm around her, but before I can contemplate the wisdom of attempting a bold move like that, she pulls away.

"My plan is for us to brainstorm the next song we'll work on while we pick praying mantis egg sacs off these pines and collect them in the buckets. What do you say?"

I look down into her warm, dark eyes. She's done so much for me in the past few days, it's time I return the favor. "Sounds like a plan. I'm in," I say. "But we should add some stakes to make it more interesting."

Paisley tilts her head, and I can't resist giving her a devilish smirk.

"Isn't the fact that you're on a supertight deadline high enough stakes for you already?"

I shrug. "That's business; this is for fun."

"Okay, what are you thinking, Kash?" she asks in her no-nonsense voice. I can tell she wants to get started gathering the eggs—Paisley's not a procrastinator like me.

"I dunno," I say. It's not like I've had time to think this through. "Whoever picks the most praying mantis egg sacs . . ."

"Is a rotten egg?" she says.

"What are you, like, six?" I ask, teasing her with her own words.

She smirks. "I'm rubber, you're glue."

"Next thing you know, we'll be double-dog daring each other . . . That's it!" I clap my hands together. "Whoever picks the most praying mantis egg sacs has to follow through with the winner's choice of a double-dog dare."

"I dunno," she says.

"C'mon. The odds are stacked against me. You're a pro and this is my first time as an egg sac exterminator."

Paisley's nostrils flare in apparent horror. "We aren't going to kill them, Kash. We're just going to relocate them. Praying mantises are one of the few natural predators of spotted lanternflies and—"

"Whoa," I say, giving her arm a gentle tug. "Hold your horses. I was just trying to point out that out of the two of us, you have a significant advantage."

She gives me the once-over and rolls her eyes. "Okay, fine," she says. "You have a deal."

PAISLEY HANDS ME A bucket and a pair of gardening shears. "Readysetgo," she blurts, grabbing a bucket and racing to the closest tree. She moves fast, snipping and dropping an egg sac into the bucket. "Cut off a piece of the branch it's on," she calls over to me. "But not too much or you'll mess up the shape of the trees."

It takes me a while to find my rhythm, but soon we're dropping egg sacs in our buckets at a steady clip, my one for every two of hers.

Thud. Thud thud.

Thud. Thud thud.

I need to pick up the pace if I have any chance for a win.

The breeze whispers through the treetops. A bird sings and Paisley pauses to glance up at it. She whistles a short tune, and I'm pretty sure the bird tweets it back.

I start humming the song, the melody evolving as I work my way down the row.

Thud. Thud thud.

Beside me, Paisley joins in, humming a line of harmony. Her lips curl up into a smile. "Is this our next project?"

"You think there's enough here to make it work?"

"I think there could be."

I know we're talking about a song, but in the back of my mind I can't help but wonder if maybe there's something happening between us and if there's enough for a deeper relationship with Paisley.

TRACK 15

It Makes Me Wonder

Paisley

NOVEMBER 21

THE PAST WEEK has been a blur.

I've been juggling farmwork with songwriting, and it feels like I'm constantly getting pulled in a million different directions. Kash and customers and refrains and receipts. On repeat. It's a good thing there are so many kids visiting the farm lately, or I'd worry that Dunder and Blixem might suffer from lack of attention.

The second song for Kash's demo is taking more time to work out than our first co-writing attempt did. Thankfully, we still have about six weeks to finish the remaining five songs. Every morning, we meet up in the loft to spend a few hours working. Part of the reason it's taking so long is because we can't quite figure out what the song should be about. We have everything sorted but the lyrics. Another part of it is that I'm finding it hard to focus on the task at hand whenever Kash is nearby. I should be thinking more about whether we should use a broken chord in the reprise than how Kash's calloused fingers feel when they happen to brush over my skin. Which seems to be happening more frequently lately.

As much as I hate to admit it, I think I've developed a crush on Kash Murray.

Turns out, he's not so bad after all. Aside from our first few interactions, he's been respectful and kind. He makes me laugh. And he's not hard to look at. Just thinking about the way his piercing eyes study me has my pulse dancing.

I flip my lyric notebook closed (because Kash has also inspired me to start writing my own stuff again) and slide it back onto the shelf. I head downstairs and slip outside, taking a moment to enjoy the quiet calm of the morning. In a few hours, Hidden Acres will be a flurry of activity. It's the only Saturday between Halloween and Christmas that we're closed to the public for our annual Morgan family holiday hoedown.

I head over to the large barn, where the gathering will be held, and pull open the whitewashed barn door. Dad repainted it a few weeks ago, and the fresh white pops against the barn's red siding.

Sun filters in from the windows, and there's a church-like echo in the giant, empty room. Soon, Mom, Dad, and Halley will arrive to start setting up. Mom's already in the kitchen working on prepping the turkeys: one for the oven and one for the grill.

In this rare moment of solitude, the silence calls to me. I take a deep breath, and for the first time in months, I allow myself to take up space when I sing.

DAD AND I ARE setting up the banquet tables when Halley strolls in.

"Morning, fam. Happy hoedown day! Who wants fresh apple cider doughnuts?" She sets down a bakery box and bustles over to give us each a bear hug.

Dad kisses the top of her head.

"I've missed you," I say when it's my turn to squeeze her extra tight.

I haven't seen her in person since she dropped by with a box of emergency chocolates for me in May. She's got a summer farm tan and blond highlights, but otherwise she hasn't changed much. She inherited Dad's light brown hair and hazel eyes, but we have the same smile and button nose. There's no mistaking we're sisters.

Halley gives me a playful squeeze. "Apparently, I've missed a lot." She drops her voice to a low murmur and whispers in my ear, "What's this about a boy you've been spending time with? Mom told me that you two are as thick as thieves."

"It's not like that," I whisper back, but there's no hiding the heat that rushes to my face.

Halley steps back and flips open the bakery box. She grabs two doughnuts and hands me one. "I can't wait to meet him."

"Stop it," I say, smacking her arm. "He's here to work on a demo. The label asked me to help."

"Sure," she says with a glint in her eye.

How is it that you can love someone and hate them so much at the same time?

"Don't worry," she says, bumping her hip against mine. "I'll play nice."

"You better," I warn. Not that there's much I can do about it if she doesn't.

Mom formally invited Kash to the party and he actually filled out the RSVP card, so it's inevitable that he and Halley will meet sometime today.

We've finished getting the tables and chairs set up and are about to get started assembling the stage when I look up to find Kash standing at the door, a shadowy silhouette against the bright daylight behind him. As usual, he's dressed in his signature dark T-shirt, but instead of his standard choice of fitted black pants, he's opted for some relaxed-fit faded blue jeans. Some days he wears a cowboy hat, but today he has a black baseball cap with gold letters pulled down low over his brow. Turns out, Kash makes the boy-next-door aesthetic look good.

Dad carries over an old wooden pallet and adds it to the stack leaning against the wall where the stage will be. "Oh good, you're here," he calls out as Kash strides over, his heavy work boots thudding over the floor. "Do you think you can help me with these pallets?"

"Sure, Mr. Morgan," Kash says. He gives me a nod and then gets to work.

I finish sweeping the dance floor, but it's hard to keep the broom moving when Kash is right over there lifting things and being all strong. I hadn't noticed the muscles in his arms before, probably because he's never had a reason to flex them, but they definitely exist.

"Keep staring like that, and you'll be mopping drool before

you know it," Halley whispers as she walks by with a crate full of cloth napkins and wooden napkin rings.

I snap my jaw shut and turn away from Kash and his distracting deltoids. Blistering heat creeps up my face and burns my ears as I attentively sweep the dirt pile into a large, rusty dustpan.

Close friends and our extended family start arriving around two.

Uncle John sets his steel guitar into one of the stands I carried over from the Hideaway and goes to help Marty Mitchell set up his drum set.

The Rowes show up with a giant Crock-Pot full of sweet potatoes, a glazed spiral ham, and their banjos.

Soon, the barn is bustling as everyone lines their instruments along the wall and sets their side dishes on the serving tables. Mom and Dad timed it so that the turkeys would be ready by three, and most everyone we're expecting has arrived.

"The invite said this was supposed to be a small gathering," Kash says when he comes to stand next to me.

"This is small," I say. "At least, it is compared to some of the other gatherings we host during the year." Our Spring Fling Hoedown easily has at least three hundred musicians descending on Hidden Acres. There aren't more than fifty or so people here today.

Dad takes the stage, carrying a microphone stand. He sets it front and center. "Testing, testing. Can y'all hear me back there?"

I give him a thumbs-up.

"First off, I'd like to thank you all for coming to our annual Thanksgiving dinner and good old-fashioned country hoedown. Each and every one of you are here today because you mean so much to our family. We're grateful to have you in our lives. And, not going to lie, I'm thankful for all the side dishes, too," he says, rubbing his belly.

A soft rumble of laughter fills the barn.

"Now, it's time to eat up before we kick our feet up." Dad pulls a cowbell out of his back pocket and clanks it like a dinner bell.

Uncle John lets out a "yeehaw," and a line starts to form at the buffet table.

Dad, Mom, Halley, and I take our positions at the serving side of the table, oldest to youngest. I'm spooning a heap of mashed potatoes onto a plate for Jim Atchley when Kash steps up beside me. "Put me to work, boss," he says.

Halley kicks my shin under the table, and when I look over at her, she's waggling her eyebrows at me. I shake my head and give her a "cut it out" stare.

Older sisters are the worst.

TILDA AND BILL ROWE kick off the musical entertainment portion of the gathering with their rendition of "Dueling Banjos." Steve Scruggs plays the spoons with his brother, Sam, on the washboard. Then Marla and the Magpies play a few traditional bluegrass numbers. Next, Uncle John plays an original piece on his steel guitar. Most everyone is saving the boot-scootin' songs for later, after we've had time to digest.

"I can't believe how much talent there is in this room," Kash says, leaning forward with his elbows resting on the table. "I wish I could play like that."

"Mom says Uncle John's been playing like that since they were kids."

As we listen to the folk, bluegrass, and country music being played, Kash gradually shifts closer. I feel the body heat radiating off him before his knee brushes against mine. His elbow crawls across the table until it touches mine. Out of the corner of my eye, I catch him glance my way a few times and electric tingles spread from my belly to the tips of my toes.

I'm so distracted by his proximity, I don't see Halley slip away from the table. It's not until I watch her step onto our makeshift pallet stage, my Fender in one hand and her old Martin in the other, that I realize what she's about to do. My hands curl into tight fists as tension fills my body.

"Hi, y'all." Halley beams. "I hope everyone's having a good time."

There is a smattering of hoots and hollers in reply.

"Us Morgans are big on tradition," she continues, with a nod of acknowledgment to Mom and Dad. "And, as all but one of you know," she says, turning her focus to Kash, "one of our family traditions at the Thanksgiving Hoedown is what we like to call the Sister Song."

I let out a low groan. I am not prepared to step up on that stage.

"Paisley, can you please join me?" she asks.

I glare at Halley and then glance around at the people sitting in the barn. Uncle John taught me to play the guitar. Tilda gave me my first banjo. Marla, Steve, Sam, Joe, Clive and Carol, Becky and Jim. These people have been in my life for years, encouraging me. Teaching me. Playing music with me. I know they won't judge me.

But still, I can't seem to make myself stand.

My mouth grows as dry as a bare-branched Christmas tree.

"C'mon, Paisley," she prompts. "We hardly ever get the chance to play together anymore."

Sister guilt is the worst.

I'm tempted to fake a bout of food poisoning or a fainting spell, but that won't help with the fact that all eyes are on me. The attention is bad enough now, but it would be so much worse if people thought I was having some sort of medical event.

"You got this," Kash whispers in my ear, pressing his shoulder against mine. The flutter in my stomach from his breath on my ear blends with the flutter from the performance anxiety butterflies that have taken up residence there already.

I'm not sure that I do.

It's nice to know he has faith in me, however misplaced it is. I still haven't told him about my connection with Six String Justice, but at least he won't be comparing my previous performance to what's about to happen here, thank goodness.

With wobbly legs, I push my chair back from the table. I might as well get this over with before Halley does something really stupid. I wouldn't put it past her to force my hand by telling embarrassing stories from our childhood.

It feels like a mile of wet concrete separates me from the stage, but somehow I manage to make it over to stand beside Halley. She smiles at me, and when I force myself to grin back, I make sure she can see the death stare I shoot at her.

"What song do you want to do?" she asks sweetly, handing me my guitar.

I try not to let anyone see the way my arms shake as I pull

the strap over my head. "This was your brilliant idea," I mutter back.

If I'm lucky, she'll pick a song with an arrangement that doesn't require anything more from me than rhythm guitar.

I'm not lucky.

Halley leans into the mic and says, "We're going to play 'Mockingbird,' a song that was written by Inez and Charlie Foxx, in the style of Carly Simon and James Taylor." Of course she goes and picks a call-and-answer duet for us to sing. After this, she'll be lucky if I ever speak to her again.

I force down a swallow and wonder if I'll bomb just like the last time I stood on a stage.

Did Halley pick this song because she knew Carly Simon had to get over her stage fright to perform it live? Is this special torture supposed to be inspirational?

If that Paisley girl don't sing . . .

I glance over at Kash and he gives me an encouraging nod.

Here goes nothing.

TRACK 16

Take My Hand Two-Step

Kash

NOVEMBER 21

PAISLEY STANDS NEXT to her sister, Halley, and gives everyone a tepid smile. Every so often, her gaze lands on my face, like I'm the beacon of a lighthouse in a stormy sea. This time, in her passing glance, I catch a glimpse of the sheer terror that seems to be swirling inside her.

The next time she looks my way, I nod. *You've got this.*

Halley tilts her head toward the mic, trying to get Paisley to step closer. Paisley purses her lips. She clearly does not want to be up there.

Halley turns and gives the room a big smile. "This is a song we used to sing a lot when we were younger. Let's give it a whirl." Halley starts playing and I don't miss the flash of panic followed by the look of pure, unadulterated loathing Paisley casts her sister.

Halley's voice is sharp and twangy when she sings, the sound filling the space.

Paisley, on the other hand, sings in an almost-whisper. It's nothing like the full, vibrant voice she had when I caught her singing before.

Halley looks over at her sister, her face pinched with pain, as if it hurts her to see Paisley so petrified. I don't have any siblings, so I can't say for sure, but I don't think she's trying to be mean. It's more like she wants to share Paisley and her talents with the group gathered here.

She shifts closer to Paisley, who's an inch or so taller, and leans her head on her shoulder. Halley's voice is still punchy, but she's toned it down a bit.

Paisley's response is slightly louder this time, with a definite warble. She strums her guitar like a robot, without any heart and soul. It's hard to see her up there, a shell of the person I know. It's like someone hit the dimmer switch.

At the table next to me, a guy with a handlebar mustache turns to the woman next to him and says something about a "boost of confidence." He waits for Halley to sing the next line, and then, when it's Paisley's turn to reply again, he stands up, points at her, and belts out "Yeah" in a deep, booming bass. Then he sits down and twirls the ends of his mustache like he's pleased with a job well done.

Paisley's eyes glisten and the side of her mouth curls with a faint, bashful smile.

Halley sings the next line, and a woman on the other side of the room stands and sings "Yeah" in a breathy voice when it's Paisley's turn. She blows a kiss to Paisley and then sits back down.

Paisley's mouth twists into a deeper, less reluctant smile. She steps forward with a bit more confidence and starts strumming her guitar with a more relaxed vibe.

People continue to chime in when it's Paisley's turn to sing, offering up their own style of encouragement. Soon, Paisley's voice—while still timid—is clear enough to hear without any bolstering. The warmth and soul that I heard when she was singing to herself isn't there, but a chunk of the Paisley I've come to know and admire is back. By the end of the song, I think there are only a handful of people who haven't chimed in to sing along with her.

Paisley strums the last chord to a round of applause. Her shoulders droop with relief when the song is over. Halley pulls her into an enthusiastic hug, though Paisley's reluctant to reciprocate. Halley whispers something in Paisley's ear. Paisley stiffens and shakes her head.

A man in a dapper tan suit vest and pants combo steps onstage with a fiddle. After a quick chat, Paisley and Halley step off the stage. They disappear, and I wonder if Paisley's planning on coming back to the table. I shift, hoping to catch sight of her, my eyes scanning the room, but I can't find her. The man onstage points to the guy who was setting up the drum kit and the woman sitting next to the guy with the handlebar mustache and curls his finger to beckon them to join him on the platform.

While everyone is getting settled onstage, the man steps up to the microphone and says, "Hey, y'all."

"Hey, Clive" is the response.

"Now, who's ready to really get this shindig started?"

Hoots and hollers echo up to the rafters.

The man next to the drum kit holds up a jug. The woman at the upright bass plays a short riff. And, much to my surprise,

Paisley steps back onto the stage with a banjo. She picks a quick series of notes with her thumb, index, and middle fingers, and then strums a few chords.

"Here are some 'Clinch Mountain Blues.'"

The man nods to Paisley and sets his fiddle on his shoulder. He counts off the beat, and Paisley kicks it off at a blazing bluegrass speed. They play and people clap along. No one's dancing yet, but there's an energy shift in the barn. Paisley's fingers fly over the banjo as she picks the notes, and the longer she's up there, the more the tension drains from her shoulders. There's a moment or two when she even gets lost in the music, her eyes squeezed shut in concentration and her mouth curved up at the edges.

She's radiant up there and I can't seem to take my eyes off her.

The song ends and someone to my right calls out, "Play 'Black Mountain Rag.'"

Couples stand and make their way to an open area, which must be the dance floor. They dance as the impromptu band plays, flatfooting even as the music changes from one energetic song to another. I don't recognize most of the tunes, since I haven't spent much time listening to bluegrass, but I like the hard, driving boom-chuck rhythm and the twang of the instruments.

"I don't know about you," says the man with the fiddle after a particularly brisk song. "But I'm parched. It's someone else's turn to entertain y'all now."

MARLA AND THE MAGPIES take the stage and the size of the dance floor expands. Paisley helps Mr. Morgan fold up some of the tables to make more room, while Halley and Mrs. Morgan clear the buffet tables. I make my way over to help.

"You were great up there." I grab a few folding chairs and follow Paisley as she lines them up against the wall.

"Thanks," she says, but I don't get the sense she believes me. I wish she could see how amazing she was, more than holding her own against a bunch of older musicians with years of experience on her.

We finish clearing the tables and chairs. Paisley sets her hands on her hips and surveys the barn. Aside from Halley, Paisley and I are the youngest people here by at least a few years. It makes me wonder why none of her friends are here, if this hoedown is for the Morgan family's nearest and dearest.

The people dancing are having a blast. Some are doing a disorganized line dance, while others are twirling their partners in a two-step. Most everyone is smiling and laughing. When I glance over at Paisley, she's chewing on her bottom lip.

Looks to me like she could use some smiling and laughing herself right about now.

A version of Tim McGraw's "I Like It, I Love It" starts up and I spontaneously grab Paisley's hand. "C'mon."

She resists for a moment, giving me a critical once-over, and then lets me lead her to an open spot on the dance floor. I'm not much of a dancer, but that doesn't seem to matter in the good-natured chaos surrounding us.

Granny taught me the two-step when I was younger, and it's pretty much the only dance I know besides the country waltz.

She'd put on "Sunny Side of the Mountain" by Porter Wagoner or Patti Page's "Tennessee Waltz" and we'd dance around the living room with her quietly counting out the beat for me. Sometimes Granddad would cut in, and I'd watch him spin her around and around.

My chest pinches at the memory, and I squeeze Paisley's hand as we join the circle of dancers moving counterclockwise around the dance floor. It takes us a few spins to coordinate our steps, but soon we're moving in sync. The other couples laugh and chatter, and it's hard not to get caught up in the fun. Paisley's smile is so bright it's dazzling.

My heart skips a beat and I miss a step. We trip over each other's feet as I try to get us back on track. Paisley giggles as she stumbles into me, her forehead bumping into my chest. My hands go to her waist to steady her, and she looks up at me with a dimpled grin. Our faces are so close and her lips are so irresistible, I'm tempted to lean down and kiss her right here and now, but before I do, the music stops. She blinks and pulls away, clapping.

We join in on a few line dances. She's just as uncoordinated as I am. We turn left when everyone else turns right, kicking our legs when we should be hitching them. We're a mess, but this is the best time I've had in ages.

We totally mix up a spin and end up facing each other. Wispy strands of hair frame Paisley's flushed face, and her nose does that adorable crinkle thing that drives me wild. She looks around at the other people dancing in lockstep and tosses her hands up in defeat.

I grab her hands and spin her around before pulling her

down into a dip. Our foreheads brush and my breath catches in my chest. Paisley's eyes go wide in surprise and then twinkle as I set her back upright.

The next song is slower. Paisley lifts her hands to my shoulders and snuggles into me. I set my hands on her waist and we sway together to the beat. "Are you having fun?" she asks.

"Yeah, are you?"

"Kinda. I . . ." She takes a deep breath. "I have a pretty bad case of performance anxiety, so getting up there . . ." She looks over at the stage.

"That's why you don't sing in public?" I glance down at the top of her head. The soft light from the twinkling white strands strung on the barn's rafters above us makes her hair gleam.

Paisley leans closer and rests her head on my chest. I wonder if she can hear the way my heart skips a beat or feel the surge of adrenaline as it races through my veins.

"One of the reasons," she says.

"And Halley knows that and she still had you get up there?" *That's kind of a jerk move.*

"Yeah." Paisley snorts. "Everyone knows."

"I didn't know."

But I do now.

It strikes me that I want to know everything about Paisley. To know her better than anyone else does. I want to watch her favorite movies together. Memorize her go-to coffee order. Learn how it feels to tuck her close on a winter day as our foggy breaths mingle in the cold.

I pull her in closer as I picture it and rest my chin on the top of her head, catching the faint scent of pine trees in her hair. I can't believe I was stupid enough to think my time here would be easier without her. I can't believe I almost missed out on all *this*.

Paisley melts into me, and we spin in slow circles. The music winds down, and soon we're one of the few couples left on the dance floor.

When the music stops, Paisley pulls away. My arms feel empty without her. She tucks a strand of hair behind her ear before wrapping her arms around her waist.

Does she miss me holding her, too?

Mr. Morgan gets back on the microphone. "First, I'd like to thank everyone for coming out and spending the better part of your day with us. I've said it before and I'll say it again—we are so grateful for your friendship and the time we spend together. Thank you for celebrating an early Thanksgiving with us." He brushes a hand through his salt-and-pepper hair and shifts his weight. "Second, I know some of you have to leave soon, but just know there's an urn full of fresh coffee and plenty of pie back there." He points to the banquet tables. "So make sure to help yourselves before you go."

People separate into smaller groups, pulling metal folding chairs into circles while they chat and eat dessert. Paisley's uncle John plays his lap steel guitar, and someone pulls out a harmonica. A few other people grab instruments, and they all start improvising.

"I'll be right back," Paisley says.

While she's gone, I listen to the impromptu jam session, awed by the song that they're playing with no prior plan or practice. I wish I could do something like that.

A minute later, Paisley's back carrying her acoustic guitar. "Here." She hands it to me. "You should join them."

"I don't know . . ." I say.

"You don't have to, but I can tell you want to."

She's right. It's been a while since I sat and jammed with Six String Justice. Even after everything, it's one thing I miss.

"You coming?"

She shakes her head. "I'm going to help Mom clean up. Have fun." She gives my arm a gentle pat, and my skin tingles beneath her palm.

When I walk toward the circle, the woman playing spoons shifts her chair back so I can sit next to her. Everyone keeps playing, and eventually I join in. It's challenging, to play by ear and predict what everyone else will do, but it's also invigorating. There's a give and take, a push and a pull, a sharing of sounds and a bit of the soul. In this moment, I'm reminded of why I love music so damn much.

A good meal. Paisley's company. Fantastic music. It all adds up to tonight being one of the best nights of my life.

TRACK 17

I Really Want to Kiss You Right Now

Paisley

NOVEMBER 23

I SHOW UP at the barn with my guitar just before nine a.m.

The tables have been returned to the storeroom, the chairs folded and put away. The pallets are in a pile out back and the floor has been swept clean. Everything's returned to the way it was before the hoedown.

Everything but my heart. Which seems to have set itself on Kash Murray.

I don't know when it happened exactly. It could have been when he gave me an encouraging nod during "Mockingbird." It might have been when he grabbed my hand and pulled me out on the dance floor. All I know is that by the time he spun and dipped me, I was well and good on the way to falling for him.

Having these feelings for Kash is complicated in so many ways. Obviously, it's not a great idea to get involved with someone you work with. If it goes well, then there's the constant distraction of wanting to kiss and cuddle and make moon eyes at someone. If it doesn't, well, that's a whole other problem. Like it or not, the trajectory of both our music careers will be impacted by Kash's demo. We need to stay focused on writing and recording demo songs and not get caught up in romantic entanglements.

And that's assuming Kash's flirtations mean something. What if he doesn't feel the same way? What if I misread the signs?

Still, there *was* a moment—when he held me in his arms as we slow-danced to Marla and the Magpies' rendition of Kacey Musgraves's "Golden Hour," and he tipped his face toward me—I was sure Kash's lips would brush over mine. My knees went the good kind of weak, and I had a fluttering of those pre-kiss butterflies in my belly. But he didn't kiss me and my knees recovered and the butterflies flew away. Who knows, maybe I dreamed it all up.

It's possibly, probably, *definitely* for the best that we didn't kiss.

As I climb the ladder to the loft, my nerves buzz with anticipation and apprehension. I haven't seen Kash since the hoedown. His grandfather drove up yesterday morning from Nashville so they could spend the day together, and I was busy supervising an afternoon reindeer "petting zoo" with Dunder and Blixem and then, later, helping out at the gift shop.

Kash is already in the loft when I arrive. He's sitting sideways in the sleigh, legs stretched out across the bench seat, with his electric guitar on his lap. I take a minute to study his profile, the straight length of his nose, the soft part of his lips, the squareness of his chin.

He turns, eyes lighting up when he sees me. "Mornin'," he says.

"Hi." I set my guitar case down by the chairs. Thankfully,

Mom and Dad decided to get the barn insulated and had a heating system installed a few years ago, when we started hosting regular holiday events and arts and crafts activities. I pull off my coat and hang it over the back of the chair. Kash slides out from the sleigh and settles himself into his usual seat.

"Do you want to keep working on the song we started last week?" I ask, pulling my guitar from its case.

"Sure. But first, listen to this." He adjusts his guitar in his lap and then plays a C-G-D chord progression with the root note string played first before he strums the rest of the strings in a classic country strumming pattern that reminds me of the slow walking gait of a horse or an old Hank Williams song.

"Okay," I say, letting my body sway to the loping, lazy rhythm. "What are you thinking for a melody?"

Kash shrugs. "I haven't gotten that far yet."

"What's the song about?" Sometimes knowing the theme helps with developing the melody. At least, that's been my experience when I don't have something solid in mind. What Kash has so far feels lighthearted and optimistic, the kind of song you'd write about the perfect fit of blue jeans or returning home after a long absence.

"I'm not exactly sure," he says, his brow furrowed. "But I think it should be about looking forward instead of dwelling on the past."

Kash might be plucking the guitar strings, but the theme is really tugging at my heartstrings.

I pick up my guitar and strum along with him. I add a few arpeggios to see if that inspires a melody. We play the chords over and over until we're no longer thinking about them.

First I hum, trying to find the notes that feel right. Then I mumble nonsense sounds. It's hard to explain, but sometimes writing music is less about theory and following the rules, and more about capturing a feeling in an organic way. Most people listening to a song aren't going to think: "Wow, that E minor transition was really an interesting choice in the reprise." They're looking for a hook. Something to comfort their sadness, celebrate love, move their bodies, or even see the world in a different way. At the end of the day, a song can be technical as can be, but if it doesn't sound good and make you feel something, it's just a bunch of notes strung together. It's kind of like the difference between a house (the structure) and a home (the feel).

"What are you doing?"

"Looking for a melody," I mumble-sing, picking out some random notes. "Da, da, trying to write a song."

Kash's eyes dance with amusement. A chunk of his hair falls into his face and he tosses his head to move it.

"Got a deadline coming soon, mmm-hmm," I continue. "So I hope it doesn't take too long."

Kash laughs. "I don't know about the lyrics."

"The words are just fillers right now. This is a way to find the notes that feel right. You try."

We repeat the chord progression a few times, and then Kash starts singing. We go back and forth, using made-up words and random sentences. Eventually, we've both shifted to the edge of our seats, close enough that our knees brush. Close enough that I can feel the warmth of Kash's breath on my cheek. See the dusting of gold flecks in his brown eyes.

Suddenly, Kash stops playing as if he's just realized something important. His whole body stills, but he doesn't break eye contact when he reaches out and takes hold of my strumming hand.

"What is it?"

Has he come up with a melody?

Realized he left the oven on in the Hideaway?

Remembered the moment we first met?

"You're singing with me." His words are quiet, just above a whisper, as if saying it out loud would be like spilling a secret.

Oh. Wow. I hadn't realized.

But now I do.

I drop my hand from the fretboard. Let my pick fall to the floor.

This is the first time since May that I haven't felt like there were hummingbirds darting around my insides when someone else was around to hear me sing. It's the very first time I've felt comfortable—truly comfortable—singing around anyone.

No, not anyone. Kash.

"Yeah," I acknowledge, still stunned at the revelation. I study his earnest face, the way his eyebrows peak in surprise over his intelligent eyes.

He exhales. "Why me?"

"Because I trust you." The answer is out of my mouth before I can stop it. Before I realize what it means.

"Thank you," he whispers, like I've given him a gift.

But it's a gift that comes with a heavy price. Because if I trust him, I have to come clean about our shared history. And when I do, things will inevitably change between us. Once the cat's out of the bag, he won't look at me the same way he's looking at me now, with tenderness and care. How could he?

My heart races, my palms are clammy, and if I stood up right now, I know my legs would wobble and my weak knees would not hold my weight. I have all the same feelings I do before I'm about to go onstage, except this time, it's not performance anxiety that's got me wound up like a spring. It's knowing that I've unmistakably fallen hard for Kash Murray, and this time when I make a fool out of myself in front of him, there's no way he'll forget.

I don't realize I'm crying until he reaches up and brushes a hot tear away from my cheek with the pad of his thumb. My skin sizzles under his touch.

"It's okay." His voice is low and soothing.

The tears only fall faster. "It's really not. I have something I need to tell you. I should have told you before."

The weight of my confession hangs heavy on my tongue. My mouth is as dry as dust.

"The first time I met you . . . it wasn't here, on the farm. We actually met backstage at Ballad FM's Music Showcase." I take a deep, shuddering breath and continue. "I was the second opener for Six String Justice. After Chet Bryant."

I watch Kash's face for an aha moment to strike, but there isn't the slightest muscle twitch. I pick at a jagged cuticle and forge ahead.

"My set was an absolute train wreck. Performance anxiety got the better of me. I stepped offstage, completely decimated, and then Six String Justice comes along. Y'all thought I was a groupie. One of the guys grabbed my lyric book and started autographing it. It got passed around. And then you broke the spine, handed me back my notebook, and winked at me . . . I felt so small and stupid."

I press my eyes closed and let the hot tears burn watery tracks down my cheeks.

"There were videos. And social media posts, including some really harsh ones from Six String Justice. People whispered and stared and made me the butt of every joke, or at least it felt that way. I was embarrassed and hurt and angry, and I felt so helpless." I choke up. Kash reaches out and wraps his hand around mine, giving it a squeeze. "I wanted someone else to blame for that night, and the members of Six String Justice were an easy target."

I force down a swallow and brush the back of my free hand over my eyes. Kash's thumb traces a slow and steady circle over the back of my other hand.

"After graduation, I basically became a hermit. I deferred college. Stopped writing. Stopped *singing*. I just . . . stopped. And then you showed up, out of the blue."

I glance over at Kash with watery eyes. There's a darkness in his eyes I haven't seen before. Anger? Disappointment? Hurt?

He doesn't say anything, but I have to keep going. I have to get it all out if I have any hope of moving forward instead of dwelling on the past.

"I thought I hated you. I hated what you represented. I couldn't separate you from that night. But when you arrived, you didn't recognize me. And you didn't want to work together, so I thought . . . I thought it didn't matter. I figured you'd be long gone by the time you found out our connection, *if* you found out at all. But then things got complicated. We started working together and my feelings evolved, and somewhere along the way you went from being the enemy to . . . something more." I've confessed so many things already, I might as well add that star to the top of the tree.

My heart races like I've run a mile. I give a watery sniffle and sigh.

There. I did it. I fessed up to everything I needed to. And, surprisingly, it didn't kill me.

Kash leans in, lifting a hand to cup my cheek. His action is so unexpected, I freeze like a deer in headlights. "Thank you for telling me."

I'm not sure what's happening here, but it seems like I'm more surprised by how he's taking all this than he is at my confession.

"I'm really sorry for the hurt I caused you, Paisley. I had no idea, I swear."

At one time, a sincere apology was all I ever wanted from Kash. Now I have it, but it's a hollow victory.

I lean into the feelings swirling inside and let them wash over me. Maybe now I can let them go.

"Now you know, so . . ."

This is where we part ways. Kash will go off to finish his demo, and I will try to reassemble the pieces of my broken heart and figure out if there's a way to salvage my songwriting career.

Kash moves his hand to my chin and gently tilts my face toward his. "I've known about most of this for a few days now, Paisley. I overheard someone talking at the hoedown. I wasn't gonna say anything. I felt so damn bad about it all. I know what it's like to go out onstage and bomb. I've had some horrible sets, and it flat out sucks. At one of our first shows, Six String Justice was actually booed offstage. But at least when we tanked, I had a band to share it with. You were brave to step out there and do it on your own," he says.

"Why didn't you say something?"

Kash shrugs. "We were having such a good time, dancing and . . . I didn't want to ruin the moment. I didn't want to open old wounds and hurt you all over again. Plus, I thought maybe you were starting to like me?" His eyebrows rise and he has a hopeful look in his eyes.

"I do like you."

Kash lifts both his hands to my face, his thumbs caressing my damp cheeks. He drifts closer until his forehead brushes against mine.

"I really want to kiss you right now."

My heart feels too big as it pounds against my rib cage. I really want to kiss him, too. So I do.

My lips press against his and I melt into him. Kash is warm and steady, anchoring me in place as I'm caught up in a torrent of emotions. His hands slide to the nape of my neck, and he deepens the kiss. Our noses brush and the backs of my knees tingle. Kash makes a low moaning sound in his throat before he pulls away.

"I think I just came up with the perfect melody," he says with a small smile. "But it can wait."

And then he leans in for another kiss.

TRACK 18

I Could Need Someone Like You, Baby

Kash

NOVEMBER 23

KISSING PAISLEY IS like diving into a cold creek on a hot summer day. At first, there's the shocking, tingly feeling that bubbles up over your skin as you disappear under the surface. Then that buoyant surge as you drag in your first breath of air after you rise, the thrill of the water rushing over you and the sweet relief from the stifling heat.

Paisley's lips are soft and smooth. She leans into me, her hands wrapping around the back of my neck as she pulls me closer, her acoustic guitar nestled in her lap between us. I'm reluctant to pull away, even as my lungs burn for air. We both inhale at the same time, but unlike mine, her breath is shaky and uneven. Her dark eyelashes glisten with lingering tear droplets, and a line of uncertainty appears between her brows.

A gust of wind rattles the windowpane, followed by the *plop*s of a few large raindrops as they smack against the glass. The loft grows dim beneath the dark November sky, making the space seem to shrink around us.

"What happens now?" Paisley asks in a ragged whisper.

"More kissing?" I brush my lips over the soft curve of her cheek.

"I'm serious," she says on a sigh that seems to hold the weight of the world.

So am I.

If I had my druthers, I'd spend the rest of the day up here in this loft, kissing Paisley until our lips go numb and our eyes grow drowsy. I'm tempted to do just that.

But she's right. We have to figure out what happens next.

I reach over and brush her hair back from her face, letting my fingers linger over the shell of her ear. The strain of the melody that I heard when her mouth first pressed against mine plays on a loop in my mind. It's similar to a line that's been running through my head for at least a week, but I couldn't figure out where it was going. Now it's clear as day.

I never understood the concept of a muse. I know there are plenty of artists who talk about a certain someone who's the source of their inspiration, and I always thought it was bogus to rely on one person like that. I didn't need a muse when I was with Six String Justice. I had my boys and we were making it happen. But now I'm wondering if I was looking at it all wrong. Maybe a muse isn't the source of inspiration. Maybe a muse is like a magnifying glass, taking something that was always there inside you and helping you see it better.

"Look," I say, locking eyes with her. "I'd like to continue working on my demo with you. I think we make a great team, and nothing that's happened changes that for me. I can't go back and fix what happened in May, but I promise I'll do my very best to support you and make sure you feel seen from here on out. I like spending time with you, I like kissing you, and I'd really like to see where this thing between us goes. But it's your call, Paisley. I want it all, but I'll take what I can get. And if I have to settle for nothing, I'll find a way to deal with that, too."

Paisley chews on her bottom lip as she studies my face. Worry, hope, concern, and possibility all flicker in her eyes.

Rain patters steadily on the metal roof, and my heart beats just as fast as I wait for Paisley to decide. Her lips part and it takes all my self-control to hold back and not pull her into another sweet, irresistible kiss.

"We can't lose focus on the music," she finally says. She reaches out and fiddles with a tuning peg. "You need to deliver a demo in a few weeks, and this is a huge opportunity for me to get my songwriting career started."

"Agreed," I say.

"My family's counting on me to help out on the farm, especially with the holidays coming up."

"I'd never ask you to blow off your family or your commitments." I thread my fingers through hers and give her hand a gentle squeeze. "I won't be around later this week—I'm going to spend a few days with my granddad—but other than that, you can always put me to work when we aren't writing music. I can help."

Paisley clasps my hand tighter. "Are you sure about this *us* thing?" She worries her bottom lip.

I lift our intertwined hands to my mouth and brush a kiss

over her knuckles. "Very, very sure. In fact," I say, my mouth curving up into a sly smile, "I'm so sure about it, I could sing."

And I can. Because I know the song now.

It all comes together like a musical epiphany. I drop her hand and reach for my guitar. As soon as the first note is strummed, I'm sure I'm onto something. I can feel it in the way the strings vibrate beneath my pick. In the way the rain on the roof adds a muted percussion background hum. In the way I don't have to think about it, the music just flowing through me.

"The past is gone,
What's done is done,
I never thought I could need someone like you, baby."

Paisley's eyes light up when she hears how the lyrics fit with the melody we've been noodling over for a while now. She straightens in her chair, sets her fingers on the fretboard of her guitar, and bobs her head gently to the rhythm. Soon, she starts accompanying me, the warm notes of her acoustic guitar filling in the gaps and rounding out the sharp, tinny sounds coming from my unplugged electric.

As I sing, she hums lines of country-style harmony as she tries to match my phrasing.

"Gotta look ahead,
Or we'll fall behind,
You came up fast on my blind side, baby."

In the places where I haven't figured out the lyrics yet, I mumble like Paisley suggested, letting my subconscious work on the puzzle. Hints of words and phrases roll off my tongue, things like "tenderness" and "making plans."

When the last notes are played, we sit in stunned silence.

"That was good," she says.

"Really good."

There's still work to be done, but we're so close I can taste it. Apparently my stomach can, too, based on how it grumbles in agreement.

"Crap, what time is it?" Paisley glances at her watch. "I'm sorry, Kash, I've gotta run. I told Mom I'd help restock the gift shop before it opens."

I stand with her as she starts packing up. "Anything I can do to help?"

She shakes her head and zips her guitar into its case. "Not really. Why don't you keep working on your song—"

"Our song. We're a team."

Paisley pauses in the middle of shrugging into her jacket. I reach out and help it on. The vibrant orange-and-red plaid fabric sets off the auburn highlights in her hair. I sweep a loose strand out of her face, letting the back of my hand brush over her cheek.

She sighs and presses up on her tiptoes to kiss me. Our lips meet and I pull her in close, loving the way she feels in my arms.

Paisley pulls back and nibbles her bottom lip. "I can meet you in the studio later tonight. Around eight?"

Eight hours seems like forever to have to wait to see her again, especially after everything we just shared. But I said I'd take what I can get and I meant it.

"I'll be there," I say.

NOVEMBER 24

GRANDDAD'S DRIVING UP FROM Nashville to pick me up first thing tomorrow morning, so we're under some pressure to get the tracks for the demo of "I Could Need Someone Like You, Baby" recorded today. If we're able to finish it up before I go, then we'll only have four songs left to work on when I get back. Barry hasn't checked in lately, but it would be nice to have something ready to go just in case the folks at Exit 12S get anxious for another sample.

"I could try to have Granddad drive me back on Friday," I offer. But based on how busy Hidden Acres has been over the past few days, I don't expect Paisley would have much time for me anyway, if I did. The farm's schedule for Thanksgiving, Black Friday, and Small Business Saturday is chock-full of activities and events.

Paisley's standing in front of the studio's recording equipment, plugging the XLR mic cable into the audio interface. "I appreciate the offer," she says, grabbing a quarter-inch cable from a pegboard behind her. "But I think we have it under control."

"I want to be helpful," I say.

"I get that. And I appreciate it. But what do you know about making wreaths from fresh tree trimmings?"

"Er."

"How do you feel about plaster of Paris?"

My brows knit in confusion and Paisley laughs.

"Exactly. No offense," she says, coming over to wrap her arms around my shoulders. Her fingers tangle with the hair at the nape of my neck. "I think . . ." She pauses, as if looking for a polite way to say what's on her mind.

"I'll just get in the way?"

"Maybe a little." She lifts onto her tiptoes and presses her mouth to mine.

I tug her closer and deepen the kiss, tasting traces of the vanilla chai latte she had earlier. I pull away long enough to mumble, "Probably a lot."

Because I know nothing about making wreaths or plaster of wherever.

"You know," Paisley says, looking up at me from beneath her lashes. "I do have something you can help me with on Sunday."

"Count me in."

"Don't you want to know what it is?" she asks with an adorable, dimpled grin.

"Will you be there?"

"Yes."

"That's all I need to know." I kiss her on the neck, just below her ear, and she giggles and pushes me away with a smirk.

"Suit yourself. You're gonna want to wear a pair of old jeans and a flannel shirt, though."

I bite my tongue before I tell her I'd happily put on a Santa suit and drive a sleigh if she asked me to.

Paisley gets back to setting up the recording equipment, and I grab the paper where I've scribbled down the lyrics for "I Could Need Someone Like You, Baby."

This song came together so fast. If only they could all be that way, but I know that's wishful thinking. We still have a lot of writing to do—four whole songs' worth—before the end of the year. So, while Paisley's working hard here on the farm, I'm hoping I can come up with a few more ideas so that we can hit the ground running when I get back.

NOVEMBER 25

PAISLEY'S PREPPING DUNDER AND Blixem for today's holiday photo shoot when I find her to say one last goodbye before I take off for Nashville. We already said (kissed) our goodbyes last night, after we finished recording in the studio. It was the kind of kissing you don't do in front of reindeer or grandparents or families looking for the perfect fresh-cut Christmas tree. Because while it was sweet with a dash of mild salsa spicy, kissing in front of any of them would be ridiculously awkward.

"Granddad should be here soon," I say, shoving my hands into my front pockets as I sidle up to the corral. I hitch my foot up on the bottom rail and lean my weight against the fence.

Paisley glances up from Blixem, her nose and cheeks rosy from the cool air. Her hair is wavy and loose under a red cowboy hat with a green band.

"I hope the two of you have a great visit," she says.

A couple walks by, heading in the direction of the tree lot, a handful of younger kids chasing after them. A woman with a toddler in a stroller walks over and starts filming a video. "Say hi to the camera, peanut. Ooh, see the reindeer."

Blixem, who's a bit of a diva, shifts as if to say, "Oh yes, look at me."

"Hold still," Paisley says as she finishes attaching the jingle bell harness.

Dunder, who's waiting for her turn, comes over, her ankles clicking with each step. The beat snags in my brain and I grasp at the early tendrils of a song.

She's a real country girl.
Faded jeans, dusty boots, dirt under her nails.

Dunder sniffs at me through the fence, probably wondering if I've brought her a treat. I slip her a handful of the raisins I stashed in my pocket. Her chin tickles my hand as she snarfs down the dried fruit.

Paisley brings Dunder's harness over and sets it on the reindeer's back. She glances around to make sure we're alone and then jumps up on the fence to brush her lips quickly over mine. A second later, her feet are back on the ground. "See you Sunday, Kash."

A cold gust of wind nips at my skin and I pull up the collar of my leather jacket. It's cold now, but I have a feeling Nashville is going to be a whole lot chillier without Paisley around. Hopefully thoughts of her will keep me warm.

TRACK 19

It's Just Not Christmas for Me Without a Spruce Tree

Paisley

NOVEMBER 29

I'VE BEEN UP to my ears in work since Kash left with his grandpa for Thanksgiving in Nashville. It's been one thing after another on the farm, and I can feel the exhaustion in my bones. If this year is like any of the previous years, we'll be going full tilt until Christmas Eve. It's a great thing for Hidden Acres' bank account, but it doesn't leave a whole lot of time for much else.

While I know that I wouldn't have had much time to spend with Kash if he'd stayed, it's still hard knowing there's a distance between us, even if it's only about thirty-five miles. It turns out that even when you're busy as a bee, you still have plenty of time to think. And I've done a heckuva lot of thinking about Kash Murray.

Ringing up sales at the gift shop and thinking about the way Kash's laugh rings in my ears.

Sweeping up the barn after a craft event and thinking about

the crafty way Kash dipped me when we were dancing there at the hoedown.

It seems like Kash has infused a bit of himself everywhere I look, everywhere I go. He's hidden a piece of his soul in every piece of Hidden Acres.

Missing Kash doesn't make him arrive any sooner. I try to stay focused on what needs to be done so I can spend time with him once he gets back. Right now, that means creating casts of reindeer footprints with plaster of Paris.

Reindeer footprint casts are particularly popular at the gift shop. So popular, we built a special walking path for Dunder and Blixem for the sole purpose of impression casting. This past morning, while the ground was still damp from an overnight rainstorm, I led the ladies side by side through the mud.

I've already set forms around the imprints—old tuna cans with the bottoms cut off—so that we get a nice, round edge for the casts. We used to use a bucket to pour the plaster, but that got messy, since I was always spilling it everywhere. Now I use a houseplant watering can with a spout and an old shoehorn. I work my way down the path in a low crouch, holding the shoehorn over the impression to spread the plaster evenly over the hoofprints. I've just about finished when I hear someone come up behind me, their boots scattering rocks as they stride over.

"This that plaster stuff you were going on about?" Kash asks, grinning down at me with those impossibly kissable lips of his.

My heart skips a beat. He's wearing his cowboy hat, the shaggy ends of his dark hair curling around his ears and the nape of his neck. The hat's brim is tipped up so that it casts a faint shadow over his face.

"Welcome back." I finish pouring the last impression and stand on unsteady legs. I'm not sure if they're wobbly from all the squatting or because my knees always seem to get weak whenever Kash is around. "How was your Thanksgiving?"

Kash wanted us to text while he was gone, but I'm still not wild about carrying my phone around. To prove my point, I'd unearthed my phone to show Kash what my notifications looked like. Part of me thought maybe things would have died down enough since the last time I checked that it would seem overly dramatic to be afraid of my phone, but no. Seth released another video—Thanksgiving themed this time—and I'll never in a million years be in the mood to read any of the comments or texts about how hilarious it is that my head's been replaced with a pale and wobbly, featherless, trussed-up turkey carcass. I suppose I could just block everyone, but it seems so much easier to leave the phone hidden away in my Grinch sock.

After I handed him my phone, Kash powered it off almost immediately, his mouth curled into a snarl as he tossed it onto the couch. "I get it," he said. "No texting. No social media. I'm cool with that." And then he wrapped me in his arms and rested his chin on top of my head. "How 'bout we just catch up the old-fashioned way, over a cup of coffee when I get back?"

"Sounds good," I said, snuggling into him. Letting the warmth of his embrace ease my tension, breathing in the subtle scent of his cedarwood-scented bodywash.

I blink away the memory. Now he's back, standing before

me with two cardboard coffee cups in his hands. "It was good," he says. "How was yours?"

"Busy." I motion for him to follow me to a spigot. "I have to rinse out the watering can so the leftover plaster doesn't set," I explain.

When I'm done, he hands me a cup.

"Thanks." I take a sip and a warm, spicy, creamy taste fills my mouth. "You got me a chai latte?"

"I wasn't sure what kind of coffee you drink," he says with a shrug. "But you had one of those the other day."

If it's possible for a heart to melt when it's forty-four degrees outside, then mine does. "It's my favorite warm beverage, other than hot cocoa."

I weave my fingers through his, and we wander into a grove of eastern white pines. I wasn't sure how it would feel to see Kash again. If what happened before was random and unrepeatable after our time apart. But when Kash squeezes my hand and looks down at me with soulful, seductive eyes, all my worries float away and we pick up exactly where we left off.

"HERE," I SAY, HANDING Kash a pair of worn work gloves and a handsaw. "It's time to deliver Mrs. Larson's tree."

I already have the perfect Norway spruce picked out for her. I tagged it "reserved" the morning after my conversation with her, and it's here in all its six-foot glory when I lead Kash through the maze of other trees to find it.

"Have you ever cut down a Christmas tree before?" I ask.

"No."

"Well," I say. "Today's the day. You're about to become a lumberjack."

He looks the part, with the collar of a black thermal shirt peeking out from the V of his heavy flannel shirt with a black-white-and-green plaid houndstooth pattern.

Kash eyes up the spruce with the same look of determination he gets when he's about to tackle a tricky part of a song we're working on. His forehead creases, his mouth presses tight, and the set of his jaw makes his chin more pronounced.

Hello, weak knees.

I blink as heat flows through me. "Mrs. Larson wants a four-foot tree, but we need to cut a foot-long handle—that's the branch-free part of the trunk—which we can trim later, so we're aiming to cut down five feet of spruce tree."

"Uh, isn't this tree too tall? It's almost as tall as me."

Kash has an inch or so on the terminal leader on the top whorl. He stands next to the spruce, the green in his shirt nearly the same deep pine color as the needles, and reaches out to gently flick the tip.

"Spruces are a great tree for stump culture. We can get another tree to grow from the stump after we cut this one down, if we do it right."

I push down a few of the lower branches to locate the bare stem that's been pre-trimmed for a handle and then help Kash position the blade where it should go. The first time he passes the saw blade over the bark, the teeth bounce over. It takes a few tries for him to figure out how much pressure he needs for the teeth to catch, but then he finds his groove.

Most people who want a Norway spruce wait until just before Christmas to cut it, since these trees don't have great needle retention. It's still early in the fresh-cut season, so it's just the two of us and the scent of spruce in this grove. The rasp of the saw moving back and forth reminds me of the rhythm of the "Wellerman" sea shanty.

"There once was a guy who felled a tree,
And the name of the guy was Kash Murray.
That spruce grew tall, till the sawing was done,
And we'll take that tree and go."

Kash gives a little chuckle and then joins me at the chorus with a low, rumbly "Da-da-da-da-da."

I PARK "LITTLE BLUE"—OUR old farm truck affectionately named after the beloved picture book character—in Mrs. Larson's driveway and cut the engine. I was obsessed with *Little Blue Truck's Christmas* when I was little. The fact that the book had actual battery-powered lights in it was wild to me. Plus, it was all about Christmas trees and we'd just moved to a tree farm. What more could a six-year-old ask for?

Kash and I hop out of the cab. He works on untying the tree while I pull the wreath and a handsaw from the truck bed. Mom made the wreath up fresh last night, and I fluff the red velvet bow as I walk toward the front porch to ring Mrs. Larson's doorbell.

Mrs. Larson answers right away. "Hello, dear," she says. Dressed in a thick housecoat and with her hair in curlers, she looks like the granny-next-door. But with her bright red lipstick and glitter-coated ballet flats, Mrs. Larson takes being an octogenarian to the next level.

"Hi, Mrs. Larson."

Kash hefts the blanket-wrapped spruce tree, which probably weighs around forty pounds, onto his shoulder with a grunt, his gloved hands wrapped around the handle to hold it in place. With his dark hair falling into his eyes and dressed in his work jeans and a flannel shirt, he makes a very sexy Christmas tree delivery boy as he carries the tree up the walkway to her front porch.

"I see you brought some muscle," Mrs. Larson says with a nod of approval. I hand her the wreath, and she arranges it on the gold metal wreath hook hanging on her front door.

"I did promise you concierge service," I say, forcing myself not to stare at Kash.

His boots thump up the short flight of stairs, and Mrs. Larson steps back into her house to hold the door open. "Come on in," she says.

Kash gives me a slow, seductive smile as he passes by. Immediately, my face grows as hot as the wood fire in the farmhouse's cast-iron stove. I reach out and grab the tail end of the tree, making sure it doesn't bump against anything in Mrs. Larson's house as we shuffle as a group to her living room.

She already has a tree stand set up in the corner. I help Kash lay the tree on the floor and then grab the tree stand. I slip it over the handle to make sure there's enough space for presents underneath the bottom branches, but not so much space that the tree will look unbalanced with too much trunk showing.

Mrs. Larson's stand has a deep well, so the length works well. But Kash cut the trunk at a slight angle, so it doesn't fit flush on the bottom.

"Okay, we just need to trim it up a bit," I say, pulling a plastic shopping bag from my pocket. I slip one handle over the trunk so the bag hangs below. It should catch the dust, bark, and bits of spruce when I saw.

Soon, Kash is helping me tighten the screws to hold the tree in place. We tilt the tree until the stand sits squarely on the floor and the tree is upright. Kash helps me unhook the bungee cords and we carefully unwrap the tree, trying to fold the blanket as we go so we don't get too many needles or bits of bark on the floor.

"How's it look?" I ask, stepping back.

Mrs. Larson says, "It's tilting a little to the left."

Kash holds the tree and the blanket while I adjust the screws until Mrs. Larson is satisfied.

"It looks marvelous and smells just as good," she says, clasping her hands together. "I know you're supposed to wait to cut spruce until it's closer to Christmas, but I simply love the way they smell. It's just not Christmas for me without a spruce tree."

That would be a great line for a song.

Kash and I make eye contact, and I know he's thinking the same thing. I doubt Exit 12S wants Kash to write a Christmas song for the demo, but that doesn't mean we can't work on one for a future recording. My heart does a little giddyup at the thought.

TRACK 20

In the Blink of an Eye

Kash

DECEMBER 9

THE FIRST FEW days of December pass in a flurry. Between writing music, helping out around the farm, and stealing quiet moments alone with Paisley to just hang out together, the days fly by in the blink of an eye. We've managed to finish writing and recording "She's a Real Country Girl" and "Lonesome Hearts" since I got back from Nashville. Which means we only have two songs left to finish before the end of the year. I'm still worried we won't meet the deadline, but I'm also grateful to Paisley for helping me get this far. I couldn't have done any of this by myself.

In our morning writing session earlier, Paisley and I played a bunch of random chord progressions and tossed some melody ideas back and forth, but nothing seemed to stick. It all felt dull compared to the songs we've already got. I don't know if we've hit a rut or we just need a little more time for an idea to develop, but we don't have time to waste. Something has to change.

While Paisley's working at the gift shop this evening, I head to the studio to see if I can shake some ideas loose—literally. Maracas. Tambourines. Clappers. I even try a pair of castanets (olé!), but no ideas are sparked.

A little voice in the back of my mind whispers, *Writer's block.*

Nope.

The problem is that I'm trying too hard. I'm putting too much pressure on myself—trying to be creative on demand—when I just need to let inspiration find a way in.

I sink into the chair Paisley sits in when she's working on the mixing part of the process and drum my fingers on the table. Maybe what I need is silence.

What you need is an idea.

I'd really like the voice in the back of my mind to either say something useful or shut the hell up.

My eyes scan the desk and catch on the soft glimmer of gold-stamped flowers on a green, clothbound book tucked beneath a stack of blank music staff pages. I tug it out, careful not to scatter the loose papers resting on top.

There's no name scrawled inside the front cover, so I flip it open to a random page to see if it's some sort of recording logbook or maybe a guest book, where people leave notes to future musicians.

It's neither of those things.

Neat handwriting in dark blue ink fills the lined pages. At the top of the page are a few notes.

Weather: Rainy
Mood: Pensive
Theme: Hope
Style: Folk

Below that is a short poem:

Last night I fell asleep to the sound of rain falling on the roof.
The sweet drip-drop lullaby that I found swept me away to a peaceful slumber.
I dreamed of June and our promises, of all those things we thought would last.
And woke smiling in the morning light, thoughts of you lingering.

It looks like a journal. Curious, I flip to another page, which has a similar setup.

Weather: Overcast
Mood: Bittersweet
Theme: Growing up
Style: Country

The Goodbye Girl

Said goodbye to those childish things.
Set my sights on other things
Like I was supposed to.
Traded paper rings for gold
Bought the lies that I was sold
Like a good girl.

Wow, this is good stuff. I'm tempted to keep reading, but it feels too intrusive. Dishonorable. Just because someone left this journal lying around doesn't mean I should keep reading words like this without their permission.

But the stuff I've seen so far is really good. Too good to be hidden away in this journal. It's inspiring and I'm desperate for inspiration. I run my thumb over the bottom corner of the pages.

Just another peek.

I'm really starting to hate that devil's voice in the back of my head.

Reluctantly, I set the open book down on the table and the pages automatically flip to a more creased section in the middle of the journal where the spine has been cracked. I don't mean to look, but the fact that this page has different handwriting in thick black ink catches my eye. Everything else about this journal is neat and organized, whereas this page is full of chaos. Unable to help myself, I lean in and my heart stops.

There it is, written in a hasty, thick black Sharpie scrawl.

Ka$h Murray

And then realization hits me like a ton of bricks. This isn't just some journal. This is Paisley's lyric book.

DECEMBER 10

MY LEG BOUNCES AS I wait for Paisley in the recording studio. I was really hoping to get this over and done with last night, but she ended up working late and wasn't able to meet up with me like we'd planned.

Now I've had all night to work myself up into a good lather. Even though I didn't intentionally do anything wrong (it's not like I stole the journal or kept reading it after I realized what it was), it still feels like I trespassed on Paisley's personal space. If she'd wanted to share it with me, she would have. And she didn't.

Even worse is that things have been going so well with us. We're writing music. Spending time together. I'm falling for her, hard.

I roll a pick back and forth over my knuckles, looking for an outlet for some of this pent-up worry. There's a good chance this will open up old wounds and change everything between us.

I have that same feeling of dread in the pit of my stomach as I did when I was younger, that time I accidentally broke my mom's stained glass butterfly. She was working late and I sat next to those tiny glass shards for hours, knowing I had to own up to it but hating every minute that passed until I could. Paisley's journal sits closed on the table in front of me, and I'm about to make another uncomfortable confession that I know will hurt someone I care about.

I could slip her journal back where I found it. Cover it in blank pages and pretend it never happened. Paisley would never know.

But I'd know.

The door to the studio bursts open and Paisley breezes in at nine a.m., punctual as always.

"Good morning," she says, setting her guitar case on the floor by the door. She wipes her boots on the entry mat as she pulls off fuzzy red mittens. "Sorry about last night. Everything gets so chaotic around here in the run-up to Christmas and . . ." She shoves the mittens into her coat pockets and pauses to study me. "Is everything okay?"

I take a deep breath and walk over to her. My heart is racing. I want to wrap my arms around her. I want to kiss her. I want to take the easy way out.

"I found your lyric book," I say, tilting my head toward the table where her notebook is sitting in plain sight.

Paisley sucks in a sharp breath. She glances at the notebook and then back at me. "Oo-kay," she says slowly, her forehead creasing as if she's preparing herself for bad news.

"It was under some papers on the desk." My voice is raspy and I force down a swallow.

"I was wondering where I left it."

A weighted silence settles into the space between us. I know I have to keep going.

"I didn't realize it was yours at first. There was no name inside the cover. As soon as I saw the page with my autograph on it . . ." The more I talk, the more the words seem to get stuck on my tongue. "I stopped."

Paisley clenches her jaw. "How much did you read?" She looks up at me with a dull, wary look in her eyes.

"Not much," I rush to assure her. "A few sentences here and there."

Her fingers play with a gold-and-green beaded bracelet on her wrist. She must have a whole drawer full of them, seeing as how she always seems to be wearing a different bracelet every day. "Thank you for telling me." Her words slice into me like paper cuts. Her tone is cool and impersonal, like she's talking to someone she doesn't know. Already, there's distance building between us.

"Look, Paisley. I wouldn't have looked if I'd known." I reach out and grab the journal from the desk. "This is yours," I say, holding it out to her. She wraps her fingers over the spine, letting the side of her hand brush against mine. Her skin is cold against the warmth of mine, but she doesn't pull away. Our eyes meet. "From what little I read . . . your words, they're really good. And I hope someday you choose to share them with the world. But they belong to you, and that should happen on your time."

Paisley bites on her bottom lip. She stares down at the notebook, and I can tell there's an internal debate raging inside of her. I drop my hand and step back to give her some room to think. I made a promise that I would do my best to support her and make sure she feels seen. If that means giving her time and space, I'll do it, even if it feels like my heart's getting ripped out of my rib cage in the process.

"You really think they're good?" she asks.

"They're amazing, Paisley."

"Thank you. But I'm not ready to share them yet."

"Okay."

"Okay." Paisley looks up at me with watery eyes, her face softening.

She takes a deep breath and slips the notebook into a pocket in her guitar bag. Then she comes over and wraps her arms around me.

"I appreciate your honesty," she says.

I pull her close, grateful that she's still willing to hug me. I savor the way she feels in my arms, how she smells like cookies and evergreens. How she makes me want to be a better person, even when it's difficult.

DECEMBER 11

"WHAT IF WE REPEAT the first two lines of the first verse here as a bridge and then build intensity for the final chorus using a whole step modulation?" Paisley asks, her eyes narrowed in thought.

She has that adorable crinkled-nose thing going on again, and I can't resist brushing a quick kiss over it. "Let's try it."

We run through "In the Blink of an Eye" again.

"It's better," she says, "but it's not quite there."

"What about a post-chorus?" I ask.

Paisley nods. "That could work."

We play it over and over again, making tiny adjustments. It's better, but there's still something missing. We've been at it for hours now and haven't made much progress.

My phone buzzes and I swipe it off the table.

"It's Barry," I mumble. Lately he's texted me, but this time he's calling. Paisley lifts her eyebrows and I shrug. I have no idea why he's calling. "Hello?"

"Hey, kid. How's it going?"

"Going well," I say. Barry doesn't sound like he's about to drop bad news, but that doesn't stop my stomach from twisting into knots. "How are things?"

"Good, good. Well . . ." he says with a dramatic pause.

Here it comes.

"What are you doing New Year's Eve?"

"Um . . . turning in my demo?"

Barry laughs. "What a jokester."

Thing is, I'm serious.

I know Paisley and I only have two more songs to go . . . but they aren't done yet. Time's a-ticking, and according to our contract, the demo has to be delivered on or before midnight on December 31. I don't want it to take that long, but right now, it looks like I'll need every minute between now and then to finish.

"I'm talking New Year's Eve night. Do you have plans?" Barry asks.

"Nothing solid yet."

I've been so busy focusing on getting through the demo, I hadn't really spent much time making plans for after it was done. I guess I kind of figured Paisley and I would finally have time to just hang out, with Christmas tree season over and my demo turned in.

"Wanna play the *Live, from Nashville!* New Year's Eve Ball? It'll be part of a countrywide broadcast for the Country Music Network. There have been some scheduling snafus, so they're looking for local musicians. Won't have any set times for at least another week or two, but it would be a good opportunity."

It feels like I've been launched in a rocket ship headed to the moon, and I grab hold of the chair to make sure I don't fall out because *holy crap*. This is a huge opportunity. "Yeah, it sounds great," I manage, because I am basically stunned in the upper atmosphere at this point.

"So, you in?"

"Yes," I say, giving Paisley a goofy grin. I can't wait to tell her the good news.

"Love to hear it. Another thing." Barry clears his throat.

A moment ago, it felt like I was launched into space, but now the ground is rushing up at me.

"The original headliner dropped out, and the producers for *Live, from Nashville!* are looking for a replacement. Exit 12S would like to throw your name into the hat. But . . ." Barry's pause has me holding my breath.

"What's the catch?" I ask, sitting back in the chair. If Barry dangled a carrot that's about to be yanked away, I'm going to be pissed.

"To be considered for that spot, you'll need to submit an all-original song by December eighteenth."

That doesn't give us much time. Maybe one of the songs we've already written will work.

"Decisions will be made the following week so the house band will have time to learn it. The theme is 'A Boot Scootin' New Year,' so they're looking for some songs that'll make people want to get up and dance," Barry says.

Maybe not.

So far, Paisley and I have written three country-rock songs and a country ballad, none of which have that "get up and dance" quality Barry's talking about. We still haven't got "In the Blink of an Eye" figured out, but there's definitely not a country dance song hiding anywhere in that one.

Another day, another impossible task.

I pinch the bridge of my nose. What is with all these tight deadlines? I willfully ignore the fact that I brought some of them upon myself.

"So, kid, what do you say? Think you can send me a contender?"

How could I possibly say no?

TRACK 21

Christmas Trees & Weak Knees

Paisley

DECEMBER 12

Weather: Cloudy and cold
Mood: Wistful
Theme: Trust
Style: Folk pop

Title TBD

The other night when we were talking
Your words sank down deep into my soul
They found a place inside of me I didn't want to go.
Trust isn't something freely given
But I've put my trust in you

My favorite blue gel pen hovers over the lined page while I stare out the window in thought. I want to come up with the next line, but all I can think about right now is Kash and how it felt to see him holding my journal again.

When he first confessed to finding my notebook, it was almost like I had an out-of-body experience. All my extremities went numb and there was a constant ringing in my ears. Things had been going so well with Kash, both musically and romantically, and there I was, facing the very strong possibility he was about to annihilate me.

Writing songs together requires a certain level of trust, both with Kash and with myself. And while I've let myself open up to him in the time we've spent together, I've kept parts of me closed off. There are things in my lyric book I've never shared with anyone else, and I'm not sure I'm ready for Kash to see the messiest, sharpest, most vulnerable bits and pieces of me. The words in my notebook are mine and mine alone.

Time nearly stopped as I stood there, waiting for the ax to drop. I could hear every heartbeat. Could feel the slow pulse of my blood chugging through my veins. Would he still look at me the same way? Would I still be able to look him in the eye, knowing what he'd read?

His eyes were so earnest, so regretful, there was no doubting his integrity. He'd owned up to it. He'd apologized. And then he'd given me space to decide how to handle it. Of all the things he could have done to solidify my faith in him, that was it.

I TUG THE FLEECE-LINED Santa hat down over my ears and grab a crate of battery-powered flickering LED taper candles. The

Carols by Candlelight walk starts in the main parking lot and follows a meandering path among themed displays before we weave through the Christmas tree groves and end up at the cocoa stand.

Kash is already in the parking lot when I arrive with the last crate of candles. He's dressed in a puffy black jacket and has a thick wool knit cap on his head. Kash looks like a ski bum ready to take to the slopes, not a country rocker about to take the stage at the *Live, from Nashville!* New Year's Eve Ball. It's a different look for him and one I could definitely get used to.

"Here," he says, taking the crate from me. He stacks it next to the other crates in Little Blue's truck bed and jams his hands into his pockets. "Brrrr."

There's nothing more I'd rather do than snuggle into Kash right now, but people are milling around, waiting for us to start. At 5:00 p.m. on the dot, Dad signals for us to begin handing out the candles. Then he hoists himself up onto the truck bed and gives a two-finger whistle. The murmurs quiet and everyone turns to face him.

"Welcome to Carols by Candlelight. Tonight, we'll be singing some holiday favorites as we walk around Hidden Acres. The path we'll be taking is not paved and can be uneven in places, so please watch your step. And please stay with the group. Tonight we'd like to keep this confined to a singing party, no search parties necessary."

A few people chuckle. Most of them play with the on/off switch on their battery-powered candles.

"Okay, y'all," Dad says. "Grab a candle"—he jumps down off the truck and holds up a giant staff with a glowing white orb at the top—"and follow me." Strands of green leaves and red berries are wrapped around the stick to make it look festive.

"That looks suspiciously like a wizard staff," Kash whispers, his warm breath brushing over my cheek.

"It was. Mom picked it up at an after-Halloween clearance event and now it's a wassailing staff."

Lifting the wassailing staff high in the air like the Christmas tree farm tour guide that he is, Dad leads the sizable group toward the shed. It's hard to count how many people are here, but there must be at least seventy or so participants. I recognize some faces, but there are plenty of strangers here, too.

Mom's put up a Nativity scene in front of the shed, so the first song on the set list is "Away in a Manger." Kash joins in with the rest of the carolers in his familiar raspy tenor.

Dad leads the carolers onward to serenade Dunder and Blixem, who are munching on their feed when we arrive, so they're treated to dinner and a show. Lucky ladies.

Tiny white flakes start to flutter down on us during "Silver Bells." The snow falls faster, glistening in the candlelight during "Jingle Bells." By the time everyone starts singing "Winter Wonderland," it feels like we are literally in a winter wonderland snow globe. The twinkling white lights and the sparkling snow make it feel like there's magic in the air.

Kash reaches out and grabs my hand, playfully pulling me into a whirl during an enthusiastic, albeit off-key, version of "Rockin' Around the Christmas Tree." Laughing, we spin around a white pine until we're hidden from view, and Kash takes the moment to dip me and steal a kiss.

"Hey," I say, glancing around to make sure we're alone. "I'm supposed to be working."

Kash flashes me a mischievous smirk and pulls me back into our position at the tail end of the group so quickly, I'm sure no one even noticed we'd disappeared. I give his hand a squeeze, wishing our fingers weren't separated by our gloves. Wishing it was just the two of us in this magical holiday greeting card landscape that surrounds us.

Dad stops the group in front of the tallest tree on the farm, one he's growing in the hopes that it will someday be chosen as the Tennessee state capitol Christmas tree. Currently, this one is about eighteen feet tall, so it seems massive compared with the others in the lot, but it needs to surpass at least thirty feet before it can even be considered. The carolers sing "O Christmas Tree," many of them linking arms and swaying back and forth.

Kash sings more enthusiastically as we continue on. He has a huge grin on his face. "This is so great," he says. "I can't remember the last time I sang just for fun. Man, it's great." Kash opens his arms wide and belts out "Fa la la la la la la la la." People turn and stare. I duck my head and step to the side, not wanting any unnecessary attention, but Kash eats it right up. His fa-la-las get more animated and off-key as the song continues.

How is Kash so relaxed? He clearly doesn't care that he's belting out the wrong words in a pitchy voice. It's hard to believe this tuneless wonder is Kash Murray, up-and-coming musician about to make his big solo debut on national television.

I wish I could be that carefree when I sing. To not worry about what people think if I'm out of tune or if I start to strain on the high notes. Flashes of May swirl through my mind like the flakes of snow swirling at my feet and I shiver.

Kash turns to me with such joy on his face it makes my heart squeeze.

I'm glad he's found his passion, but I'm gonna stick to songwriting from here on out.

THE SNOW HAS SWITCHED over from tiny, glittering specks to large, fluffy flakes by the time we get to the courtyard. There's already a line forming at the hot cocoa stand, so I need to get to work right away. Kash joins me behind the counter, and we start pouring cocoa from large insulated beverage dispensers. Kash hums while he works like he's having the time of his life. It's hard not to get caught up in the festive energy he radiates.

Over the past few years, Carols by Candlelight has been well attended, but we generally don't have this many people stick around for the hot cocoa portion of the evening. None of us were prepared for the volume, and soon, the beverage dispensers start to gurgle and sputter. We're about to run out of cocoa and we still have . . . a lot of people waiting.

"We have a problem," I say to Kash, explaining the situation.

He surveys the line of people whose patience will only last so long and nods. "You make more cocoa," he says. "I'll handle the carolers." He gives my hand a quick squeeze and then strides from the cocoa stand, the half door swinging shut behind him.

"How's everyone doing tonight?" he asks like a game show host as he walks along the queue.

I quickly start heating up more water, grateful that Dad opted to spring for outdoor plumbing for the cocoa stand so we wouldn't have to lug water over from the farmhouse.

"I don't know about you," Kash continues, really leaning

into his inner showman. "But I had a great time caroling with y'all tonight. Now, Paisley over here"—he points at me and I give a tiny, awkward wave because *why, Kash, why?*—"is making up some fresh hot cocoa, and it's gonna be delicious. But it's gonna take a few minutes. So I figured, why not sing a few more songs while we wait? What do you say to an encore?"

A few people clap.

A particularly feisty attendee calls out, "Quit yer yappin' and start singin'," which draws a few chuckles. I can feel the carolers' impatience begin to recede.

The water boiler makes a chugging sound as it heats up. Kash glances at me with a broad grin and then launches into a Broadway-style version of "Let It Snow." Big sweeping arm gestures. Extra animated facial expressions. He holds the attention of every person in this captive courtyard audience. Even I can't seem to look away. I've never seen Kash perform before, and he has that innate magnetism that all good stage performers have.

There's not a lick of it in me, that's for sure.

I'm so mesmerized by him, I forget all about the boiling water and hot cocoa I'm supposed to be preparing. My fingers brush against the giant metal carafe, and while I don't get burned, it's a wake-up call. I can't afford to get so caught up in Kash that I lose sight of everything else.

I quickly mix the hot water with cocoa powder and hoist the insulated dispenser onto the counter. I have another pot of water heating, just in case we run out again, but this fresh batch will at least get the line moving.

Kash glances over and I give him a thumbs-up. He winks. Unlike the last time he winked at me, I don't hate him. Not a bit. In fact, my feelings are very much headed in the opposite direction.

Kash starts a boisterous rendition of "Holly Jolly Christmas," but when he gets to the part about having a cup of cheer, he inserts the word *cocoa* and jogs back to the stand, singing all the way.

And he doesn't stop singing. He keeps it up as we pour and serve. I'm pretty sure some people sneak back in line for seconds. The line sure doesn't seem to be whittling down at all, but there's a steady stream of people wandering into the gift shop and then back out with bags full of purchases, so who am I to stop the merriment?

Kash finishes the song he was singing, and people start calling out requests. They're a lively bunch tonight, probably because of all the sugar we're pumping into them. I make up another vat of cocoa and set another pot of water to boil.

"Sing 'Baby, It's Cold Outside,'" someone calls.

"With Paisley."

"Duet! Duet! Duet!"

It feels like someone just dumped a bucket of ice down the back of my shirt. I stiffen and freeze, my heart racing.

Kash gives an overly bright laugh and looks over at me. There's plenty of concern in his eyes but also a spark of hope that I just might say yes.

"It could be fun," he says gently. I can tell he really wants me to sing with him, though I can't quite figure out why. He's heard what I sound like onstage, and he knows how much of a train wreck I am because of it.

I shake my head and give a sharply whispered "No." Singing in public will never be fun. Especially not when it's in front of a bunch of strangers. I turn my back to the crowd and busy myself with making more hot cocoa.

"Okay," he says, backing up so he's even with me but still facing the line of thirsty revelers.

"Duet! Duet!"

Kash sighs. "Now, hear me out."

My heart hammers even harder. After everything, I can't believe he's about to pressure me into singing with him.

"How do you feel about lip-synching?" he whispers, stopping my spiral of doubt in its tracks.

Wait, what?

"I think we can give them what they want but also give you what you need. All you have to do is pretend to sing. No actual sounds need to come out of your mouth."

The idea is so out of the blue and bizarre, I let out a surprised snort-laugh.

"What do you think?" He waggles his eyebrows.

"I think you've had too much hot cocoa."

"Or not nearly enough," he says with a crooked grin.

"It's a bad idea."

"It's the best idea," he says. "They'll be too hopped up on cocoa and Christmas spirit to know the difference."

I doubt that.

Then Kash uses the one card he has to force my hand. "I double-dog dare you." He says it in a teasing voice, but it's a double-dog dare all the same.

I just knew that losing that praying mantis egg sac-picking contest was going to come back to haunt me. And here it is with a resounding *Boo!*

"No singing," I say.

“No singing,” he confirms. “And, Paisley, you don’t have to do this.” There’s such sincerity in his eyes, it makes my heart pinch.

I nod and turn to face the line. As much as I regret it now, a deal’s a deal. “Let’s just get this over with,” I say through gritted teeth.

TRACK 22

Worth the Wait

Kash

DECEMBER 12

I GIVE PAISLEY a reassuring nod. "You've got this."

She looks at me with doe eyes and I can tell her stage fright is surging. "I won't be mad if you change your mind. Or if you decide to sing," I tease, giving her a playful nudge.

She swallows hard.

"No matter what, I'll be right here next to you. I won't let you down." I link my fingers with hers and squeeze.

The people waiting in the hot cocoa line grow antsy.

"You know what? I've got an even better idea than a duet," I say to the crowd. "How about we get everyone involved? If you were born on an even-numbered day, sing with Paisley. Everyone else, sing with me. Show of hands. Who's singing with Paisley?"

A bunch of gloved hands lift into the air. It looks like about half the group, so hopefully it won't be too apparent that she's not actually singing.

“Excellent. And who’s singing along with me?” Different gloved hands shoot into the air.

“Ready?” I ask Paisley.

Her fingers squeeze my hand in a vise grip.

“Here we go. A-one, and a-two, and-a, one, two,” I say.

Paisley looks at me with uncertainty, and then we both share a wide-eyed “oh crap” look. She’s realized the same thing that I have: Traditionally, for this duet, the female singer goes first. And in order to get the crowd singing together, someone needs to get the ball rolling. And that someone needs to be me.

Now what?

I guess we’ll have to flip the script.

“Three, four,” I finish. And then I launch into the first line of “Baby, It’s Cold Outside” to save Paisley from having to sing first. I’m loud and spirited, doing as much as I can to draw as much attention away from Paisley as possible.

Thankfully, the carolers are in it to win it. They sing along loudly and boldly with me, their voices echoing around the courtyard. Paisley mouths her lines, and everyone is so busy having a good time, they don’t notice she’s not actually singing. My shoulders sink with relief, and I throw myself wholeheartedly into the next line.

Paisley turns away from the counter to mix up another batch of hot cocoa, and I can swear I hear her humming along. Her cheeks are bright red and her lips are rosy. My heart swells.

When she comes back to the counter, I’m sure I hear the soft, whispery tones of her voice mingling with the other carolers. I catch her eye and her mouth twitches with a sheepish half smile, like she’s been caught sneaking a Christmas cookie from the plate left out for Santa. There's something irresistible and magical about this night, here under the twinkling lights surrounded by the scent of warm, creamy chocolate and the sounds of friends, neighbors, and strangers sharing in a moment like this.

The song ends, and the majority of carolers head toward the parking lot.

I don't want Paisley to stop singing. I want her to find peace with a part of her that's been left battered and bruised.

"Are you going to say anything?" she asks. "I know you heard me singing."

There's no one left in line, so she pours out two last cups, one for each of us. We toast and sip, leaning back against the counter, the side of our hips touching.

"I'm proud of you," I say, bumping my shoulder into hers. "You didn't have to do it, but you did. It was brave."

Her brow lifts with skepticism.

"It took courage to stop lip-synching and start singing," I insist. "You didn't have to."

"Even if you were the only one who heard me?" she whispers.

"Did it scare you?" I ask.

She sighs and twirls the cardboard cup in her hand. "Yes."

"Did you do it anyhow?"

"Yes."

"Then it was brave." I reach over and adjust her hat, giving it a jaunty slant. "If a Christmas tree sings in the forest, and no one's around to hear it, is it still brave?"

Paisley laughs and my heart is as warm and toasty as a flaming marshmallow.

Her face grows serious again and she sighs. "I've never really enjoyed singing or performing. And after everything that's happened, I'm more convinced now than ever that I want to be a songwriter. Tonight was . . ." She narrows her eyes and scrunches her nose. "Fun adjacent, but I truly never want to set foot on a stage again. It's just not for me."

"I respect that," I say, giving her hand a squeeze. "I'm glad you want to stick with songwriting, 'cause you're really good at it. The world deserves to hear your music and lyrics."

Paisley squeezes my hand back.

Fine, delicate snowflakes shimmer down from the branches above. White lights twinkle. The air is crisp and refreshing.

I take our empty cups and toss them in the trash. Then I wrap Paisley in my arms. "Sing with me," I say, leaning back so I can look her in the face. "Just one song. Just for us."

Paisley looks around at the near-empty courtyard and then looks into my eyes. "I just told you, I don't like singing."

"Even with me?"

Paisley tucks her bottom lip between her teeth. "I don't *hate* it."

"I promise, I'll sing every word with you," I say.

A flicker of temptation flashes in her eyes. "What song?"

I press a quick kiss to her lips and grin. "Taylor Swift wrote this song about a Christmas tree farm. Ever heard of it?"

Paisley rolls her eyes but rests her head on my shoulder. "One song. And then you have to help me clean up."

My heart soars. Because here I am, singing carols with a beautiful girl in my arms, on the verge of a major career breakthrough. I'm the luckiest guy in the world.

DECEMBER 14

WE'RE BACK IN THE studio Monday morning trying to find a way into an upbeat country dance song. It's not going well, and again, there's this ticking time bomb in the back of my mind, reminding me that if I don't meet yet another deadline, this opportunity goes *poof*.

We've tried playing different chords. Drumming different tempos on the body of our guitars with our knuckles. Speeding up "She's a Real Country Girl" and "Lonesome Hearts" but nothing is right. Nothing is good enough.

I groan and massage the back of my neck. There's a tangled thread of worry wrapped around my chest that seems to grow tighter by the minute. How am I supposed to deliver a country dance song catchy enough to get me the headliner spot when I've never written one, let alone played one, before?

"This is impossible."

Paisley sighs and sets her acoustic guitar in a stand. "It's not impossible. It's just challenging. We'll figure it out."

I could use a bit of her optimism right now.

She stands and stretches her arms over her head. When she brings them down, she gives a little shimmy-shake. "What we need is a little perspiration."

"Don't you mean inspiration?"

"That too." Paisley claps her hands together. "Okay, I've got an idea."

She goes over to the studio computer, opens a screen, and

then types something in. A second later, "Boot Scootin' Boogie" by Brooks & Dunn starts playing on the speakers.

"Get your butt up," she says, holding out a hand. "It's time to dance."

This seems like a waste of time, dancing to other people's songs. But she does that shimmy thing again and grabs my hand, tugging me up and out of my seat.

"I guess we're doing this," I say.

"Oh, we're doing this." She knocks her hip into mine as I come to stand beside her. I dig deep for some of that extrovert energy I was drawing on during Carols by Candlelight the other night. I'm pretty outgoing, but there are times when my well dries up, especially after a performance. My tank's pretty empty right now.

Still, Paisley's not asking for a lot here. I asked her to sing with me and she stepped up, pushing past her fear to do that for me. The least I can do is scoot my boots with her.

"I don't know how to line dance."

"So? It's just the two of us here, and we're trying to shake some ideas loose," she says with an exaggerated wiggle. "Come on, Kash, you gotta loosen up." Paisley bobs her head to the beat and then starts dancing. "Right foot, left foot. Right foot, left foot." She moves to the left and then does a kick, kick, kick.

"That seems complicated."

"More complicated than writing a song?" she asks.

Maybe.

The song ends and she sighs. "Let's try a different song."

By the time she plays Beyoncé's "Texas Hold 'Em," I've loosened up enough to be silly. Paisley giggles as I pull her into a do-si-do, and my heart thuds to the beat. I'll never get used to the way my insides go all gooey when she laughs or how good it feels to be near her.

We twist and twirl and do some heel digs, and I even manage a few dramatic dips with a quick kiss or two.

After a few more songs, I've worked up a sweat and Paisley's winded. She stops the music and sets her hands on her hips while she catches her breath. "Well, that was invigorating," she says. "But was it inspiring?" Her eyebrows lift as she looks at me.

"Well . . ."

Unfortunately, I don't have any great ideas for another song, but I am feeling better. Something about moving around and getting the blood pumping helps me ignore the doom-and-gloom voice in the back of my mind. Might be the exercise endorphins. Might be having Paisley in my arms. I'm thinking it's a bit of both.

"Okay," Paisley says, shaking her arms by her sides to loosen up like she's preparing for a shadowboxing match and she's about to beat the song from the ether. "Let's try something else." She sits in the chair in front of the laptop and pulls up the recording software. "There are some pre-recorded drum beats that came with the mixing program," she explains, selecting a MIDI file. "Does this rhythm seem dancy enough to you?"

I pull a chair over to the desk, scooting closer until my knee touches hers. The sample has a strong beat. It's got a decent rhythm. I suppose it could work, but I don't think it's the one. "Meh."

Paisley opens another file to play. "How about this one?"

"Too bouncy."

"This one?"

"Too disco."

"Okay, what about . . . ?"

I listen to the steady, driving *chugga-chugga* train beat, and it's definitely got me wanting to tap my toes. "This could work."

I don't have an idea yet, at least nothing tangible, but I can feel it just out of reach as I listen to the beat.

DECEMBER 15

I'M NOODLING ON MY electric guitar, trying to pin down a memorable riff, when Paisley breezes into the studio a little after nine a.m.

My fret hand slides down the neck of the guitar and the strings squeak. I have to do a double take to make sure it's really her in that getup.

She's dressed in a festive elf costume—a knee-length green dress with fluffy white fur trim and shiny gold accents over red-and-white-striped leggings tucked into fur-lined, shiny black ankle boots. Unlike her usual minimal-makeup, fresh-faced look, she's gone big and bold with bright scarlet circles of blush on her cheeks, shimmery gold eye shadow dusted across her eyelids, and ruby-red lipstick that makes her mouth look full and enticing. A green felt Santa hat with jingle bells spaced out along the brim is pulled down over her bright red wig, which is a riot of corkscrew curls.

"Sorry I'm late," she says, passing me a cardboard to-go cup, her jingle bells jangling as she moves. "Trisha called in sick this morning, so I need to cover for her at the reindeer photo op. It took me a while to get all elfed up."

Our fingers brush when I take the cup from her. "You're worth the wait," I say. And *BAM*. It hits me like a bolt of lightning. I have an idea for a song. It's still just a tiny spark, but I know that if I let it smolder a bit, it'll catch fire.

"I look ludicrous," she says.

"Nah. You look cute," I say before taking a sip of hot cocoa. "Very Dolly Parton meets Buddy the Elf."

"Just the look I was going for," she says with that dimpled grin that makes my heart soar. "Though, I'm hoping no one will recognize me." She slides on a pair of red cat-eye novelty glasses with rhinestones all over them. "Think I can pull off the Clark Kent/Superman, hidden-in-plain-sight thing?"

"I think you can do anything you set your mind to, Paisley," I say. The mood in the room goes serious. I wasn't trying to kill the playful back-and-forth we had going, but I want her to know how incredible I think she is.

Paisley's familiar brown eyes meet mine, and she blinks her eyelashes bashfully behind those ridiculous rhinestoned glasses. "Thanks," she says so softly, I almost can't hear it.

"So, I think I might have just gotten an idea for a song. What do you think about this?"

Paisley's eyes light up as I tell her what I'm thinking. Her jingle bells shake as she nods. "I think it could work. Let's give it a try."

TRACK 23

Laying Down Tracks

Paisley

DECEMBER 15

IT HAS BEEN the longest day of the year, even though we're only a few days away from the winter solstice and the amount of daylight is dropping on a daily basis. I crawled out of bed when it was dark. I haven't crawled back into it and it's dark already. And I didn't get a lick of rest all day.

I shouldn't complain. Hidden Acres needs a solid fourth quarter to float the tree farm for the rest of the year, even with the extra boost of having the Hideaway booked for Kash's stay. I'm finally living my dream of being a working songwriter. And I'm definitely not mad about getting to spend time with Kash.

But I feel like I'm being pulled in a million different directions. Mom needs me at the gift shop. Dad needs my help selling trees. Dunder and Blixem need attention. And Kash is counting on me, too. At the end of the day, there's not much time left for me.

I glance over at my lyric book, sitting on the shelf. It's only been a few days since I cracked it open to put down my ideas, but it feels like it's been forever, given how many snippets of music and phrases are floating around in my mind. I know I should probably try to write them all down before they disappear, but I just don't have the energy. I'm spent.

As much as I'd love to make it all happen, I can't be in two (or more) places at once. It wasn't too hard to juggle it all before, but now I feel like I'm constantly rushing around, about to drop the ball and let someone down. And with Trisha out sick, now I'm pulling double duty as Holly Parton, the elf. It's exhausting.

My feet ache from the blisters that I got from wearing Halley's old boots around all day. Even though I took the elf hat off hours ago, I can still hear the constant ringing of jingle bells. I am *not* feeling very merry about that at the moment.

Bah humbug!

I glance at my watch. I told Kash I'd meet him in the studio if I got done before nine. It's just past eight now. I wish we could just take the night off and sip hot apple cider and watch a classic Christmas movie, but his deadline is coming up quick. We don't have time to take it easy.

While I might not have a lot of energy left to give, I can at least show up.

Ten minutes later, I push open the recording studio door. Kash is sitting in a chair with his back to me, his electric guitar in his lap and a pair of headphones over his ears. I close the door on a gust of wind, and he shivers before turning to face me.

"Hey," he says, his smile lighting up the room.

I'm like a solar panel, soaking in the rays and converting them to energy to repower my batteries. It's not enough to get me through a 5K road race or a strenuous Christmas cookie-decorating marathon, but it'll power me through another writing session with Kash.

"Hey, yourself," I say.

I hang my coat on the hook by the door. When I turn around, Kash is there, ready to wrap me in his arms. We share a quick kiss, and then I sink into his embrace.

"Long day?" he asks.

"Mmm-huh," I mumble into his chest. His T-shirt is soft as a pillow, and I close my eyes and savor this rare moment of rest. "How did the writing go?"

"Okay," he says, but I can tell he's disappointed with his progress by the flat tone of his voice.

"Wanna show me what you have so far?"

Kash nods and grabs his guitar.

I sit in the chair next to him and listen as he plays a catchy riff that reminds me of the opening guitar parts from "Footloose" and "Chattahoochee." The longer I listen, the more I like it.

"I think that's a great opening."

Kash sighs a breath of relief. "I was hoping you'd think so."

He plays me what he has for the chorus and some lines of melody that might work for the verses. We toss ideas back and forth, and by the time we have something that we're both satisfied with, it's already eleven.

"I have to be up early tomorrow to feed Dunder and Blixem," I say, groaning at the thought of another predawn wake-up. I am so making Halley feed them on Christmas morning as a present to me.

"Hey," Kash says, giving my knee a gentle squeeze. "Just

worry about one thing at a time. And right now, that's getting some sleep."

DECEMBER 16

WE'RE BACK IN THE studio again at nine a.m., and I'm hoping that we can make some more progress today. Kash and I have managed to work out most of the music for "Worth the Wait," but we still need to finish the lyrics and lay down tracks for the demo. This song will need more layers and mixing than the other ones we've done if we want to give Kash the best shot at being selected as the headliner for the New Year's Eve Ball. While the previous songs we've recorded for the demo were pretty bare bones, we're both thinking we need to add more instrument tracks and some backing vocals to round out the sound and pump up the "wanna dance" factor.

Unfortunately, that's going to take time, which I'm short on at the moment. It's only a little over a week until Christmas, and Hidden Acres is hopping with customers from the minute we open until we lock up the gift shop for the night. Plus, I can't seem to shake this nagging feeling in my gut that there's some unexpected emergency waiting for me on the horizon, something that will pop up and pull me away right as we're scrambling to finish the song by our deadline.

Ice storm?

Mouse infestation?

Stomach flu?

I know I can't plan for every possibility, but that doesn't

mean I can't put some guardrails in place to keep this train-beat song on track, just in case.

"I should show you how to do some basic mixing. Just in case I won't be available to help as much as I'd like," I say. "That way, you can add backing vocals and other tracks when I'm not around."

Kash looks up from the sheet of paper where he's been scrawling down lyrics.

"I haven't done any mixing before," he says. His lips press together with uncertainty.

"That's okay," I say. "You have a good ear. I can teach you the rest."

We set up the studio so we each have a vocal mic and guitar input going to the audio interface. "We'll do a quick run-through of 'Worth the Wait' so I can show you how to record and then mix when you have multiple voices and instruments to deal with."

We settle into position, chairs side by side, a music stand between us so we can each read the lyrics Kash has written. "You can try out one melody on the first verse, and I'll join you singing the chorus and the alternate melody on the second verse. That way, you can use my track as if it's backing vocals so you can practice mixing multiple voices. Then we can decide which melody sounds best, and you can use that one when we record all your vocals tomorrow."

"Sounds like a plan," he says.

We each slide on a pair of closed-back headphones—one ear covered and one ear free—so we can hear the train-beat track he picked for this song and what we're playing at the same time. I retune my guitar while Kash double-checks the tuning on his.

"Ready?" I ask.

"Ready," Kash says.

I hit record.

After four measures of the train-beat track, Kash comes in on his electric guitar, playing a riff that repeats a few times before I join in strumming acoustic rhythm guitar. My toe taps with the beat as we play a few more measures, and then Kash plays the electric guitar lead-in and kicks off singing the first verse in his rough-around-the-edges-but-smooth-when-it-wants-to-be tenor.

"One, hold your horses,
Two, hold the train,
I'm standing out here in the pouring rain.
Three blocks down
Four over from Main
I'm waiting and waiting for you again."

Kash gives me a grin when he's done the first verse. Now that it's all coming together, there's a different vibe in the studio. I can feel the unbridled energy radiating off him.

I scan the lyrics on the page, trying to decipher his chicken scratch and prepare for this impromptu duet as we play the interlude. My pulse skyrockets as I get ready to sing. I'm not sure I can do this. What if I go pitchy or flub the lyrics or am so focused on what my mouth is doing that I mess up what I'm playing on the guitar?

I'm sitting in a chair next to Kash, but once again I'm transported back to the May Music Showcase. My throat starts to close up. Did someone turn up the thermostat?

I can't do this.

But then Kash gives me an expectant, hopeful smile.

This is just for practice.

No one's going to hear my singing but Kash. Tomorrow, we'll record his actual vocal tracks. I can do this. I will.

Kash improvises a lick and then plays the lead-in electric guitar riff. I drag in a shaky breath and attempt to sing harmony on the fly while Kash takes the melody line.

" 'Cause you're
One, two, three minutes late,
Four, five, six, then seven and eight.
Other guys, well, they might be irate,
But you—
You're worth the wait."

Just like that steady train drumbeat, it's full steam ahead. I warble my way through the second verse, but Kash doesn't seem to mind how I sound. He's lost in the music, his pick flying over the strings.

"Five o'clock shadow,
Six o'clock news,
Coolin' my heels, no time to lose.
Seven for a secret,
Eight lucky horseshoes,
If you leave me hanging, baby, I'll be blue."

We repeat the chorus. Kash "ooh-ooh-oohs" his way through the bridge, plays a solo with a few improvised licks, and then we finish the song on a double chorus that leaves us whispering "You're worth the wait" over and over to the train drumbeat. For our first full run-through, it was pretty good—if you ignore all the times I went pitchy or flat or breathy. So basically, any of the sounds that came out of my mouth.

I stop recording.

Thank god that's over.

Kash beams at me. "That was so good. Do you think we should add a fiddle track? Or maybe a train whistle?"

For the first time since we started working on this song, Kash is pumped up. He sounds like a kid in a toy store, asking for everything he sees. Unfortunately, we have a budget (like most shoppers do, except our wallet is low on time), and I'm not sure we can make all that happen in the hours we have left. Still, I don't want to dampen his fire.

"There are some MIDI tracks that might work," I say. "Maybe you can pick a few out and we can try them tomorrow, when we're mixing the final submission?"

"Okay."

"Here, I'll create a folder where you can save all the tracks for this song," I say.

I pull up the four tracks we recorded—two vocal tracks and two guitar tracks—and the MIDI file for the train drumbeat. Kash scribbles down notes as I explain how the software works.

"The first step is to create a static mix. Basically, you're just trying to balance the instruments and vocals. Think of it like the bird's-eye view of the song." I sweep my arms open in a big arc. "To create a static mix, you can either work with the tracks from the ground up, starting with the drums," I say. "Or you can mix from the top down, starting with lead vocals or the lead guitar. No matter which option you choose, you want to set the levels around that element. I like to keep it around here," I say, pointing to the –10dB marking on the on-screen meter. "Because that leaves some headroom to work with later."

I show Kash how to look at the levels in each track at different points of the song and how to adjust them with the different toggles, slides, and knobs available in the software.

"First, we'll zero out the mix," I say, instructing Kash to drop all the faders to their lowest position on the software console.

We spend a good hour like this, hunched over the laptop while Kash learns the basics of the DAW—digital audio workstation—program.

"How do you feel?" I ask after I've finished the tutorial.

Kash glances down at the loose-leaf pages of notes he's taken on college-ruled lined paper and blows out a deep breath. "A bit overwhelmed."

"It's a lot," I say. "But the more you play around with it, the easier it gets." I press a kiss to his cheek and the wrinkle in the center of his brow disappears. "You've got this," I say. "And if you run into any trouble, there's a searchable digital manual."

TRACK 24

Good News Has Me Singing the Blues

Kash

DECEMBER 17

"GIVE THIS A listen."

I press the play button on the mix I created for our first attempt at "Worth the Wait" for Paisley. I worked most of the day and late into the night on it, figuring out what I liked and didn't like and then making adjustments.

When I'd gotten it as far as it could go based on Paisley's lesson, it didn't feel done to me, so I watched a few how-to videos to learn about panning instruments to get a more three-dimensional sound, equalization to clarify the sound, and how to finish it off with some compression and reverb.

The final cut isn't sleek or sexy, but it has depth and a whole lot of character. I like the old-school, gritty feel of it. It reminds me of Six String Justice's early songs, chock-full of heart and barely contained energy. It's definitely not highly processed, like most radio-ready songs are these days, but it's ours and I'm proud of it.

Paisley closes her eyes and nibbles on her lower lip as it plays. Her eyebrows dip and rise with the intro music. She tilts her head when the first verse hits, and the edge of her mouth twitches into a smile when I start singing. Even though I was thinking about recording a doubled vocal line track, I kind of like the way my voice sounds all by itself against the guitars. Her head starts bobbing when we reach the chorus, which sounds bigger with two voices since I've managed to do a decent job of blending our tracks so it sounds like she's singing backup vocals.

When the second verse starts and Paisley's breathy, slightly hesitant singing voice comes out of the studio monitors as if she's singing a solo, all the color drains out of her face.

She might not like it, but I love the way her voice sounds. The way it floats over the melody, the perfect contrast to the whine of the electric guitar and the driving train beat.

Paisley frowns. A deep crease develops in the center of her forehead as the verse progresses and it stays there throughout the chorus. At the bridge she finally takes a breath, and a bit of color comes back into her face. Still, she sits as rigid as a rock until the final few bars of the song.

I'm almost afraid to ask her opinion. I thought it was great for my first attempt at mixing, but I'm pretty sure Paisley doesn't feel the same way about it. Still, I need to know what she thinks in order to improve. "Well?"

She clears her throat. "I can tell you spent a lot of time on it."

That's like the equivalent of a parent trying to figure out a way to say something nice about their kid's art class project when it's an absolute eyesore. I know this because I sucked at art, so I got a lot of *This must have taken a lot of time* and *I can see you put a lot of effort into this* from my mom.

Being a performing musician requires a thick skin when it comes to feedback, but mine's feeling onion-skin-thin and just as brittle at the moment. "Right."

Paisley's face falls. "No, that's not what I—" She reaches out and takes my hand. "I think you did a great job with what you were working with. You have a great ear, and you took the mix so much further than I expected in such a short time."

"YouTube," I say.

"I just . . . I didn't expect to hear my voice so prominently featured."

Oh.

I'm such an idiot. Paisley wasn't criticizing me. She was laser-beam focused on how she sounded. I should have seen it coming, knowing how self-conscious she is about her singing voice. I wish she could hear herself sing the way I do, because I think her voice is beautiful and nuanced and vulnerable. It's the imperfections that make it stand out and make you want to keep listening.

But how am I supposed to tell her that?

"I get it," I say. "I was just messing around with the song, seeing how it might work as a duet, and I liked how it sounded."

She gets a thoughtful, faraway expression on her face. "Actually, it does work well as a duet. I wonder if Exit 12S has a singer they can pair you up with."

Only if it's you.

DECEMBER 18

AFTER PAISLEY HELPS ME set up the studio to record the different tracks, I spend the majority of the day recording lead vocals, doubles, harmonies, and ad-libs until my voice hurts, and electric and rhythm guitar parts until my fingers are numb. Then I spend some time looking for the perfect MIDI track for a bass guitar and a few percussion embellishments to give it a little something extra. There are so many tracks saved in the Ka$hTrain file when I finish, I'm not sure how I'll keep them all organized.

Once I start mixing, I don't stop. Well, I break for coffee and Easy Mac and snacks, but otherwise, I'm the Little Engine That Could, chugging along through the night. The song's due today, and I'll catch up on all the lost sleep once it's done and turned in to Barry.

I'm bleary-eyed and bone-weary when Paisley arrives at the studio.

"Whoa," she says, sweeping her eyes over me and the disaster zone that once was the studio desk. Now it looks more like a pack of raccoons broke into a 7-Eleven and had a field day. "Okay, how are you, Kash?" she asks in the same kind of voice you use on a wild animal you don't want to startle.

"I'm fine. I'm tired. I'm sorry about the mess." I rub my eyes and stretch. "But I think I finished it. Wanna give it a listen?"

"Yes," she says, like there are no other possible answers.

I yawn and press play.

Today, when she listens to the mix, her eyes sparkle and gleam like ornaments on a Christmas tree. She sits there, paying rapt attention to the music, as if she can hear every note I sing, every vibration of a guitar string, every detail. She smirks at the train whistle and claps when we get to the end. "That was fantastic, Kash."

"You think?"

"I know," she says. "They asked for a country dance song, and you're about to deliver that and more."

I pull her into my lap and wrap my arms around her midsection, letting my head fall onto her shoulder. She brushes a lock of hair from my face and presses a kiss to my forehead.

"You did it," she says.

"*We* did it," I reply, my voice hoarse from all the singing and lack of sleep.

Paisley places her palms on my cheeks and tilts my face up so she can look me in the eye. There's a bittersweet look in her eyes, like she's proud of our accomplishment but also sad that all this is coming to an end. "You're going to take Nashville by storm."

"Can I take you with me?" I don't realize how serious I am about it until the words come out of my mouth. Paisley and I make a good team. I don't want to lose what we have, personally or professionally.

Paisley blinks in shock. "That's just lack of sleep talking," she says, pushing my shoulder playfully.

"What if it's not?"

She sighs and slides out of my lap. "I'm not cut out for Nashville."

"It's not just for performers. Plenty of songwriters are there."

"Look, Kash," she says, picking up wrappers and shoving them into the trashcan that was under the desk. I hadn't noticed it before. "You're about to hit the big time. You're gonna go on *Live, from Nashville!* and blow them all away. The last thing you need is me hanging around."

. . . not the direction we're going in . . .

It's nothing personal . . .

Am I getting dumped? Again.

"Hold up," I say, bolting from the chair. "You're talking like you want to end whatever this is." I motion between us.

"No. What I'm saying is I don't belong in Nashville." She bites her bottom lip. "But that doesn't mean *we* don't belong together. I'm not ready to leave Hidden Acres, but I don't want to lose you."

I pull her in for a hug. "I don't want to lose you, either. I like what we have going on."

"Me too."

"Hidden Acres is only a short drive from Nashville. Well, unless a big rig spills a bunch of lithium-ion batteries," I say wryly.

Paisley's shoulders give a little shake of laughter. "True."

"I'm going to need someone to co-write more songs with me for a full-length album."

"True."

"And I'm probably going to need to book time in a recording studio."

"Makes sense."

I step back and take her hands. "I want to see where this goes with us, Paisley."

"Me too."

I sway on my feet, the exhaustion catching up with me.

"You need sleep," she says, her lips skimming over my cheek.

I nod. "First, I have to send the song to Barry. Then sleep."

Paisley looks at the clock and screws up her face. "I have to get over to the cocoa stand. I'll see you later?"

"You can count on it."

We kiss goodbye, and then she's out the door.

I turn to the computer, quickly select the file from the Ka$hTrain folder, and drop "Worth the Wait_Kash" into SoundCloud. I also upload the folder with the other five demo songs Paisley and I wrote. I set the playlist to private and shoot the link over to Barry with a note: *"Worth the Wait" should get toes tapping on New Year's Eve.*

Done and done.

DECEMBER 22

NOW THAT MY DEMO and dance song have been turned in, I direct my attention to helping Paisley around the farm. There's more than enough to do, but at least we can do it together. From slinging cocoa to helping haul a cut tree to a customer's car in the parking lot, I'll volunteer for any job that will give me an excuse to spend more time with Paisley.

Right now, I'm taking a break from lumberjack duty to help Paisley cut strips of ribbon for a wreath-making event in the big red barn. Neither of us wants to talk about the fact that I'm heading back to Nashville in a few days or that I don't know when I'll be back. Instead, we're making first date–style small talk. Not gonna lie, I kinda love it.

It's my turn to ask a random question. "Crunchy or creamy peanut butter?"

"Ooh," she says, pausing to think. "Depends on the application. Crunchy for sandwiches, creamy for candies."

"Solid answer. Your turn."

She snips a length of shiny green ribbon. "Okay, is *Die Hard* a Christmas movie?"

I'm about to answer "Of course" when my phone buzzes.

"It's Barry," I say.

Paisley and I share a wide-eyed look. Barry's either calling with good news or bad news, or maybe it's a mixed bag of news. Either way, our afternoon is about to be shaken up like a snow globe.

"Heya, kid," Barry says as soon as I answer the phone. "Got a minute?"

My heart thuds. "Sure."

"The team over here loved the demos you and Paisley put together. There's some good stuff in there. We'll work on getting some session musicians scheduled for early next year so you can record them with one of our producers."

I flash Paisley a huge grin and a thumbs-up. "That's great."

"I can tell you that we're all very happy with what you've delivered so far, and we're looking forward to more good things to come. You know, since you're already on a roll, you might want to think about coming up with a few more songs to round out a full-length album."

"I'll get right on that."

"I did want to ask you about the duet you sent over."

Duet. What duet? "Uh?"

Suddenly, I'm filled with all this nervous energy that I don't know what to do with. I need to move. I get up from the chair and pace across the floorboards in the barn.

"We kinda had you pegged as a solo artist and hadn't considered a collaboration like that. But I gotta tell ya, kid, it works."

My stomach clenches. I have a very, very bad feeling about this. "That's great, Barry," I say, trying not to choke on the panic that's rising inside me. "But, um, I didn't send you a duet." I glance over at Paisley, who's turned her attention back to measuring and cutting ribbon.

"Are you kids calling it something else these days? A collab, maybe? I can't keep up with all the new lingo. All I know is, you sent in 'Worth the Wait,' and it's got two vocalists. I'm gonna guess it was you and Paisley?"

Oh. Shit.

"Barry," I say. "That song's—"

"Incredible. I loved it."

"Barry."

"I sent it to the team over here, they loved it," he continues, completely ignoring me.

"Barry," I try again.

"So they sent it right over to *Live, from Nashville!* They loved it, too. In fact," Barry continues like a steamroller without brakes, "you and your duet partner will be the headliners for the New Year's Eve Ball. Merry Christmas, kid!"

"Barry, it's not a duet," I say.

"Of course it is, kid."

"No, I mean, Paisley won't sing it with me."

"She's gonna have to. That's what they're expecting."

"Barry," I say, but it's no use.

There's a muffled announcement in the background. "I

gotta run, my flight's about to leave. I'll get you the details next week. Stop by the office on Monday when you're back in town, and bring Paisley with you. We'll all talk then."

Barry disconnects the call and I stare at the phone in a daze.

How the hell did Barry get my practice file and not the demo track?

TRACK 25

It Was an Honest Mistake

Paisley

DECEMBER 22

"WHAT'S UP?" I ask, arranging the random curls of ribbon in front of me into a neat stack.

"So, there's good news and . . . less-good news."

I glance up at him. "Like, bad news?"

He scrunches up his face. "Eh. I mean. I guess it depends on how you look at it. Some people might say it's all good news."

Well, that's not cryptic or anything.

Instead of taking the seat across from me, where he was before, Kash pulls out the chair next to mine and turns it to face me. I set down the ribbon and give him my full attention.

Kash leans forward and rests his elbows on his thighs, letting his linked hands droop in the space between his knees.

"Start with the good news," I say.

He puffs out a slow stream of air, like he can't believe what he's about to tell me. "The label likes the demos. They're really happy with what we put together. Barry says they're going to book recording time with a producer and some session musicians to record with me early next year."

"That's great, Kash," I say.

We worked so hard on those songs. I was worried that they'd feel rushed or they weren't what the label was looking for, but now Kash is going to get his album, and I'm going to have some songwriting credits to my name. This is a win-win for both of us.

"It's huge," he says, his eyes lighting up with excitement. "And Barry wants more songs from us for a full-length album. He didn't say how many, but I'm guessing another handful or so."

"What?! That's amazing." I hold up my hand for a high five, and Kash smacks his palm into mine.

"Is there a deadline?"

"Not yet," he says.

We both share a relieved smile.

"More good news," I say. "Now we can take time to develop our ideas and enjoy the holidays with our families."

"Yeah, about that," he says, scratching his jaw. "It's kind of a funny story . . ."

Oh.

In my experience, most stories that start off that way are not funny at all.

I slowly breathe in through my nose and release through my mouth. "So, is this the less-good news you're about to tell me?"

Kash sits back and rubs his palms over his thighs. "Barry absolutely loved 'Worth the Wait.' Thought we hit it out of the park. And the label loved it." Kash shrugs. "And apparently, *Live, from Nashville!* loved it, too."

"Oh my god!" I jump out of my seat, nearly knocking it over, and wrap my arms around Kash, smooshing his face into my midriff. "I knew they would! As if there was any doubt. You're the headliner, right? Oh, this is great for you. For your career. Probably mine, too, when other music publishers find out I co-wrote it with you . . ."

Kash wraps his arms around me but doesn't hold me as close as he usually does. It feels more like he's treating me like a delicate piece of crystal that's in danger of breaking.

"Thing is, I accidentally sent the wrong file," he says, his words muffled.

"Say what now?" I ease back so I can see his face. His brow is creased with worry. "Did you just say you sent the wrong file?"

Kash looks up at me and swallows like it's painful. I hope he's not coming down with something. "Yeah."

"I mean, who hasn't done something like that? I once sent my English term paper to my science teacher. Accidents happen."

"I sent Barry the practice file."

"So, it wasn't the one with the mixed tracks?"

Kash's eyes narrow like he's in physical pain. Gosh, I hope it's not the flu or COVID. "Oh, it was mixed all right. It was just . . . it was the duet version."

I get this sinking black hole of a feeling in the pit of my stomach that radiates outward toward my extremities. The ringing in my ears is so loud, I couldn't possibly have heard him correctly, because I thought he said . . . "Duet?"

Kash nods. "Yeah."

My feet are on the floor, but it feels like I'm trying to balance on stilts. My legs go wobbly and I drop back into my chair.

I absolutely *hate* the way I sounded in that recording, my voice so flat and whiny. I'm not a singer. I don't want to be a singer. And I sure as hell don't want anyone outside of my trusted circle of family and friends to hear me sing (and not even them sometimes).

Don't panic.

I suck in a deep breath. "That's definitely not great," I say. "I can see why you referred to it as 'less-good' news."

"Definitely not up there with the really good stuff," he says.

"Obviously you told Barry it was a mistake," I say. "That it's not supposed to be a duet. You're going to send Barry the correct file and get it all sorted out, right?"

Kash winces. "Um, well, I tried, but . . . thing is, they want *us* to perform it live at the New Year's Eve Ball."

I let out a surprised laugh, because yeah, right.

But Kash isn't laughing. In fact, he looks pretty darn serious.

Whoosh. The air in my lungs rushes out of me.

"You told Barry no, right?" I wait for him to answer, and it's like someone took a giant vacuum and sucked all the oxygen out of the barn, because I can barely breathe. "Kash. You told them no, right?"

He scratches the back of his head and looks a little lost, like he's not quite sure how to process everything. "Barry didn't give me the chance. He just said they loved it as a duet and that I should stop by the office with you on Monday to work out the details."

"Call him back," I say. The sooner we get this straightened out, the better.

Kash frowns. "He was about to get on a plane. And what am I supposed to say? 'Hey, Barry, thanks for the offer of a lifetime, but we're going to pass'?"

I groan. "I can't believe this."

"I'm sure we can figure something out. Although . . ." He

studies me from beneath his long, dark bangs with thoughtful eyes. "It's not a bad idea." He says it like he thinks we *should* just show up to the *Live, from Nashville!* New Year's Eve Ball and perform a duet.

Onstage.

In front of other people.

Together.

I shake my head in disbelief. "You can't be serious?"

Kash knows how terrible my stage fright is. He knows how badly I bombed in May. He knows better than to ask this of me.

He shrugs. "I think we should at least consider it."

What is there to consider? How many different ways I could possibly screw it up? I mean, this is such a bonkers idea, I don't even know where to start.

"I—I can't do it."

"I know you can, Paisley. You sang at the Thanksgiving hoedown," he says.

"That's completely different. That was in front of close friends and family. And if you recall, I didn't want to—Halley forced me," I say, spitting her name out like a four-letter word.

"You sang at Carols by Candlelight," he says.

"It was a double-dog dare. Half the time I was lip-synching."

Kash takes my hands in his. "Paisley, I have faith in you. I know you can do it."

Maybe I can. Maybe I can't. But I sure as hell don't *want* to.

I bite my bottom lip as the black hole in my stomach swirls into a fierce tornado of angst.

"I'll be right there with you," he says.

I tug my hands away. How can I trust that when it doesn't

feel like he's here with me right now? He knows how much I hate singing in public. Why won't he just listen to me? Why does Kash want this so badly?

"Why do you even want me to sing with you?" I ask.

"Why wouldn't I?" Kash's brow wrinkles like he's surprised by the question. "We sounded really good together on the recording. The song works better as a duet."

"That was just you and me in the studio. You know I'm a mess onstage."

"Actually, I *don't* know. Every time I've heard you sing, you've been great."

"Yeah, right," I huff.

"Paisley, one bad set isn't the end of the world. It's not even the end of a career. It happens. I've had plenty of bad sets with Six String Justice, and we still booked gigs after."

Tears spring to my eyes. How nice for him, that he doesn't know how it feels to be ridiculed and jeered at. How awful it is to discover another Seth Carpenter video making the rounds on social media. How it feels to have all your hopes and dreams teetering on the edge of disaster, ready to be completely crushed with one more misstep.

"You were there," I say, spitting out the words like an accusation.

"I wasn't watching."

"I'm sure you've seen the videos."

"No. I haven't." Kash shakes his head like he's not sure what to do. "I didn't pay you any attention back in May, and I wasn't searching for videos of you. My focus was on other things. Do I wish things had gone differently for you? Yes. Do I wish I remembered meeting you backstage that day? Hell yes." Kash sighs.

"When I finally found out about what happened, we'd already spent time together. It didn't seem right to watch the video. Why would I want to?"

"Why wouldn't you?"

Everyone else seems to find it hugely entertaining.

"Because I don't care what happened back then—"

"You don't care?"

"You didn't let me finish. That's the point I'm trying to make, Paisley. Of course I care. But I care about what's happening now."

"You have a funny way of showing it."

Kash's mouth drops open. "What's that supposed to mean?"

"How is pressing me to sing a duet with you in public caring?"

"I'm only asking you to take a beat and think about it. This is a huge opportunity," he says. "For both of us."

My eyebrows rise. "Both of us?" My fingernails dig into my palms as I try to stay calm and not let my emotions spin any further out of control. "This isn't an opportunity for me; it's a setup. Because there's no way I won't crash and burn. It was bad enough flopping on a local stage. I don't need to do it live on national television. Not to mention, I could ruin both our careers."

"You're not going to ruin my career," he says, like I'm being ridiculous. Like there's no doubt in his mind that he could survive the fallout.

He's probably right. If the show goes well, great. If not, even better. Nothing goes viral faster than a train wreck. And what could be more enticing for the online masses than a train wreck set to a train drumbeat? They'll eat it right up, and he'll get his name out there. I'm sure the label's PR team will know exactly how to spin it to sell more of his albums. They'd probably make it look like I was drunk or something equally awful to gain some pity purchases. A sale's a sale, after all.

A bitter taste fills my mouth.

I'm in a no-win situation thanks to him. If I show up to the New Year's Eve Ball and fail, I'll be the butt of every joke for ages. And if I don't show up, I'll probably be labeled as difficult to work with. Songwriters in Nashville are a dime a dozen, and word of mouth could quickly make me a persona non grata in the industry. "No matter what, my music career is shot," I say.

Why can't he see that?

"Paisley," he says, reaching out to rest his hand on my forearm. All I hear are the echoes of the promises he made not so long ago: *I'll do my very best to support you and make sure you feel seen from here on out.*

That big, black swirling storm in my gut burns with betrayal. This is him supporting me and making me feel seen?

I'm so stupid. I always knew he had big dreams and big goals, but I got caught up in his country-rock vibe, with his dark hair and dark eyes and that makes-your-knees-all-weak smile of his. When he kissed me, I thought I was special. I thought I was seen. I thought I could trust him. With my words and my music. With my fears and my failures. With my heart.

And that right there is the worst part of it. Not only has he potentially put my songwriting career at risk, but he's also shattered my heart.

I shrug off his hand and push my chair back, standing so I'm out of his reach. His eyes are pleading and his mouth is parted and my heart aches like my chest is packed full of snow.

“I can’t do it,” I say with such icy force that the temperature in the barn drops at least twenty degrees. I shiver and wrap my arms around myself for warmth. “I won’t do it.”

“Let’s just talk about it.”

I’m done talking. Why bother, when he won’t even listen?

“If they insist on a duet, find someone else for New Year’s Eve, Kash. It’s not going to be me.”

“Paisley,” he says.

But I shake my head. “I need some time.” Burning-hot tears threaten to spill over as I storm away.

“Paisley,” he calls out after me, his voice pleading.

But it’s too late to stop this ’ship from sinking. We’ve hit the rocks and we’re going down.

TRACK 26

All My Mistakes

Kash

DECEMBER 22

THE BIG RED barn goes dead silent in the wake of Paisley's departure.

What the hell just happened? Did Paisley just dump me?

I scramble up out of my seat and race to the door to go after her, but the parking lot's filled with families and onlookers when I get outside. Enough eyes are already trained on Paisley as she races toward the farmhouse, the last thing I want to do is bolt after her and draw more attention. Plus, it doesn't seem right to force her to talk to me, when she clearly wants nothing to do with me right now. As much as I don't like it, I need to give her some space.

Every misstep I made to get to this point runs through my mind as I head back to the Hideaway. It all started with me sending the wrong file. If I hadn't done that, then none of this would have happened. Paisley and I would probably be celebrating the good news right now.

But sending the wrong file was just the inciting incident. Paisley probably could have forgiven me for that part of it. The real problem is how I handled everything that came after.

I push open the recording studio door and sink into a chair, letting my head flop back until it whacks against the headrest.

I should have cut Barry off immediately.

I should have insisted that "Worth the Wait" isn't a duet.

I should have demanded to be heard.

Thinking on my feet has never been my strong suit, and talking with Barry always throws me off-kilter. I always feel like I'm a beat or two behind, rushing to process everything he throws at me so I can catch up. There was a lot to process on our last call, but even then, that's just an excuse. I knew I needed to say something, but I didn't try hard enough.

And then I just got it in my head that maybe "Worth the Wait" should be a duet. Paisley and I sound so good when we sing together. Our voices just meld together, her smooth, breathy sound complementing my rougher tenor.

I love singing with her. I love how it makes me feel when our voices harmonize. But I never should have pressed Paisley to sing with me on New Year's Eve.

She's right to feel let down and overlooked. I promised that I would support her and pay attention to her, and the first chance I got to prove it, I failed.

I wouldn't be surprised if she thinks I was actively choosing my career over hers . . . over her. I'd probably be thinking the same thing if I were in her shoes. I wish I could try to explain, to say I'm sorry, to try to repair the damage, but Paisley deserves more than excuses and apologies and a cheap off-brand bandage.

She deserves better.

I can't just say I want to be better for her. I actually have to be better. All I have to offer her right now are words, and words just won't suffice. I have to do something meaningful to show her just how much she means to me and how sorry I truly am.

The wind whips up outside as I pull out my cell phone. I scroll to my last text message with Barry and start to type.

Today, 3:46 PM

Kash:

I know you're traveling, but I need to talk with you.

Please call me when you land.

Or as soon as you can.

I SET THE PHONE down on the desk and watch it as if I could will it to ring. Which is dumb, because Barry's on a flight and I have no idea where he's going or how long it'll be before he lands. I could sit here, staring at my phone all night, and he might not try calling me at all. I might as well do something constructive with my time while I wait.

DECEMBER 23

WHEN THE CLOCK IN the studio ticks over to 9:00 a.m., I half expect Paisley to come bursting in to start another writing session. Somehow, the space seems hollow without her. There's no pop of color on the wall next to the door, where she usually hangs her bright orange-and-red plaid coat. There's no piping-hot cups of cocoa to scald my tongue. No laughter to sink into even the smallest crevices.

It's lonely in here, where it's just me and all my mistakes.

I rub my eyes and stare at the disaster in front of me. Much like it looked the other day, there are wrappers and cups strewn all over the desk. Somehow, one of my socks ended up hanging from the corner of the percussion cabinet. And there's a damp spot on the stack of guitar tabs I was scribbling on that could either be from drool or tears. It was a long night and I had a lot of emotions to process.

The sky is a wintery gray, perfect for my current mood: cloudy with a side of melancholy. It's the kind of day when you can't really decide if sunglasses are beneficial or not. With my lack of sleep, it makes me squint, so I tug the curtains closed.

I grab my wayward sock, take a swig of what's left of my cold and bitter coffee, and sweep the trash on the desk into the basket below. I only have a few hours until Granddad arrives, and I still have a lot to do before he gets here.

Originally, the plan was for him to drive up here to get me on Christmas Eve morning, before my parents' flight is scheduled to land at Nashville International Airport. I figured I could introduce him to Paisley and maybe even pick out a live tree for the four of us to decorate (instead of the fake tree he got after Granny passed). But now that the demo is done, and Paisley and I are . . . whatever we are . . . there's no point in staying here another night.

By the time I lock up the studio and head to the apartment

side of the building, it's nearly three. I'm hungry, tired, and in sore need of a shower. Plus, I can't stop thinking about Paisley and how badly I messed everything up.

I take the stairs up to the bedroom two at a time and pull my empty suitcase out of the closet. I set aside a fresh outfit and then toss in clothes, not bothering to separate the clean ones from the dirty ones. I hate doing laundry, but Granddad hates when people are late, and I was in the studio longer than I'd planned.

I rush through a shower, barely towel-drying my hair, and then dump my toiletries on top of the clothes and zip my suitcase shut. I double-check that I haven't left anything behind. Well, nothing besides my heart. That's been Paisley's since that day I found her singing my song up in the loft. It's hard to believe it was only a few weeks ago, given everything that we've shared in the time in between.

I knew leaving Paisley and Hidden Acres would be hard when the moment came, but under the present circumstances, it's brutal. Before, I was worried about the *when*s, not the *if*s.

When will I be back at Hidden Acres?

When will I get to see her again?

When will I get up enough courage to tell Paisley how I really feel about her?

Now it seems the *if*s are all I have left to cling to.

Headlights shine through the windows, and there's the familiar sound of gravel crunching under car tires. I hoist my bag off the bed and grab my guitar case, neither of which is nearly as heavy as the gaping hole in my chest.

The evening air is cool and smells like snow. Patchy, thin

gray clouds are scattered over the cobalt-blue sky. My boots are heavy as I make my way down the front steps of the Hideaway, probably for the very last time.

Granddad pops the trunk from the front seat of his silver Lexus, and I toss my luggage in.

"Hey, sport," he says when I slide into the passenger seat. Warm air blasts from the vents, and the pale dashboard light highlights the wrinkles in his face.

"Thanks for coming to get me on such short notice," I say, since I'd only called him this morning.

"I'm glad you called," he says. "I could use some help getting everything ready before your parents arrive tomorrow."

Granddad shifts the car into gear and steers us to the lane that leads back to the main road. We pass families carrying handsaws in one direction and families carrying back cut trees in the other. White Christmas lights cast a soft glow over the shed and the barns. Everywhere I look, there's a reminder of Paisley.

The corral where she harnessed Dunder and Blixem.

The loft of the big red barn where we shared our first kiss.

The grove where we picked praying mantis egg sacs off the trees.

My chest aches as my mind flips through the memories.

"Do you mind stopping by the farmhouse?" I ask. "I need to drop off the key and check out."

Granddad pulls up in front of the farmhouse. The porch is decked out with evergreen garlands, giant wreaths, and fluffy red bows dusted with a fine layer of snow.

It looks so inviting. So festive. I know I have to leave for Nashville, but I really don't want to.

I pause with my fingers on the door handle and take a deep breath.

"You okay?" Granddad asks.

I shrug and pull open the door. Cool air sweeps over my skin as I step out. "I screwed up and I don't know how to make it right," I say, ducking down to talk, with one hand on the roof and the other on top of the door. "I'll tell you about it on the drive."

Granddad nods. He grabs his phone and pulls up the navigation app. "We're going to want to make a stop at Carson's for a milkshake on the way home, then," he says, tapping on the screen.

I shut the door and climb the stairs that lead to the massive porch. I consider knocking, but everyone's probably out working on the farm, given how busy it is. Cars trickle up and down the driveway and the sound of laughter and chatter carries over from the courtyard near the gift shop.

There's a pull-down through-the-wall drop box next to the door, with a hand-painted slate sign hanging above it:

HIDDEN ACRES & THE HIDEAWAY
KEY RETURN
MONEY FOR TREES
COMPLIMENTS & CRITIQUES
THANKS FOR STOPPING BY!

I reach into my front pocket and pull out the key for the Hideaway. The wooden key chain is smooth and warm. There's a reverberating clink of metal hitting metal when I drop it in the box. A small, poorly wrapped package crinkles as I tug it from my inside jacket pocket. I didn't have any wrapping paper handy, so I used a sheet of blank guitar tabs from the studio and then tied the thin, square package up with an old electric guitar string that was lying around. For the tag, I used a piece of cardboard cut from the lid of a cereal box. On it is written, in my messy penmanship, *For Paisley*.

It's ugly as homemade sin, but it's the best I could do. It's not fancy, but it's from the heart, so I hope that counts for something. I pull open the flap and slide the gift into the drop box. It lands with a soft *thunk*.

I turn and jog down the stairs to the waiting car. Granddad hits the gas as soon as I hop in, and then we're bumping along the unpaved road, getting farther and farther away from Paisley and the mess I'm leaving behind.

TRACK 27

Cold Hard Kash

Paisley

DECEMBER 23

MY EYES ARE puffy and red from another long night of crying, and there's a hollow ache inside me that no amount of comfort food can fill.

I somehow managed to survive today, forcing myself to put one foot in front of the other while I chomped on candy canes like they were about to expire. My teeth ache from the sugar, but it's nothing compared to the constant dull pain in my chest. I don't know how I'm going to make it through the next few days being friendly and jolly with all our last-minute shoppers when I feel about as festive as a fart.

The Grinch?

Ebenezer Scrooge?

They've got nothing on me. I am a living, breathing pendulum of anger and anguish.

I tug open a packet of gold under-eye patches and press the

cool gel pads onto my skin. They promise seemingly impossible things like *removes puffiness* and *eliminates dark circles*, which I definitely need so I don't look like a ghoul. I'm pretty sure I gave one little kid nightmares last night, based on the teary-eyed, fearful look they gave me at the Photos with the Reindeer station in the courtyard. I wish these eye patches could also tackle impossible tasks like "mends broken hearts" and "turns back time."

Out my bedroom window, I watch a steady stream of red taillights disappear down the road, and then the white Christmas lights turn off for the night. If only it was as easy to flip a switch and turn off the thoughts in my head.

I yank my lyric notebook from its spot on the bookshelf and pull it open. My hand shakes as I lift the blue pen and try to channel everything I feel in this moment onto the blank page. These crushing feelings weigh heavily on me—the heartbreak, the disappointment, the loss of so many hopes and dreams I had—and if I don't spill them out, I might implode.

Weather: Icy and Bitter
Mood: Disconsolate
Theme: Betrayal and Heartbreak
Style: Country ballad

<u>Cold Hard Kash</u>

You stole a kiss and took my heart,
My emotions left torn apart,
'Cause I couldn't help falling into you.

Hit the brakes, I've got to stop.
What you see is what I've got.
It's clear now that you never really saw me.

You're asking far too much of me,
I'm not the girl you want me to be, no.
Endless tears that I have cried,
You said you cared, you must have lied, oh.

Spun golden tales to ease my fears,
Those pretty words, they disappear
Turns out it was only ever about you.
Trapped in this cage, I can't break out,
Left with heartache, left with doubt.
It's clear now that you never really knew me.

Squealing tires on the road,
Left before the corpse was cold,
Keep on running.
Buried my feelings,
Buried our dreams,
Buried our future,
Bit back my screams.
Keep on running.
You can't lose and I can't win,
Mourning all that could have been,
Sink down deep under my skin,
Again, and again, and again, and again.

DECEMBER 24

CHRISTMAS EVE.

The last day of the season for Hidden Acres Christmas Tree Farm, and I've never been so glad for it to be over.

Harried families rush around, trying to find the perfect tree they can decorate "right quick." Last-minute shoppers pop into the gift shop hoping to find a gift for an unexpected guest or a neighbor who's "fixin' to drop by with a present later today." Racks stand empty where handmade wreaths and centerpieces were on display before we sold out. The bins at the Festive & Free stall are picked bare, with only bits of pine cones and sawdust left.

At five p.m., Mom flips the OPEN sign to CLOSED in the gift shop window. For the first time since Thanksgiving, Dad chains off the parking lot and puts out our SEE YOU NEXT YEAR! road sign.

I clip leads onto Dunder and Blixem and guide them out of their temporary pen. Blixem grunts and paws at the ground, shoving her snout into a clump of pine needles. "C'mon, ladies," I say, giving the lead a gentle tug.

They don't seem in any rush to get back to the barn, and I'm in no rush to get back to the farmhouse. Everyone's been so busy with Christmas stuff, it's been easy to slip in and out without anyone noticing. But Halley's home now, and we'll be spending plenty of family time together. I just know she's going to have a million questions I don't want to answer.

The reindeers' harnesses jingle as we walk, their feet *click, click, click*ing as we mosey along. A slow, lazy rhythm that reminds me of Elvis's "Blue Christmas." In my head, I can hear his deep bluesy timber, the way his tone is so melancholy and sad.

I lead Dunder and Blixem to a small thicket of trees surrounded by a picket fence and bring them inside. The ladies have worked hard this month; they deserve a little treat. When I unclip their leads, Dunder bounces and happy-trots to the other side of the enclosure, her rear end and legs swaying back and forth like the pendulum on a clock. She digs at the ground with her front hooves, puffing and snorting as she sniffs a patch of fescue. Blixem rubs her antlers against a tree trunk and then starts nibbling on some of the gray-green lichen growing along its side.

I lean back against the fence and sigh as "Blue Christmas" plays on a loop in my mind.

"I'm right there with you, Elvis," I mumble as I brush a stray tear from my eye.

DECEMBER 25

CHRISTMAS MORNING ISN'T NEARLY as frantic as it was when Halley and I were younger. Now when I pad downstairs at sunup, I head straight for the coffeepot instead of the stockings hung from the mantel with care.

"Merry Christmas," Halley says, not bothering to look up at me from the bench in the entryway as she pulls on a pair of dusty old work boots and tucks her PJ pants inside.

She's up early to feed the reindeer, and I'm up because tossing and turning in bed was getting old. Mom and Dad are still asleep, as they should be after such a nonstop month. They deserve every minute of rest, though I do miss the wilder days when Halley and I would race down the hall and into their room to jump on the bed and gush about the presents under the tree until they finally agreed to get up.

"Morning," I say. My voice is hoarse from another night of sobbing into my pillow like a fool, but thankfully those eye patches really do help reduce the swelling.

I set the oven to proof and pull two trays of homemade cinnamon rolls I stress-prepped last night from the fridge. Once they rise, there will be enough here to feed a small army, but it wasn't nearly enough work to distract me from the "Blue Christmas" earworm or the way my mind wouldn't stop gnawing on my memories of Kash as I kneaded and rolled out the dough.

Halley finishes lacing up her boots, and then her hazel eyes bore into me as I flip on the coffee maker. There's a gurgling rattle as the heating element kicks on and the water starts to heat.

"What?" I ask. I spin to face her and cross my arms over my chest, leaning my hip against the counter.

She purses her lips, as if debating what to say. "Kash gone?" she asks.

I *so* don't want to do this right now.

I turn away and grab a coffee mug from the cupboard, clinking it on the counter when I set it down with too much force. "Yup."

Halley stares at me, her eyes narrowed into a pensive expression. "Want to talk about it?"

"Nope," I say, popping the *p*. I pull a container out of the fridge and splash a heavy-handed pour of salted caramel creamer into my mug.

Halley comes over and wraps me in a huge hug. "I don't know what happened. I'm not going to push you to tell me. But just know I love you." She gives me an extra-tight squeeze and then pulls back to look me in the face with a feisty glimmer in her eye. "You know what these boots are made for?"

"Walkin'."

"That's right, Nancy. And I'll walk these boots all the way to Nashville to kick his ass if you want me to."

I can't stop the snort that sneaks out. "You have a car. You could just drive there."

Halley heaves a frustrated sigh. "I think you're missing the point, Paiz."

"I love you, too," I say, and bring her in for another bear hug.

The oven beeps and we pull away. I really don't want to talk about it, but it's nice to know she's got my back.

I STARE DOWN AT the printer-paper and guitar string wrap job and frown at my name, written in Kash's now-familiar scrawl. *For Paisley.*

Someone had slipped it under the tree with all the other presents. I wasn't prepared to open it earlier—downstairs with my family in the living room in front of a roaring fire—and I'm not sure I'm prepared to open it now.

The house is quiet.

Mom's on the phone in the kitchen, catching up with Aunt Betty.

Dad's watching football, though he's probably napping in his recliner.

Halley's in her room, trying out the new nail polish she got in her stocking.

My pounding heart seems to thunder in the silence.

Even though I know Kash's present isn't a prank jar with a snake spring or a jack-in-the-box, I'm still hesitant to unwrap it. A jump scare is one thing, but I'm just as nervous about the feelings that might jump out at me when I open what he left for me.

I untwist the guitar string and set it on my bedside stand. Slide my nail beneath the edge of the paper and tear the tape. Inside is a plastic CD jewel case with a piece of lined notebook paper folded up inside it.

I pull open the case and stare down at the note.

Paisley,
I wasn't sure how to get this to you since you never check your messages. Your phone is probably still wrapped up in your sock drawer and out of battery, not that I blame you. There are things I should have said and done differently. I know I let you down. I'm sorry. Please just give it a listen and give me the chance to make it right.

~Kash

He's scrawled a shortened URL under his name.

I grab my iPad from my desk, minimize the GarageBand

app, and pull up the browser. After typing in the URL, I wait for the page to appear. A YouTube video loads and starts to play. I recognize the loft, with its mountain of boxes and the old sleigh pushed against the wall. One of the rickety old wooden chairs is set in the center of the room, where the light from the window is the brightest. There's some rustling in the background, and then Kash walks into the frame carrying an acoustic guitar.

He's wearing his usual outfit of dark jeans, dark shirt, and dark black jacket. His hair is longer than it was when he arrived, and his stubble looks a few days old. Dark circles beneath his eyes make them look even darker.

In the video, he sits in the chair and settles the guitar in his lap. Strums an open chord and then looks at the camera. Looks at me. "I'm not sure if you'll ever see this, but I hope you do. I'll give you as much time and space as you need. I'll wait for you. As long as it takes."

Kash strums another chord, and a lock of hair falls into his face. He tosses it back and bites his bottom lip. "I wrote this song for you. It's called 'All of My Mistakes.'"

My pulse spikes as Kash plays the intro. As he strums, he taps the heel of his hand on the body of the guitar to give the song a percussive beat. My heart stutters when he starts singing, the raw emotion in his voice piercing me.

"I'm not perfect,
I never claimed to be.
But I made promises,
Promises I tried my best to keep."

Tears spill down my cheeks as the music seeps into my skin. He looks into the camera with eyes full of sorrow and regret.

"Here I am, the sum of my mistakes,
Wanted more for us than ending in heartbreak.
I don't deserve forgiveness
or any more of your time.
But just know I've given my heart to you,
And it's no longer mine."

I listen to the rest of the song, and my heart aches for Kash and for what we had. I don't know how to repair the damage, but I know it hurts. It hurts so damn much.

Tears rack my body. I flop face down onto the bed and let out an anguished sob.

TRACK 28

Lonesome Hearts

Kash

DECEMBER 31

IT'S BEEN A whirlwind week in Nashville. Between meetings, rehearsals, and sound checks, I don't think I've had so much packed into my daily schedule since I graduated high school. The breakneck speed at which everything's been going makes my head spin. Even the busiest days at Hidden Acres, when I was pulling double duty co-writing with Paisley and then helping her out on the farm, seem like a walk in the park compared with this.

I really wish she were here.

Because even though this is what I've been dreaming about for years, it feels like a hollow victory without her to share it with.

The venue they booked for the *Live, from Nashville!* New Year's Eve Ball is one of the biggest I've ever played, with a main stage area that has the capacity for seventeen hundred ticket holders and an indoor/outdoor rooftop deck with a second stage and a view of the Cumberland River. The venue even has enough greenrooms available that each performer or group gets their own, which is wild to me. On tour with Six String Justice, we usually ended up hanging out in the back of the van or crammed into a tiny room the size of a phone booth until it was time for our set. Now I have an entire room with an attached, sparkling clean bathroom all to myself.

And yet . . .

If the guys were here, Johnny and Ryder would be goofing off like always. There's a bowl of M&M's on the refreshment table, and I can picture Ryder trying to toss M&M's into Johnny's mouth from across the room. They'd whoop and holler whenever one made it in. Justin would be sitting in the huge armchair in the corner, updating Six String Justice's social media accounts and messing around on his phone. He'd ignore us until it was time to head out to play and then bark orders at us as if we were incapable of preparing ourselves for a show. Thing is, I can't picture what *I'd* be doing if we were all here in the greenroom.

Justin's words come back to me, but in a whole different light. *What do you bring to the table?*

What *did* I do when we were still a four-person unit?

It hits me now that maybe I had outgrown them. As much as it hurt at the time, Justin did me a favor. It was time for me to move on.

I think I have moved on.

Paisley helped a lot with that. All those hours helping me write songs, teaching me how to mix music, sharing her keen ear and the insights that made me a better songwriter and a better musician. I wish it had also made me a better man.

I sigh. If Paisley were here, she'd probably be reminding me to drink plenty of water. She'd have her legs curled up underneath her on the couch, playing with one of the many bracelets on her wrist, gently snapping the elastic or twirling the beads. I'd probably say something stupid and her laugh would fill up the room.

My heart pinches in my chest, and I blink back to a greenroom where it's just me and some furniture. Here I am, with my dreams coming true. I never expected it to feel so lonely.

There's a knock on the door, and then Barry pokes his head in.

"Hey, kid," he says, stepping all the way inside and pulling the door shut behind him. "How you feeling?"

Nervous. Excited. Sad. Elated. Worried. Determined.

"Fine," I say, because Barry doesn't have all day to hear about the roller coaster of emotions I'm riding on.

"Excellent. You're going to do great out there."

I sure as hell hope so.

While I'm excited about being the headliner, it also means I'm the last to play. It's a lot of waiting around and stressing out, especially now that the rehearsals and sound checks are over.

"I have the latest set list," Barry says, handing me a bright green sheet of paper. On the top, in bold lettering, it reads: TENTATIVE SCHEDULE.

There are three columns on the page: *Time*, *Main Stage*, and *Rooftop*.

I scan down to the bottom of the third column where, at 11:55 p.m., I'm set to perform "Worth the Wait" as a solo act—not a duet—on the rooftop right before the ball drops. It still seems a bit like a dream, that I've managed to nab the headlining spot out of all the other performers. It never would have been possible without Paisley, and I wish for the millionth time today that she were here to share this moment with me.

As I'm glancing back up at Barry, my eyes catch on an entry for the main stage for the half-hour time slot that starts at 11:05 p.m.: ~~Leland Bellwether~~ TBD

"What happened here?" I ask, pointing it out to Barry.

"Flight got delayed 'cause of an ice storm."

"They got a replacement in mind?"

I'm not going to get anywhere in this business if I don't take every opportunity presented to me. And maybe even some I have to create myself. I can't piddle around and wait for things to happen. I have to make them happen.

Barry glances at me with a knowing grin. "You want that spot?"

Someone once told me that if I wanted to be a successful career musician, I needed to do two things: get damn good at playing and then find as many opportunities as I could to get up in front of people and play.

I nod. "Sure do."

He pulls out his phone and sends a text message. A reply comes back almost immediately.

"You think you can get me a set list in the next five minutes?" he asks.

Another good piece of advice they gave me was to always show up overprepared. I reach into my back pocket and pull out two note cards. I hold up the one in my left hand. "Covers and originals." And then I hold up the one in my right hand. "Originals only. Will either of these work?"

Barry fixes me with an amused grin. "I'll take both and we'll see which one the producers go for."

GRANNY ALWAYS SAID, *YOU can put boots in the oven, but it don't make 'em biscuits.*

Well, you can strap on a guitar at a concert, but that don't make you a musician.

The time has come for me to prove I'm cut out for this.

It's go time for my first set of the evening, the 11:05 p.m. call time on the main stage. A spike of adrenaline surges through me, and I shift my weight back and forth. I've played other solo sets since I was booted from Six String Justice, but this is the first time that my set list is all-original material. It's easy to work the crowd when you're playing familiar standards everyone already knows, but it's a lot harder to get people to warm up to songs they don't know the words to. It was easier with Six String Justice, knowing the group was in the same situation, that we'd sink or swim together. But stepping out onto the stage to play original songs with a band I've only rehearsed with once? It's a whole other level.

I've got my guitar strapped on, a pick in my hand (and an extra in my pocket), and my cowboy hat pulled down low. There's an energy buzzing through me, part nerves, part excitement. I push away all the doubts and uncertainty. I need to be one hundred percent ready when I step out on that stage.

The stage manager gives me the sign, and I walk out to my position in front of the central microphone. Already in their places are the drummer (Kenzie), bassist (Rich), acoustic guitarist (Sandy), and percussionist (Carl) for the local house band, Cumberland River Country, who were hired to support solo acts like me for the night. The members of Cumberland River Country are all seasoned session musicians, some of whom have played for the biggest stars to come out of Nashville. Of all of us, I'm the weak link.

Still, I'm betting on me, and the songs Paisley and I wrote together. If I can come out here and win over the crowd, it will build momentum for us. This could boost both our careers.

No pressure.

I flash a smile and tip my hat up to look out at the audience. The room's filling up as it gets closer to midnight, so there's a decent crowd. "Howdy, y'all," I say, stepping up to the microphone. "My name's Kash Murray, and backing me up tonight is Cumberland River Country." I turn to the other members, one at a time. "Ready?"

They all dip their heads in acknowledgment. Kenzie nods and twirls a drumstick in the air.

Yeah, if anyone's going to flub it up, it's me.

"Let's go. A-one, a-two, a-one, two, three, four." I count off the tempo and Cumberland River Country plays the intro to "She's a Real Country Girl" like they've been playing it for years.

In the monitors playing back at us from the front of the stage, the song sounds so much fuller, rounded out with drums and a bass accompanying the rhythm guitar and my electric guitar. I bet it sounds even better out on the floor.

I look out at the audience, my gaze rolling over faces, hoping to spot someone I know. Or at least one friendly face in the crowd. I hate that Paisley's not here to hear it. My eyes continue to search the room, as if I could will her to appear, but she's not there. Not that I expected her to be.

I swallow down my sadness and lean in to the mic to sing.

"She's a real country girl.
Faded jeans, dusty boots, dirt under her nails.
Oooh, she's a real country girl."

TRACK 29

No Matter What I Do, I Just Can't Get Over You

Paisley

DECEMBER 31

KASH'S SONG FOR me has become an earworm I can't shake.

Just one listen to it, and *bam*. It took up residence in my head and burrowed into my heart.

In the post-Christmas quiet that's settled down over Hidden Acres, it's been hard to ignore since that first listen. Even harder after the fiftieth. Kash's song is all I seem to hear.

What's worse is that everything here is haunted by my memories of Kash.

The loft.

The studio.

My lyric notebook.

I press my hand over my chest where it hurts the most. My heart.

My pointer finger presses play, and I watch the video again. I listen to the way his voice is tinged with so much sorrow and regret. I watch how he looks into the camera with such raw intensity, like he can actually see me.

It feels like the floor falls out from under me as the truth of it hits me. Kash really did see me. He saw the girl who was hurting and scared and hidden away on a farm. He saw the girl who dreamed of being a songwriter. Who wanted to break free from her past. He saw the good and bad of me, and he didn't look away.

I think about our fight, playing it back in my mind, and try to see it from his perspective. He'd just gotten some amazing news from Barry. The label loved his songs. They wanted more. That's huge in and of itself. But then, to find out you've been selected as the headliner for the broadcast of the *Live, from Nashville!* New Year's Eve Ball? That must have been a wonderful shock.

The earworm snags on the bridge of the song, as if my subconscious is trying to tell me something.

"I couldn't choose for you,
It's not my right to take.
And even if it hurts,
It's a choice you have to make."

I was mad at the time that he didn't tell Barry no on my behalf. But couldn't I have been just as mad if he had? Yes, sending the wrong sample was an accident. And yes, it put me in a crappy position. But now I realize Kash didn't want to make that choice for me. He wanted to give me time to consider my options. Barry was on a plane. We had time to talk about it. I had time to think.

Kash really wasn't pressuring me to sing a duet. If I think

about the tone of voice he used, along with his words, he wasn't begging or pleading. He never said "please." He was simply saying, "I know you can do it. I believe in you."

What if he wanted to sing a duet with me because the song was ours? What if he truly didn't care if I bombed because it was more important to him that I had the option to say yes?

I've been so stuck for so long, defining myself by one thing that happened in the past, I've just assumed everyone else is stuck there, too. But how can I expect anyone else to move past it if I can't?

Kash was right. The New Year's Eve Ball is a huge opportunity. Tonight could propel him to the top with a song we co-wrote. And instead of being excited for him—for us—I threw a hissy fit.

"HEY, GRUMPY MCGRUMPY FACE, wait up."

There are times when I really don't like Halley. Is it a big sister thing to constantly annoy younger siblings, or did I just win a special lottery with her?

I roll my eyes and slow my roll to a shuffle so she can catch up.

"Whatcha doing?"

As if it's not obvious, based on the crate of cleaning supplies I'm lugging back to the farmhouse, along with a bag of nonperishables I pulled from the pantry. "I just finished up at the Hideaway."

I frown down at the food, the real reason I went to the Hideaway in the first place.

When Kash is away, the mice will play.

Mice.

I probably should have deep-cleaned it sooner, but Exit 12S had reserved it until today. There was a chance Kash would be back, and then all the scrubbing and mopping I did would have to be done again. Or maybe that was just wishful thinking on my part. Maybe, somehow, things would magically go back to how they were before it all went to hell in a handbasket.

"So that's it, then?" she asks, falling into step with me when I pick up the pace.

"I'll have you know I've been busting my butt since I woke up," I say. "Not all of us can get hours of beauty sleep in the morning. Some of us have *work* to do."

I'm trying not to be bitter, but she's pushing all my buttons.

"It takes a lot of sleep to look this beautiful," she says with a cheeky grin and a pronounced drawl, reminding me of that Dolly Parton quote *It takes a lot of money to look this cheap*.

"You should probably get back to bed, then."

"Ouch." Halley shoots me a fake-wounded look, but then all the teasing fades from her eyes. "How are you doing?"

"I'm doing."

Halley sighs and takes the bag of food from me to lighten my load. "Are you still writing music?"

"A little." It had become such a routine when Kash was here, I still find myself drawn to the loft or the studio at nine a.m., ready to work on songs. Now I sit up in my room and let my thoughts and feelings spill out onto paper. I've written so much in the past few days, I've filled the new lyric notebook almost halfway, which is wild, because I'd been working on the previous one for two years.

"Are you missing Kash?"

A lot.

I'll miss him till the cows come home, because Kash isn't coming back. Not on his own. He said as much in the video. *I'll give you as much time and space as you need.*

He's leaving what happens next up to me.

We stop before the porch stairs and silence fills the space between us. In a tree above us, the mockingbird whistles the song we've been working on together, which makes me think of the song that Halley made me sing, which gets me thinking of how Carly Simon has constantly battled stage fright and still has had a long and successful music career.

I'm not the first person to have performance anxiety, and I won't be the last. I'm not sure I'll ever be able to overcome it, but I won't know if I can if I don't try.

Halley reaches out and squeezes my arm. "I'm heading into Nashville for a party tonight. I'll probably leave around seven, if you happen to know someone who might want a ride."

"THIS IS GETTING OUT of control," I mutter as I sort through the heap of beaded bracelets I've dumped on my bed. I probably should have a better organizing system than a shoe box, since it's impossible to find what I'm looking for anymore.

I glance at my watch: 6:45 p.m. There's still time. I dig into the pile with renewed vigor, tossing bracelets back into the box as I go.

"Gotcha," I say, plucking WWCKD from the mess.

What would Carole King do?

In May, I channeled some of her overcoming-stage-fright

energy and walked out onto that stage. I wonder if there's a little bit of it left for me now.

I slide the bracelet on and dive back into the pile, looking for the perfect mix of inspiration and a reminder that I'm not alone. Kash said, *I know you can.* I have to find a way to believe it, too.

I stare down at my wrist, covered in colorful beaded bracelets.

I HOPE YOU DANCE

DO IT LIKE DOLLY

MOCKINGBIRD

FOLLOW THAT DREAM

WWCKD

"Okay, Elvis," I say. "We had a Blue Christmas together. But now it's time for me to celebrate New Year's in Nashville."

TRACK 30

Two for the Show

Kash

DECEMBER 31

"YOU WERE AMAZING," I say, shaking hands with the members of Cumberland River Country after we step offstage. "Thank you."

I've never played with such professionals before, and it was a solid performance. I could jump for joy. The energy was so great out there, and they made our songs sound so good. Barry kept giving me a thumbs-up, and people were actually paying attention. I'm full of post-show endorphins, but there's a damper on my mood. I don't have anyone to celebrate this success with.

"Looking forward to playing with you again real soon," the bass player says, giving my hand a tight squeeze.

Before I can reply, the stage manager comes over, clipboard in hand. "Hate to break this up," she says. "Kash, you need to head up to the roof now."

I glance at my watch: 11:45. I have ten minutes until I make my television debut with "Worth the Wait."

I follow a runner they've sent to collect me through a maze

of hallways to a service elevator. We take it up to the top floor, and I step out into a narrow room behind the rooftop stage. The band before me is finishing up their set, and I take a moment to center myself.

I close my eyes and breathe in slowly, trying to channel all the positive energy I soaked up downstairs. I can't get caught up in the cameras or the pressure. I just have to go out there and do my thing.

The rooftop stage manager hands me an earpiece and gestures for me to put it in.

As soon as I do, an unfamiliar woman's voice says, "It's been a spectacular night here in Nashville."

"That's right, Megan," says a male voice. "In just a few short minutes, the ball will drop. And then the party will really kick off."

"It's an exciting time, Russ."

The stage manager gives me the signal.

It's go time.

I straighten my shoulders and take a deep breath. I've spent the past few days working on a new arrangement for "Worth the Wait," but in my heart, it's still supposed to be a duet. The song was meant for Paisley and me.

I press my fist over my heart, feeling how quickly it's beating in my chest.

The stage manager, with an impatient look, gives me another signal.

I nod but don't move. In the ear monitor, the hosts are making small talk as they wait for me to take the stage.

There's a bustle behind me, and the stage manager's eyes

narrow. "You're not allowed back here. This space is for performers only."

I turn as Barry's familiar voice says, "It's all right. She's with the band."

"Paisley," I say, my breath catching in my chest.

"Sorry I'm late," she says. Her eyes dart nervously around the darkened space we're standing in.

"What are you doing here?"

"Singing?" she says. She tucks a strand of hair behind her ear and takes a deep breath.

"You don't have to do this," I say, stepping closer to her.

"It's supposed to be a duet."

The bass player drifts over and gives me a "C'mon, man, what the hell" look.

"You need to be on the stage now," the stage manager says.

My heart hammers in my chest. "Are you sure?"

Paisley nods, but the way her lips are pressed into a thin line tells me she's not sure about this at all. She grabs my hand, and together we step out onto the darkened stage.

The rooftop deck is smaller and more intimate than the main stage was downstairs. Up here, there are disco balls hanging from the rafters and everyone's wearing party hats and New Year's novelty glasses. There's a different vibe, probably on account of the cameras and the fact that we're only a few minutes away from the New Year.

In the far corner, a mobile camera crew is focused on a blond woman in a long silver dress and the cowboy hat–wearing man in a suit beside her. They're both holding microphones and smiling at the camera.

"And now, to sing us into the New Year with his upcoming single, 'Worth the Wait' . . ." he says.

The woman holds up her hand to point in my direction, and suddenly I'm blinded by the mega-bright stage lights as they blast on. "Kash Murray."

The man peers down at a piece of paper Barry hands him. "And Paisley Morgan."

My heart thuds as I blink, trying to clear my vision enough to see. I give Paisley's hand a reassuring squeeze before letting go so I can play the intro.

"One, hold your horses,
Two, hold the train,
I'm standing out here in the pouring rain.
Three blocks down
Four over from Main
I'm waiting and waiting for you again."

I look out into the audience, relieved to see people dancing. They might be drunk or overexcited because the countdown is on, but they are moving and grooving. There's a change in the air, like it's been charged with energy.

Paisley stands stiff like a statue, and there's a pained expression on her face. She plucks at the bracelets on her wrist, and I nudge her to get her attention. When our eyes meet, I smile and play the pre-chorus guitar riff. I don't break eye contact with her as we both step to the mic to sing.

" 'Cause you're
One, two, three minutes late . . .

Four, five, six, then seven and eight.
Other guys, well, they might be irate."

Paisley gives me a warm smile before she looks out at the audience with wide, worried eyes. Then her eyes are back on mine as we finish the chorus.

"But you—
You're worth the wait."

As soon as I can step back from the mic, I signal for the other guitarist to vamp while I check on Paisley.

"Are you doing okay?" I ask.

She forces down a swallow and nods.

"You don't have to stay out here, you know."

Paisley looks tempted. But she shakes her head. "I want to see it through."

Still, her dark, frightened eyes don't leave mine as we return to center stage and she jumps in to sing the next verse.

"Five o'clock shadow,
Six o'clock news,
Coolin' my heels, no time to lose."

Paisley's warm, breathy voice mixes perfectly with mine. We sing facing each other, ignoring the cameras, the audience, the rest of the world. This moment is ours.

The song finishes to a round of boisterous applause and a few hoots and hollers. We've finished the song just in time, because as soon as it quiets, the countdown begins.

"Ten."

"I can't believe we did it." Paisley beams up at me. She's pale and breathing hard, but she's here.

"Nine."

"We just did that," I say, still not quite believing it's true. I reach out and brush my hand over her cheek.

"Eight."

She sucks in a shaky breath. "We did."

"Seven."

"Onstage," I say, my eyebrows raised in exaggerated shock.

"Six."

Paisley looks down at the bracelets on her wrist.

"Five."

"Carole King. Carly Simon. Even Elvis had stage fright."

"Four."

"They still performed live," she says.

"Three."

"I figured, if they could do it, so can I."

"Two."

"You're incredible, Paisley," I say. "Thank you."

"One."

I shift my guitar around onto my back, and Paisley reaches up to cradle my face in her hands, guiding my mouth down to hers.

Our lips meet as the crowd cheers, "Happy New Year!" I pull her closer, deepening our kiss.

Confetti shoots from cannons placed around the room and streamers fall from the rafters. Outside, the sky lights up with bursts of shimmering fireworks. But all I care about is that

Paisley's here, in my arms, on one of the most important nights of my life.

When we finally pull apart, Paisley's lips are plump and pink. She smiles at me as she reaches up to pull a streamer from my hair. "I'm sorry it took me so long to get here," she says, her dark eyes filled with regret.

"I'm just glad you're here now." I brush my lips over her forehead and smile. "'Cause you, you're worth the wait."

OUTRO

Kash Money Pais Off! Hot New Couple Kash Murray & Paisley Morgan Announce Tour, Share Video for New Song

"Better Together" is the final preview of their upcoming album *Two for the Show*.

By **Deva Davis**

Dynamic country duo—and Nashville's hottest couple—Kash Murray and Paisley Morgan have announced a headlining tour and recently shared a music video for "Better Together" from their upcoming debut album, *Two for the Show*. Directed by Sammy Jenks, the video was shot at Hidden Acres Christmas Tree Farm, owned and operated by the Morgan family, just outside Springfield, Tennessee. Murray was previously a member of the now-defunct country-rock band Six String Justice.

Singer/songwriter Paisley Morgan commented: "On *Two for the Show*, we wanted to blend Kash's country-rock styling with my folk and bluegrass background to create a signature sound."

Kash Murray added: "We bring out the best in each other, and I think that really comes through on the album."

Murray and Morgan share co-writing credits on all but one song on their LP, a country-style version of Frank Sinatra's classic "It Had to Be You" (written by Gus Kahn and Isham Jones). These singing sweethearts head out on a North American tour next month, where they'll be performing songs from the duo's new LP as well as hit songs "Lonesome Hearts," "I Could Need Someone Like You," and "Worth the Wait" from Murray's breakout solo album, *Worth the Wait*. The tour kicks off on October 9 in Nashville, Tennessee.

ACKNOWLEDGMENTS

I am incredibly grateful to be continuing on this publishing journey, accompanied by so many amazing people who have helped to make my third novel a reality.

To my incredible agent, Jordan Hamessley: Thank you for your encouragement and championing. I am so glad to be on this adventure with you. And to the team at JABberwocky Literary Agency for all your support.

Thank you, Alison Romig, for being the best editor an author could hope for. Working with you is a pleasure! Your keen feedback and enthusiasm are always appreciated. And to everyone at Delacorte Romance: Thank you for all you do!

To Sarah Lawrenson, my amazing publicist: Thank you for all the time and energy you put into promoting my books, scheduling author events, and more.

Alissandra Seelaus, you hit it out of the park with another fantastic cover illustration! You have an amazing talent for capturing my characters perfectly. Thank you! I'm looking forward to our next brunch!

To Diana Gallagher, for your kindred-spirit friendship. I wouldn't have been able to do this without your honest feedback, brilliant brainstorming, and voice of reason. Cold Crock-Pot Romance forever!

There are so many amazing authors who make up the supportive, positive community I am grateful to be a part of, including Andrew Sass, Kristy Boyce, Becky Dean, Kristy Everington, Sabrina Fedel, Madeleine Gunhart, Tara Hannon, Catherine Hapka, A. J. Irving, Stephanie V. W. Lucianovic, and Addie Woolridge.

To all the booksellers and librarians who have supported my books and invited me for events, thank you! Especially Cordelia Wolfe, Elisabeth Jewell, Hannah Amrollahi, Anna Bekker, and Nancy Reiter.

I am so grateful to have a great group of friends who are some of the best cheerleaders in the world, including Evelyn Cadman, Andrea Champagne, Cheryl Dicks, the Dicksons, Margitta Dziwenka, Jenna Grigalauski, Caitlin McMonagle and Wyatt Sinclair, the McMonagles, Christi Segura, and the Verocks.

To my family, for your endless love and support. Mom and Dad, thank you for always believing in me. To my sister, Samantha, and brother-in-law, Austin, for continually cheering me on (and updating my website). To Aunt Pat, for giving me the best pep talks when I need them most.

To my husband, Jody, for helping me carve out time to disappear into the writing cave. Thank you for letting me bounce ideas off you and for reminding me that I can do anything I set my mind to. I love you!

To Brooks and Madeline: Thank you for inspiring me! And for keeping me grounded. I am so proud of you both!

Coming up with an idea for a third book was a real

challenge. When the concept of having a country music storyline was first suggested, I couldn't figure out how to make it work. I spent weeks brainstorming, and nothing felt right until I hopped in the shower and started humming Taylor Swift's "Christmas Tree Farm." Suddenly, it all clicked! So, thank you, Taylor Swift, for the inspiration!

A number of memoirs, interviews, and videos helped shape this story, including those featuring musicians Sara Bareilles, Carole King, Willie Nelson, Dolly Parton, Rich Redmond, Carly Simon, and Gabi Wilson (H.E.R.).

A quick shoutout to the Christmas tree mug, the pine-scented candles, and *Narada: The Christmas Collection Vol. 1*, which I used to help capture some holiday spirit while I was drafting this book during one of the hottest summers of my life.

I also want to thank all the readers, reviewers, and recommenders who have taken the time to read my books. I love interacting with readers and am so grateful for all the notes and kindness you've shared in person and online. None of this would be possible without you!

ABOUT THE AUTHOR

KATRINA EMMEL is the author of *Near Misses & Cowboy Kisses* and *Trail Rides & Starry Eyes*. She grew up in New Hampshire, moved to the Midwest for graduate school, and is now a resident of Nevada. In addition to writing fiction, she loves science, crafts, making up silly songs for her kids, and supporting monarch butterfly conservation by planting lots of milkweed.

katrinaemmel.com
@katrinaemmelauthor

Once you love a boy in a Stetson, you'll never be the same.

CHAPTER 1

Riley

MIDWESTERN AIR SMACKS me in the face the minute I step off the plane onto the Jetway. It's cooler, damper, and greener than I'm used to. Back home—what used to be home, anyway—it's arid and dusty. Trudging up to the gate, I adjust the straps on my overstuffed backpack. The wisps of hair at the nape of my neck curl in the humidity.

Unlike the continuous chaos of our layover in Las Vegas, Eppley Airfield is quiet. There's a reason Nebraska is called a flyover state—you're not supposed to actually land here. And yet, here I am. In Nebraska.

The rest of my family snagged a row of seats together in the front of the plane, so they were able to disembark first. It irritated me to be stuck in the back near the bathroom, but honestly, I didn't want to sit with them anyhow. Their extra-chipper "we're going to have so much fun" attitude is grating on me. As if their positivity could make up for uprooting our lives and transplanting us to the Midwest with hardly any warning. I was supposed to be sunning myself on Huntington Beach and working some crap part-time job to save up money for college when I wasn't volunteering at the marine nature center or working on my art portfolio. Enjoying my summer before senior year with friends. Nowhere on the list of activities was "board a plane the day after school gets out to fly to Nebraska for some ridiculous weeklong family excursion to kill time while the moving company carts our stuff to our new house."

Instinctively, I reach for my phone, but what's the use of switching it out of airplane mode at this point? Do I really want to read all the *wish you were here* and *having so much fun* messages? Or worse, what if they've already forgotten about me?

Not Quinn, of course. Quinn would never forget about me. We've been friends since kindergarten, when we were both put in time-out for lobbing fistfuls of sand at each other at recess the first day of school. But I think a text from her right now would only make me sadder.

I spy my parents by a bank of cell phone charging stations that remind me of library study cubbies. As soon as Mom makes eye contact with me and waves me over to where they're standing, she makes a beeline for the restroom. Dad takes a moment to stretch his legs. My younger brother, Caleb, hovers nearby, his fingers flying over his phone. He'll be a high school freshman in the fall, so the move is less disruptive to his plans, since he was going to start the year in a new school anyhow.

We're quiet as we shuffle toward baggage claim. The three of them walk together like a cohesive unit and I lag behind. Ever since Mom and Dad announced the big move a few weeks ago, it's felt like three against one. Traitor that he is, Caleb pounced on the prospect of a bigger room with an en suite bathroom and the promise of a game room in the partially finished basement of our new house. How he could just sit there and take the news with a shrug and a "cool" is beyond me.

Even though the airport is air-conditioned, it's still muggy. Nebraska must know I'm dehydrated, given how much moisture it's trying to force into my skin. I don't even want to think about the humidity hell I'll have to deal with for the foreseeable future. As if to prove a point, my long bangs start to curl in my peripheral vision, taunting me.

We lay claim to a little spot of tile near the front of the luggage conveyor belt and watch it slither along its serpentine loop. I pull out my phone again out of habit, but can't bring myself to unlock it. A sharp sting of dread mixed with resignation has me slipping the phone back into my bag. I'm not sure I'll ever be ready to deal with that level of FOMO.

"The van is scheduled to pick us up at three p.m. sharp," Dad says, an excited gleam in his eye. "It's a two-hour drive to Darby and then adventure awaits."

Mom beams back at him. "We are going to have so much fun." Her eyes get misty as she wraps an arm around my waist. "This will probably be one of our last family vacations before you're off to college."

I swallow down the lump in my throat and fight the urge to remind her that I'm not going off to college next fall. If everything goes according to my parents' plans, I'll be enrolling in Alden University, where they've both accepted coveted tenure-track professorships—the whole reason why we're here in the first place. Mom's been working without a contract at the local community college for the past two years and Dad's been unemployed since his last professorship—a short-term stint to cover someone's sabbatical leave—ended. The opportunity for them both to have permanent jobs is great, but the timing just really sucks.

The screen above Baggage Carousel 2 flashes with our flight number and bags start pouring down the slide. Dad steps forward to grab Mom's purple roller bag and his navy duffel. Caleb spots his lime-green suitcase and hauls it over.

A few nondescript black suitcases glide past, a set of golf clubs, and a car seat. None of them are mine. We wait. And wait. And wait for my teal suitcase decked out with purple ribbons and butterfly patches surrounded by metallic Sharpie doodles.

Eventually, the conveyor belt grinds to a halt and the flashing light at the top of the carousel stops blinking. I glance around at the empty baggage claim area, hoping that someone might have accidentally grabbed my bag and set it off to the side, but no luck. If this were LAX, I'd assume that someone walked off with it, but there was hardly anyone here and the vibrant bag is pretty hard to miss.

My head flops back to rest on the top of my backpack, the extra weight causing the straps to cut into my shoulders. Why is the universe against me?

Mom pulls the baggage claim receipts from her purse and scans them until she finds mine. Shoving the rest back into her purse's outer zipper pocket, she signals for me to follow her over to the lost luggage office. "I'm sure they'll be able to help."

"Doubtful," I mumble, my hands clenched around my backpack straps.

The man working behind the counter gives us a pleasant

smile when we step into the room. "I take it you lost a piece of luggage?"

"Unfortunately, that appears to be the case," Mom replies in her annoyingly chipper manner. "Here's the claim ticket for the bag."

The man—Arnold, according to his employee name tag—keys some info into his computer and then frowns. "I'm afraid the bag was accidentally routed to Tampa from LAX."

Of course it was.

"It'll probably be about two days before it makes it here . . ."

Mom and I share a glance. For the first time since announcing the Great Upheaval, there's a chink in Mom's "everything is going to be great" armor.

"We're going on an Oregon Trail Adventure tour," Mom says. "It leaves Darby early tomorrow morning and won't return for a week."

"In that case, we can arrange for the hotel to hold your suitcase until your return," Arnold says.

I glance down at my ballet flats, cutoffs, and DESTROY THE PATRIARCHY NOT THE PLANET T-shirt and cringe. "I can't wear this outfit for an entire week in the middle of the Nebraskan wilderness. All my clothes . . . my art supplies . . . my perfectly broken-in hiking boots . . ." My eyes get misty and I furiously blink away tears. I've already cried enough in the past two weeks to last an entire lifetime.

Yes, I'm overtired.

And yes, I'm emotional.

bestselling author of the kissing booth
BETH REEKLES
Beach Cute
WILD About You
KAITLYN HILL
Author of Love from Scratch
ALL ROADS LEAD TO ROME
SABRINA FEDEL
Hearts OVERBOARD
Becky Dean
Near Misses & Cowboy Kisses
KATRINA EMMEL
bestselling author of the kissing booth
BETH REEKLES
Love & Lattes
Delacorte Romance
Better Than Revenge
KASIE WEST
WHILE We're YOUNG
K. L. WALTHER
DATING and DRAGONS
Kristy Boyce
Love Points to You
Alice Lin
I LOVE YOU S'MORE
AURIANE DESOMBRE
ALL'S FAIR IN LOVE AND FIELD HOCKEY
KIT ROSEWATER
ALL PATHS LEAD TO PARIS
SABRINA FEDEL
LOVE UNMASKED
Becky Dean
LOVE AT Full Tilt
JENNY L. HOWE